EVERYONE
HAS
SECRETS

To Toni
with love
Mandy
x

BOOKS BY A J MCDINE

The Baby
The Photo

When She Finds You
Should Have Known Better
No One I Knew
The Promise You Made
The Invite

EVERYONE HAS SECRETS

A J MCDINE

Bookouture

Published by Bookouture in 2024

An imprint of Storyfire Ltd.
Carmelite House
50 Victoria Embankment
London EC4Y 0DZ

www.bookouture.com

Storyfire Ltd's authorised representative in the EEA is Hachette Ireland
8 Castlecourt Centre
Castleknock Road
Castleknock
Dublin 15 D15 YF6A
Ireland

ISBN: 978-1-83525-792-0
eBook ISBN: 978-1-83525-791-3

For Adrian – for everything

PROLOGUE

One phone call. That's all it took for my life to implode. Like a storm ripping through a quiet street, the call upended everything, leaving chaos in its wake.

I had it all, you see. A cosy home, a loving husband and a handsome son who was the centre of our world. We were happy. At least, I thought we were.

As I crumpled on the sofa, my phone clutched in my hand, I knew my perfect life had been nothing more than an illusion. I'd taken my eye off the ball, and suddenly everything I cared about was snatched from under my nose. Stupid. *Stupid*.

The voice on the other end of the line still echoes in my ears as I force myself to my feet and stumble out of the house. Soon, I'm sprinting across the road, images of my son flashing through my mind. His red, scrunched-up face the day he was born. Asleep in his buggy, his thumb in his mouth. On the swing at the park as I pushed him higher and higher. Clasping my hand on his first day at school. So many memories; every single one of them tainted, now I know the truth.

I reach the other side of the road and stop to catch my breath. Our front door is ajar. Beyond it, the hallway is in darkness. I push the door open, shivering in my thin cotton top. The silence is suffocating.

I stagger through the house, still reeling with shock. How can everything look the same when nothing will ever be the same again?

'Perfect.' I stand back to admire my handiwork. Streamers and honeycomb balls hang from the kitchen ceiling and bunting and balloons adorn the walls. A huge disco ball shimmers like a sparkling diamond as it refracts the beams of the late afternoon sun. 'Joe's going to *love* it.'

My husband Noah wanders in as I'm setting out paper plates on the granite worktop. Smiling, I wave an arm at the decorations. 'Ta-da!'

He wrinkles his nose. 'It's a bit over the top, isn't it?'

The smile slips from my face. 'You think it's too much?'

'Joe's sixteen, not six.'

I pluck distractedly at the plastic wrapper on a packet of paper cups I ordered from an online party shop. I'd been inordinately pleased when I'd found plates and cups to match the blue and silver colour scheme I'd chosen for our son's birthday party. Now Noah's well and truly rained on my parade.

'D'you think I should take them down?'

He shakes his head. Shadows ring his grey-green eyes, and his shirt is creased. 'I don't know, Eve. Ask the birthday boy. It's his party.'

'He's got a match, remember.' But I pick up my phone anyway and leave a message asking Joe to call, then scan the room. Maybe the decorations are a bit over the top. I drag a chair under one of the honeycomb balls and step onto it. As I reach for the ceiling, the chair wobbles precariously and for a heart-stopping moment I fear it's going to topple to the ground, taking me with it. I shoot out an arm and grip the nearest kitchen cupboard and exhale slowly.

'What are you doing?' Noah asks.

'Toning it down a bit. You're probably right. I don't want to embarrass him in front of his friends.' I peel off the Blu Tack fixing the ball to the ceiling, climb down and move the chair along to the next. 'But the disco ball cost twenty pounds. It's staying.'

At first, I'd been reluctant when Joe asked if he could invite a few friends round to celebrate his sixteenth birthday. The last time we'd held a party for him at home was when he was five. A horde of hyped-up boys from the village had rampaged through the house, destroying everything in their wake like sugar-fuelled tornados. I was still finding unidentifiable stains on our travertine tiles weeks later.

'Never again,' I told Noah as I gingerly extricated a mouldy carrot stick from the back of the sofa. After that, Joe's parties had taken place at trampoline parks and bowling alleys, laser tag centres and swimming pools, where it didn't matter if the kids sprayed tomato ketchup everywhere or ground chips into the carpet with the heels of their trainers, because someone else cleaned it up. Expensive, but worth every penny.

Joe declared that birthday parties were beyond lame when he was twelve, and I breathed a silent sigh of relief, assuming his partying days were over.

Apparently not.

He found me in the garden hanging out some washing last week. I could tell he was after something. It was the way he shifted his weight from foot to foot, his hands thrust into the pockets of his black Nike joggers.

'Can I invite some friends round for my birthday?'

'What, like a house party?'

'Not a party, Mum.' He bent down to pick up a towel from the washing basket and handed it to me. 'Just a few mates over to play a bit of Xbox and hang out.'

'I'll have to check with Dad.'

'I already asked him. He says it's fine.'

'Oh, right.' I was stung Joe hadn't come to me first, but forced a smile. 'Who were you thinking of asking?'

'Just the usual gang. Connor and Josh and maybe a couple of friends from school.'

'And Annie?' I checked, because it wouldn't be right not to ask my fifteen-year-old god-daughter. She and Joe have known each other all their lives. Her mum, Lisa, is my best friend. We do everything together.

He shrugged. 'If she wants.'

'Let me think about it, OK?'

For a second, I thought I saw a flash of anger in his eyes, but then he smiled, leant over the washing basket to peck me on the cheek, and said, 'Thanks, Mum,' before loping back into the house.

'When were you going to mention Joe's party?' I asked Noah as we were getting ready for bed that night. 'Because I would have liked to have been consulted before you told him it was OK.'

'Eve, it's just a few friends over for some beer and *FIFA*.'

'Until he announces it on social media and hundreds of gatecrashers turn up and wreck the house.'

'He's not going to announce it on social media. He's not stupid.' Noah's jaw clenched, two deep frown lines scoring his forehead. There was a time when he would have softened his words with a smile. Not any more. These days he didn't bother to hide his exasperation, and it cut me to the quick. Couldn't he see why I was so worried?

'I know he's not stupid,' I said. 'But I'm still not sure it's a good idea.'

Noah placed his glasses on his bedside table and massaged the bridge of his nose. 'Let the poor boy have some fun.'

'I guess if we're here—'

'No, Eve.' It was almost a growl. 'We'll leave them to it. You've got to start giving him some space.' It was a tune he'd been playing since Joe hit his teens. *Take a step back. Stop smothering him. Let him make his own mistakes.*

It's easy for Noah to say. He already has a son, Billy, with Jenny, his first wife, whereas Joe is my only child, and I've spent the last sixteen years wrapping him in cotton wool. You can't let go on demand.

'Where will we go?'

'Lisa's.' Noah pulled back the duvet and climbed into bed with a grateful grunt, then glanced at me. 'You spend half your life at hers anyway. And if you're not there, she's here.' He reached across to turn off his bedside lamp. 'Or if Lisa's working, we'll go to the pub.'

'But what if something happens?' I said, picturing cigarette burns on the sofa, broken bottles scattered across the carpet and piles of vomit in the potted plants.

'It won't,' he said, turning onto his side, his back towards me. 'And if it does, we'll only be on the other side of the green.'

I didn't have the energy to argue, but now the party is just hours away I wish I'd put my foot down. I can't shake the feeling something terrible is going to happen.

* * *

Noah disappears into his study muttering something about his year-end accounts while I take down a couple of strings of bunting and unpack the shopping. As well as enough snacks to feed a dozen hungry teens, I also – against my better judgement – picked up some alcohol. Not much: just a box of beers and half a dozen bottles of cider. I did drop a couple of packs of WKD in the trolley, then changed my mind and put them back on the shelf. I know kids Joe's age drink, I'm not naive. I just don't want them getting wasted under my roof.

Equally, I know there's no point banning booze, especially with Connor Moody and Josh Duffy on the guest list. Better to provide a small amount of beer and cider than risk them smuggling in spirits or raiding our drinks cabinet.

I put the beer and cider in the fridge and find bowls for the peanuts and crisps. I'm heading upstairs to take a shower when the front door clicks open and Joe appears. His rugby kit is covered in mud and his cheeks are ruddy.

'Hello, sweetheart. How was the match?' I ask, even though I saw the result flash up on the school's social media feed half an hour ago.

'Lost sixteen-fourteen,' he says, heeling off his trainers and dumping his kitbag and rucksack on the hallway floor.

'Close, though. Any tries?'

'Nah, not today.'

'I picked up some stuff for tonight,' I say, following Joe down the hallway and into the kitchen, almost colliding with him when he stops in his tracks to gaze around the room.

'Jeez, Mum, you shouldn't have.'

'Ah, it was no trouble,' I say, smiling. 'I was worried I'd overdone it a bit, but you're only sixteen once.'

Joe reaches into the fridge for a can of Pepsi Max. 'It's not even my birthday till Monday,' he says, snapping the ring pull.

'I know, but I thought it would be fun.'

Joe takes a long draught, then peers into the fridge again. 'Is there anything to eat? I'm starving.'

'I bought you a pizza. It'll only take ten minutes.'

'What time are you and Dad going to Lisa's?'

'Half six. We'll be back about eleven.'

'Can you make it midnight?'

I reach up and ruffle his hair. He smells of mud and grass and sweat. It's been a manic week and I'm shattered. I'd be tucked up in bed with the lights out at ten given the choice. 'Seeing as you asked so nicely, midnight it is.'

'Thanks, Mum,' he says, flashing me a smile.

Out of nowhere I experience a sudden sense of unease. What if something does happen? Before my imagination goes into overdrive, I give myself a stern talking-to. Noah's right, I need to give Joe space. He's a good lad and I trust him.

I take the pizza from the fridge. As I turn the oven on and slice through the packaging with a vegetable knife, my inner voice needles me.

I might trust Joe, but can I trust his friends?

2

'D'you think we should've laid down some ground rules?' I ask Noah as we cross the village green to Lisa's house.

'Definitely not. You know what they say about rules. They're made to be broken. Anyway, Annie'll be there. She'll make sure the boys behave themselves.'

He's holding a bottle of wine in each hand, one red, one white, while I carry a chocolate tart and pot of double cream. The lights are blazing in every window of Lisa's tiny cottage, giving the illusion the place is on fire. I glance back at our house. 'I hope the kids don't light the candles in the fireplace.'

'Give it a rest, Eve,' Noah says, scowling, as he holds Lisa's gate open. I step through and walk along the path to the front door. Before I've raised my hand to rap the knocker, the door swings open and Annie breezes out. My heart lifts, as it always does when I see my god-daughter. Slim, with waist-length blonde hair and a wide smile, Annie is the spitting image of Lisa. Like her mum, she's sunny and vivacious, a stark contrast to Joe, who can be monosyllabic and moody. She is the positive to his negative. The daughter I never had. When she was tiny, we bonded over *Sesame Street* and *Peppa Pig*. These days our families are just as close. Annie and I share a love of Eurovision and cheesy romcoms. Her company always puts a smile on my face, and I feel my worries melt away when I'm with her.

'Hello, darling,' I say, handing the pudding to Noah and giving my god-daughter a hug. 'You look lovely. Pretty dress. Did you make it?'

Annie steps back and gives a self-conscious twirl. 'D'you like it? I wasn't sure about the neckline.'

'It looks amazing. *You* look amazing.' A smudge of eyeliner, a slick of mascara and a lick of lip gloss is all you need when you're fifteen, I think ruefully. Annie has teamed her forest-green velvet mini dress with opaque tights and Doc Martens and is wearing her hair in a plait. She's always had an innate sense of style, even as a toddler rooting through Lisa's dressing-up box.

'Have a nice evening,' Noah says.

'You know where to find us if you need anything,' I add.

Annie grins and sets off across the green. The security light comes on as she marches up our drive and rings the bell. A moment later the scarlet front door opens and she is swallowed into the house, as fleeting as a summer shower, and the hairs on the back of my neck bristle with disquiet, though for the life of me I don't know why.

Lisa's front door opens straight into her living room, which is in its usual state of messy chaos. Every surface is covered with interesting shells and pieces of driftwood, unpaid bills, abandoned coffee cups and forgotten library books. The radiator is bedecked with a couple of pairs of black lacy knickers and a matching bra; watercolours wrapped in brown paper are stacked against the wall by the front door and Lisa's Jack

Russell, Vincent, named after Vincent van Gogh, is snoozing on the rug in front of the fire.

Mixed in with the smell of wood smoke is the scent of coconuts and spices and my stomach rumbles. I was so busy decorating the house for Joe's party I forgot to stop for a sandwich.

'Only us,' I call as we troop through the tiny dining room into the galley kitchen at the back of the house. Lisa is snipping coriander from a plant on the windowsill but drops the herbs on the worktop when she sees us.

'I'm doing my own take on a red Thai curry,' she says, giving us both a hug. 'Did you know that some people think coriander tastes like soap? There's even an international I Hate Coriander Day. Who knew?'

'It's to do with genetic variants in olfactory receptors,' Noah says, dumping the wine bottles on the table. 'People with the variant detect a soapy smell from coriander.'

'All right, smarty pants,' Lisa says, handing him a corkscrew. 'Get that open. I need to drown my sorrows.'

'What's up?' I ask, putting the tart and cream in the fridge. I know my way around Lisa's kitchen almost as well as I know my own.

'The landlord's just announced he's putting my rent up by two hundred pounds.'

'He can't do that,' I gasp.

'I'm afraid he can.' Lisa shrugs. 'His mortgage on this place has just come out of a fixed rate and his repayments have shot up. I can't really blame him.' She takes the glass Noah offers her, closing her eyes briefly as she sips.

'But how will you find the extra money?' I ask. Things are already tight for Lisa. She ekes out a living selling watercolours and teaching painting classes in local village halls. How's she supposed to magic up an extra two hundred pounds a month?

'There's a job going at the petrol station on the bypass.

Night shifts, so I can fit it around my classes. It's minimum wage, but beggars can't be choosers.'

I can't imagine anything worse, but I bite my tongue. Lisa has taken on a range of temporary work since I've known her, from cleaning and gardening jobs to working behind the bar at the village pub, The Swan. She's plucked turkeys and picked apples, waited at weddings and mucked out at a local livery yard to make ends meet. My job as Head of Maths at the local girls' grammar school is stressful, but Lisa works harder than anyone I know and yet she still struggles to keep her head above water. Now this. It isn't fair.

'I can have a chat with the Head of Art at school if you like,' I say. 'She might have something for you.'

Lisa gives the curry a final stir and scatters over the chopped coriander. 'That's so kind of you, Eve, but don't worry. Everything'll be fine.'

And that's the difference between us, I reflect, as Lisa takes warmed bowls from the oven and sets them on the table. I'm a glass half-full person, whereas Lisa's glass is always brimming. Automatically, I check my phone, but there are no new messages.

'I'm going to nip home to make sure the kids are OK while you're dishing up,' I say, grabbing the house keys from my coat pocket.

Noah slams his glass on the worktop so violently Lisa and I both start.

'For Christ's sake, Eve, will you stop fussing?' he bellows. 'The last thing they want is you poking your nose in. They'll be perfectly fine.'

Mutinously, I replace the keys and fix him with a look. 'For your sake, I hope you're right.'

3

Noah tears off a corner of naan bread and dips it in his curry. 'This is amazing, Lisa. Is that lemongrass?'

She nods. 'I poached it in the coconut milk.'

The curry is fragrant, the jasmine rice fluffy. I eat greedily, not caring that the waistband of my jeans is biting spitefully into the doughy folds of my stomach.

'Hard to believe our babies are nearly sixteen,' I say, reaching for the bottle of Sauvignon and refilling our glasses.

Noah spoons more rice onto his plate. 'One minute you're changing nappies and the next you're looking at universities. It doesn't seem possible.'

'Is Annie's heart still set on the London College of Fashion?' I ask Lisa.

'If she makes the grades.'

'London will be expensive,' Noah observes.

'She's already talked Matt into giving her a job washing glasses at the pub three nights a week so she can start saving.'

'I wish Joe would get off his backside and find himself a job,' Noah grumbles, and I sigh inwardly as he warms to his theme. 'Kid thinks the world owes him a living. He has no idea.'

'Haven't I always said you should have sent him to the high school?' Lisa waggles a finger at us. 'He spends his days rubbing shoulders with the overprivileged. It's no wonder he thinks cash grows on the magic money tree.'

'It was Eve's decision to go private, not mine,' Noah reminds her. 'Only the best for our boy.' His voice is mocking, and I flush. It's a well-worn argument. Noah hates the fact that his youngest son sounds posher than he does. He also begrudges every penny of the exorbitant school fees Elmwood Manor charges for the privilege of attending the most elite school in the county. Thirty grand a year, which doesn't include extras, such as the guitar lessons, ski trips and school exchanges. Joe has set his sights on a Year 12 trip to China next summer which will set us back another four thousand pounds. I haven't dared mention that to Noah yet.

I have nothing against state education, but when Joe failed his eleven-plus, his choices were stark. Go to the local high school, which had recently gone into special measures, or go private. When Joe and I went to an open day at Elmwood and saw the all-weather sports pitches and the indoor swimming pool, the state-of-the-art performing arts centre and the library that looked like it was straight out of Hogwarts, the decision was made for me, even if it meant I had to return to teaching full-time to afford the fees. It was a price I was willing to pay.

After we've each demolished a slice of chocolate tart, I help Lisa wash up and we retire to the living room, taking the second bottle of wine with us. I'm drawn to the window and peer across the green. Our porch light is on, just as we'd left it, but otherwise the place is in darkness. And why wouldn't it be? The kitchen is at the back of the house. Still, I can't shift the low-level anxiety churning in my stomach.

'All quiet?' Lisa kicks off her slippers and tucks her feet underneath her as she settles on the sofa. Vincent jumps up from the rug, circles a couple of times, and curls into a ball beside her.

'All quiet,' I confirm.

'Why are you so worried?' she says, rubbing Vincent's ear absent-mindedly. 'They're good kids.'

'I know, but you read these horror stories about parties spiralling out of control. You know, when they announce it on social media and hundreds turn up and trash the house. Cigarette burns on the sofa, sick on the carpet and smashed beer bottles everywhere.'

Noah laughs. 'Sounds tame compared to the house parties I went to when I was their age.'

I join Lisa on the sofa. She's right. They're good kids, and I'm worrying needlessly. OK, so Joe's marks at school have dropped this term, but he's still predicted decent enough grades in his exams this summer. He'll never be a straight-A student like Annie, but that's fine. He wants to go to Loughborough to study sports science. Secretly, I hope he'll decide to do a post-grad certificate in education when he's finished his degree. I've always thought he'd make a brilliant PE teacher.

At ten, Lisa finds a pack of cards, and we play Hearts and Blackjack in front of the fire, moving onto Lisa's home-made sloe gin when we've finished the red wine. The evening is blurring around the edges, the alcohol acting as an anaesthetic, numbing my anxiety as effectively as a dentist's needle numbs a tooth. Noah's voice is getting louder, as it always does when he's drunk too much. Lisa's pale face is flushed. I realise just how much I've had to drink when I stand to go to the bathroom and the room starts to spin.

'Anyone want a glass of water?' I call as I walk back through the kitchen. No one answers, but I pour three anyway and carry them into the living room.

As I carefully place the three glasses on the coffee table, a phone rings. It takes a few seconds to grasp that it's mine. I stumble over to my bag, which I left by the front door, catching my foot on the corner of Noah's chair. I really have drunk too much. My head will be pounding in the morning.

Noah and Lisa's eyes are on me as I stare at the screen. 'It's Joe,' I say, looking at them in concern. 'What can he want?'

'Keys to my man cave so he can help himself to my beer, probably,' Noah says. He pats his pocket and smirks. 'Luckily I brought them with me. Are you going to answer it or not?'

I accept the call and press the phone to my ear.

'Mum?' Joe cries. 'You need to come home.'

'Now?' I frown. 'I thought you didn't want us back till midnight?'

'Please, Mum. Just come. I... I don't know what to do.'

His voice is breathless, panicked. Fear coils in my stomach. 'Joe, you're scaring me. What's happened?'

'It's Annie, Mum. Something's happened to Annie.'

4

I gaze at Lisa, fear twisting in my gut.

Her face freezes. 'What is it? What's wrong?'

'Joe says something's happened to Annie.'

'What? What's happened?' she cries. As our eyes meet, the colour drains from her face.

'I don't know. He didn't say.'

Noah's already on his feet and making for the front door. I pull on my boots and follow, not bothering with a coat, telling myself everything will be fine, that Annie's probably burnt her hand on the oven warming up the garlic bread I wrapped in foil and left on the worktop, or has cut herself sweeping up a broken beer bottle. Then I remember the panic in Joe's voice and the fear intensifies. Joe's normally level-headed like his father. I'm the worrier in the family.

We sprint out of the cottage and across the green to our house. I bang on the front door while Noah fumbles with his keys, swearing under his breath as he drops them on the doorstep.

I bend down and scoop them up, but before I can slot the key in the lock, the door swings open. A boy I dimly recognise

as Ethan Curtis, the son of our local GP, is standing in the hallway, his face as white as a sheet and his pupils dilated with fear.

'They're in the kitchen,' he mumbles, standing back to let us
pass.

I sense Lisa behind me as I run through the house calling
Joe's name. We burst into the kitchen. Annie is lying in the
recovery position on the rug in front of the sofa, Joe crouched
over her. I barely register the three other teenagers huddled in
the corner of the room, watching warily.

'Annie!' Lisa cries, dropping to her knees and cupping her
daughter's face.

I squat down beside her and pick up Annie's hand. I'm
expecting her arm to be floppy, but it is rigid, and her skin feels
hot to the touch. I press the tips of my index and middle fingers
into her wrist. Nothing. This can't be happening. I close my
eyes and press harder. Finally, I feel it: a pulse, faint but there.

'Call an ambulance!' I shout at Noah. He nods, his phone
already in his hand, and walks into the hallway to make the call.

I turn back to Annie. Lisa is stroking her clammy forehead,
smoothing back her sweaty hair. Annie's jaw is set and a thin
line of saliva dribbles down her chin. I resist the urge to reach
out and wipe it away.

'What happened, Joe?' Lisa says. 'Did she take something?'

At first, I'm not sure what Lisa means. Take what? And
then it hits me. Lisa's asking Joe if Annie has taken any drugs. I
feel a whisper of dread as Joe wraps his arms around his chest
and bows his head.

'Joe!' Lisa repeats. 'Did she take anything?'

'I think someone gave her an E,' he mutters.

'Jesus,' Lisa says, cradling Annie's head in her lap.

My stomach swoops. Ecstasy? Who would give Annie
ecstasy, here, in our house? I jump to my feet and turn to the
gaggle of teenagers who were lurking by the open patio doors
when we arrived, but they've melted away into the night.

Noah strides back into the kitchen. 'They've diverted an ambulance from another call. They'll be fifteen minutes. Is she breathing?'

I nod quickly.

'OK.' He runs a hand through his hair. 'In that case they said we need to make sure her airway doesn't become obstructed.'

I push past Joe to grab a tea towel from the drawer and run it under the cold tap. My hands are shaking as I wring it out and hand it to Lisa, who presses it against Annie's forehead. I take another and use it to mop up a puddle of water by Annie's head. It must have spilled from the upturned pint glass on the floor by my feet.

'Will you turn that fucking music off?' Noah barks at Joe. I blink. I hadn't even noticed the low bass beat playing in the background, thumping like a distant drum. Joe fiddles with his phone and the music stops abruptly.

'I'm going outside to wait for the ambulance,' Noah says. 'Call if you need me.'

I nod and watch him disappear through the door. I squeeze Lisa's hand. 'She'll be all right,' I murmur, because the alternative is too awful to contemplate. When Lisa doesn't reply, I haul myself to my feet, prop myself against the kitchen island and watch the second hand go round the clock over the range cooker. It's just after half past eleven. How long is it since Noah called for an ambulance? Five minutes? Ten?

Time has slowed to a crawl, but my mind is racing. Joe said Annie had taken ecstasy, but it doesn't make sense. Annie's the most sensible girl I know. She's on the school council; she's captain of the under-16s hockey and netball teams. She's conscientious and well-liked. A high-flier, one of those golden girls destined for great things, not the type to pop an E at a friend's house party.

I steal a glance at Joe. He's hunched in the corner of the

room, staring at the floor, his face etched with misery. It's under-standable: he and Annie are closer than most siblings. Compassion washes over me and I go to him and put my arm around his shoulders. 'She'll be all right,' I repeat.

He is stiff, unyielding. 'I'm going to wait with Dad,' he mumbles, pulling away from me.

Desperate for something to do, I soak another tea towel and give it to Lisa.

'My poor baby,' Lisa croons. 'My darling girl.' Tears are rolling down her face, but she doesn't wipe them away, and they splash onto Annie's flushed skin.

'Who did this to you, angel?' she whispers. 'Who did this?'

5

Finally, the silence is punctured by the faint wail of a siren. Relief makes me weak. Soon, paramedics will be here, taking charge, making Annie better. Everything will be all right.

'She's in here.' Noah's voice carries from the hallway. He appears, followed by two paramedics, a man and a woman.

The woman crouches down beside Lisa. 'Are you Mum?' she asks.

Lisa nods.

'Do you know what she's taken?'

Lisa glances at Joe. 'Ecstasy.'

As the paramedic clips an oximeter onto the end of Annie's middle finger, her body starts to tremble, her muscles spasming.

'She's fitting,' the paramedic calls to her colleague. 'We need to get her to hospital now.'

'I'll get the stretcher.' He shouts something into his radio and disappears from the room. He's back seconds later, and the pair roll Annie onto a stretcher and wrap her in a cooling blanket.

'Are you coming in the ambulance?' the female paramedic asks Lisa.

'Please.'

'I'll come too,' I say, glancing at Noah, who nods. 'Are you taking her to Nesborough?' It's the nearest hospital with an A&E department, a ten-mile drive from here.

'Yes.' The male paramedic's expression is grim as he jerks his head towards the front door, beckoning me to follow him, but Lisa blocks my way.

'No,' she says.

'What?'

'I don't want you to come.'

I blink. 'But I can wait with you, keep you company while they treat Annie.'

Her expression hardens. 'I don't want you to come,' she repeats.

'Lisa, please.' I hold out a placatory hand. 'You're upset. I get it. But I can help. Talk to the doctors for you, take notes, that kind of thing.'

'Who's coming?' the female paramedic asks urgently.

'Just me,' Lisa says. Her jaw is tightly clenched, as if she's unconsciously mirroring her daughter. 'This is your fault,' she snarls, her gaze drifting from me to Joe, who is hovering at the bottom of the stairs, his hands thrust deep into the pockets of his baggy jeans. 'And I will never forgive you if Annie... if she...'

The rest of her sentence is stolen by a heart-wrenching sob. When she finally manages to get her voice under control, it is as hard as a splinter of ice. 'Stay away from Annie and me.'

*   *   *

Sleep is impossible, and after we've sent a shaken Joe up to bed, Noah and I take up position on the corner sofa in the kitchen to wait for news. Not that I think Lisa will let us know how Annie's doing. I'm still reeling from the raw hostility in her voice when she left.

'We should have asked Joe about the drugs,' I say, picking up a cushion and hugging it to my chest. I'm finding it hard to believe that just a couple of hours ago I was pleasurably tipsy, enjoying a game of cards with my husband and my best friend. In the blink of an eye, my safe, predictable little world has turned on its axis.

'It'll wait until the morning,' Noah says.

'I'll make a cup of tea.' I jump up, glad to have something to occupy me, even if only for a minute or two. I set both mugs on the coffee table and resume my place on the sofa. 'I'll phone the hospital and ask how she's doing.'

'They won't tell you. We're not family.'

'We're as good as,' I counter. He cocks an eyebrow, but I ignore him, because it's true. I was four months pregnant with Joe when we moved from North London to The Old Vicarage in South Langley sixteen years ago. For the first few months I thought we'd made a terrible mistake. Although imposing, our new house, three times the size of our cosy, modern mid-terrace in Highgate, was damp and draughty. Country life was a culture shock: the terrible Wi-Fi, the lack of public transport, the ten-mile drive to the nearest supermarket. Friends who'd already made the move out of London never mentioned the stench of the autumn muck-spreading, the four o'clock wake-up call from the resident cockerel, the suspicious looks from regulars when you dared to step inside your new local.

For the first time in our lives, we were the outsiders, our noses pressed against the window, hoping someone might notice us standing in the cold and invite us in.

Everything changed when we met Lisa and her husband Craig at antenatal class in the village hall. Lisa, whose baby was due soon after ours, was from South Langley; Craig grew up in Nesborough, the nearest town. We clicked instantly, and they welcomed us into their social group with open arms. Soon, Noah was a regular at the weekly pub quiz, and I started as a reading volunteer at the local primary school. When Joe and Annie were born two weeks apart, our friendship deepened as we navigated the ups and downs of new motherhood together. I was friendly enough with the other mums in the village, but they were always so competitive. I didn't need to pretend to be someone else when I was with Lisa. She didn't mind if I was almost incoherent with exhaustion or had vomit stains on my T-shirt. She was more than a friend; she was the sister I never had. It wasn't long before The Old Vicarage began to feel like home, and Lisa, Craig and Annie part of our family.

I was devastated when Craig was diagnosed with an aggressive form of testicular cancer two years after we moved to South Langley. He fought the disease with his trademark humour and bravery, but even increasingly brutal rounds of chemotherapy couldn't stop the cancer spreading to his bones. He died in our local hospice, with Lisa, three-year-old Annie and his parents by his side, a year later.

'We're not family in the eyes of the hospital,' Noah says, pulling me back to the present.

'How else am I supposed to find out how Annie is when Lisa's not replying to my texts?' I check my phone for the hundredth time. The half a dozen messages I've sent in the last hour are showing as delivered but unread.

'She'll call when she can.' Noah drains the last of his tea. 'You should try to get some sleep.'

He's probably right. My eyes are gritty with exhaustion, my limbs leaden. I tramp up the stairs, pausing on the landing outside Joe's bedroom. The door is closed and Joe has hung the 'Do not disturb' sign he liberated from a Spanish hotel when he was twelve on the doorknob. Usually, I respect it. Not tonight. Tonight, I knock on the door and push it open without waiting for a response.

He's still awake, his bedside light casting a butter-yellow glow across his bed.

'Are you all right?' I ask.

'What d'you think?'

'Sorry, silly question.'

The room smells of sweaty trainers and Adidas antiperspirant. Long gone are the *Thomas the Tank Engine* pyjamas Joe used to love. He sleeps in his boxers now. His shoulders are broad and his pectorals defined, but he is still a boy. *My* boy. Out of habit, I bend down to pick a dirty T-shirt off the floor. It's the one Joe wore to the party. I ironed it for him this morning. It seems like a lifetime ago now. Another world.

'Have you heard from Lisa?' he asks. There's a pallor to his face that reminds me of the time he caught norovirus on a school trip to the New Forest. He was sick for a week.

'Not yet. I'm sure she'll phone as soon as she can.' I fold the T-shirt in half, my fingers worrying at a small grease mark by the hem. I'll rub some Fairy Liquid onto it before I put it in the wash. It should do the trick. I sit on the end of the bed and meet his gaze. Noah told me to wait until the morning, but I have to know now. 'Did you know someone brought drugs to the party?'

'No.'

'Did you take anything?'

He rears up. 'Of course I didn't!'

His denial is so vehement I'm immediately guilt-ridden. 'Sorry, sweetheart. I had to ask.'

He grunts and we sit in silence for a moment. On his bedside table his phone lights up with a notification.

'Who's messaging you at this time of night?'

He glances at the screen. 'Billy.'

'*Billy*?'

'I told him what happened to Annie. He's worried about her.'

The only person my stepson Billy is usually worried about is himself, but I hide my surprise. Joe worships his half-brother.

'Of course. But you still need to sleep.' I hold out a hand for his phone. 'I'll plug it in on the landing for you.'

'Mum! I'm not ten. I'll silence notifications.'

'Make sure you do.'

He fiddles with the phone for a minute, then places it face down on his bedside table. 'Will you let me know when Lisa calls?' he asks.

'Of course.' I drop a kiss on his forehead and leave the room, closing the door behind me with a heavy heart.

Somehow, I know Lisa isn't going to call. All I can do is hold onto the hope that Annie will be OK.

6

I sleep fitfully and wake with a start, my heart hammering in my chest. I shoot an arm out, seeking Noah's reassuring bulk, but his side of the mattress is empty, his pillows perfectly plumped. He hasn't come to bed. That's when I remember Joe's panicked phone call last night. Racing home to find Annie lying unconscious on the kitchen floor. The paramedics carrying her away on a stretcher.

I swing my legs out of bed and grab my phone from the bedside table, hoping with all my heart to see a text from Lisa. *Panic over. Annie's fine. See you at rugby later? Xx*

There is no text.

I pad across the bedroom to the en suite and jump in the shower. My head is woolly and my mouth feels like sandpaper. I fiddle with the temperature until the water is scalding and my skin turns crimson, but that just reminds me of Annie's flushed skin, so I turn it down until it's so cold I'm gasping for breath.

Back in our bedroom, my hair wrapped in a towel, I try calling Lisa. It rings once then goes straight to voicemail.

'Lisa, it's Eve. I'm just phoning to see how Annie is. Call me, please, when you get a moment? We're all so worried.'

On a whim, I find the number for Nesborough Hospital and I'm calling it before I can talk myself out of it. A recorded voice asks me to dial an extension number if I have one, or to hold for further options. I rub my face. My skin feels dry and tight. The voice is back. 'Please state clearly the ward, person or department you require. If you need assistance, say "operator".'

I clear my throat. 'Operator.'

The wait seems interminable. Finally, a woman with a monotone voice says, 'Nesborough Hospital. How can I help you?'

'I'm phoning for a condition check.'

'Which ward?'

'I... I don't know. It's my, um, niece. She came in last night. Well, the early hours of this morning.'

'Her name?' the bored-sounding switchboard operator asks.

'Annie Bradstock.'

'And you're her aunt?'

'That's right.'

'What's her date of birth, please?'

'The twenty-sixth of February, 2007.' I reel off the date without thinking. I know Annie's birthday as well as I know Joe's.

'I'll put you through to ICU,' the woman says, and I grip my phone tighter. Intensive care? Just how sick is she? The phone clicks, and a man with a broad Bristol accent answers.

'Oh, hello,' I say. 'I'm just calling to see how Annie Bradstock is this morning.'

'Annie Bradstock?' Am I imagining it, or is there an edge of suspicion in his voice? 'Who is this?'

'Her, erm, aunt.'

'Right.' A murmured conversation takes place and then the man is back. 'I'm sorry, but Annie's immediate family have requested that no information be released over the phone. I'm sorry I can't be of more help.'

I sit on the bed, wondering what this means. Surely Lisa wouldn't freeze me out? She knows I'm not a fair-weather friend. I've been by her side through thick and thin for the last sixteen years. I have been her confidante, her champion and her shoulder to cry on.

The need to be there for her is so deep-rooted that I almost phone the hospital back and tell the man with the Bristol accent he must be mistaken, that he's obviously muddled our Annie up with someone else in the ICU, because there's no way Lisa wouldn't want me to know how she is. Then I remember the fury on Lisa's face last night and I toss my phone onto the duvet in despair. I can't call her, in case I've got it all wrong and she's shutting me out because she holds me responsible for what happened to Annie.

Feeling sick, I tie my wet hair back and pull on some clothes. Before I head downstairs, I inch Joe's door open and peer in. He's buried under his duvet, his breathing regular and deep. It's only half eight and he never surfaces until at least ten at the weekend. I'll let him lie in.

Noah's sitting at the kitchen island, his hands wrapped around a coffee cup. The smell makes my mouth water and I head for the coffee machine.

'You didn't come to bed,' I say.

'I dossed down here.' He dips his head towards the sofa. 'I didn't want to wake you.' The cushions are scattered all over the place, and the berry-red throw I always drape artfully over one arm of the sofa is puddled on the floor like a pool of blood. I shiver.

'I rang the hospital to see how Annie is.'

Noah's ears prick. 'And?'

'You were right, they wouldn't tell me. All I do know is that she's in intensive care.'

Noah's shoulders slump. 'I've been googling ecstasy over-doses. So many kids have died, Eve. It's such an unpredictable drug; you never know how someone's going to react, and there's nothing the doctors can give them to reverse the effects.'

Normally, I'm the one who sees the risks in every situation, especially when it comes to Joe. When he was young, I catastrophised about everything. The world is a perilous place for an adventurous boy with no sense of danger. I worried about him drowning in a rockpool, or hitting his head in the playground, or running out in front of a car. So I mitigated for every potential disaster: holding his hand while he fished for crabs, standing under climbing frames ready to catch him if he slipped, keeping him close as we walked down the street.

Noah is my counterbalance. He's always telling me not to wrap our son in cotton wool. 'He needs to make his own mistakes' is one of his favourite mantras. 'He's never going to learn resilience with you hovering over him ready to rescue him every time he looks as if he's about to fail at something.'

When Joe was little, Noah let him climb trees and walk to school on his own. Later, when Joe hit his teens, it was Noah who said he could meet his mates in town on a Saturday night; Noah who let Joe take a four-pack of beer to a friend's party.

And now, just when I need Noah to reassure me, to tell me Annie will pull through and everything will be all right, he's the one over-dramatising.

I purse my lips, about to tell him to get a grip, when there is a knock at the door. We look at each other uncertainly.

'It might be Lisa,' Noah says, placing his mug on the counter and climbing down from the bar stool. 'I'll get it. You make her a coffee.'

I nod and pull another mug from the cupboard, hope blossoming in my chest. If Lisa is here, it must mean Annie is feeling better, maybe she's even well enough to be discharged from hospital. With Annie home we can put this whole sorry chapter behind us.

Noah walks stiffly back through the door. Expecting to see

Lisa behind him, I gape as two uniformed police officers step into the kitchen.

The coffee cup I'm holding slides through my fingers and smashes on the tiled floor, the sound like a gunshot in the silent room.

7

'Careful!' Noah is beside me in a flash, grabbing my elbow and pulling me back from the shards of shattered mug. 'Take everyone into the living room. I'll sort this out and be through in a sec. Can I make you a drink or anything?' he asks the two police officers.

'Tea would be lovely,' the older officer says, glancing at his colleague, who nods. 'Both white, no sugar.'

I step around the broken mug and smile weakly at them. 'This way,' I say, heading for the hallway. With the heat of their gaze on my back, I suddenly find it difficult to walk, my movements jerky as if my arms and legs belong to someone else. My tongue is glued to the roof of my mouth. I hope Noah remembers to bring me a fresh coffee.

In the living room, I gesture for the officers to take a seat. They opt for the high-backed petrol-blue sofa, and I sink into one of the slouchy armchairs opposite, immediately feeling at a disadvantage.

'I'm Sergeant Dan Harrington and this is PC Marcus Anderson,' the older officer says. 'I expect you know why we're here.'

It can only be because of what's happened to Annie. The ambulance service must alert the police when a teenager is rushed to hospital with a suspected drug overdose.

'Annie?' I say, and Harrington nods. I swallow. 'How is she?'

He answers my question with one of his own. 'I believe she was unconscious when you found her last night?'

'That's right. Is she still—?'

'She's yet to regain consciousness, I'm afraid,' the sergeant says, reaching into his pocket for a small black notebook and pen.

I wait for him to elaborate, and when he doesn't, I ask, 'But she will be all right, won't she?'

The two officers exchange a look, and the tiny glimmer of hope inside me flickers and dies.

'It's touch and go,' Harrington says. 'That's why we're here. We need to establish exactly what happened in this house last night.'

I glance at the door, wishing Noah would hurry up. I don't want to face this inquisition on my own. But the two officers are watching me expectantly, so I run my tongue around my lips and begin.

'It's my son Joe's sixteenth birthday tomorrow so we said he could have a few friends round to celebrate last night. We spent the evening at Lisa's—'

'That's Mrs Bradstock?' Harrington checks.

I nod. 'We wanted to give the kids a bit of privacy while being near enough to be on hand if anything happened.'

'Is your son in the habit of hosting house parties?' Anderson asks.

'No, it's the first time we've let him.' And the last, I think privately.

'Mrs Bradstock said Joe called you just before eleven o'clock,' the sergeant says.

'That's right. He said something... something had happened to Annie. We dropped everything and raced over, as you can imagine, and when we arrived, Annie was lying on the floor in the kitchen. My husband called an ambulance, and Lisa and I stayed with Annie until it arrived.'

'Did you know at that point what had happened?'

I shake my head. 'I suppose I thought she was drunk.' I picture Annie on the floor, her face flushed and her limbs stiff. 'Actually, no, I didn't think that. I thought she must have had a seizure, epilepsy, something like that.'

Noah finally arrives with the drinks, and once he's given the officers their tea, I take my mug from the tray. The coffee is stronger than I like but I drink it anyway, grateful for the chance to lubricate my parched throat.

'Annie was fitting, but it wasn't epilepsy,' Harrington says. 'At what point did you become aware that she'd taken MDMA?'

The two officers must register the confusion on my face, because Anderson explains, 'It's the active ingredient in ecstasy.'

'Right. Well... Lisa asked Joe if Annie had taken anything, and he said someone had given her an E.'

'Someone?' Harrington queries. 'Did he say who?'

'No. I haven't asked him, but he assured me he hadn't taken anything himself.'

'And you believe him?'

I feel a ripple of annoyance. 'Of course I believe him,' I say crisply.

'Who else was at the party?' Harrington asks, his pen poised.

I remember the pinched faces of the teenagers who slipped out through the patio doors before the ambulance arrived, but my mind's gone blank and I look to Noah for help.

'There were a couple of lads from the village. Josh Duffy and Connor Moody,' Noah says. 'They go to the high school.

And a boy and girl from Joe's school, Elmwood Manor. Ethan Curtis and Lottie Miller. Plus Annie, of course.'

'Just six of them,' Harrington says, looking up from his notebook. 'You're sure about that?'

'Well, obviously I wasn't here, so I can't say for certain, but they were the ones who were here when we came back. I'll ask Joe now if you like?'

'We do need to speak to your son,' the sergeant says. 'Is he at home?'

'He's still in bed,' Noah says. 'I'll fetch him.'

With Noah out of the room, I find myself the focus of the two officers' attention once more.

'Was there alcohol at the party, Mrs Griffiths?' Anderson asks.

'A bit, yes. Just a few bottles of beer and some cider. No spirits, nothing like that. We took the view that if we banned alcohol, they'd only bring their own or raid our drinks cabinet.' I give a nervous laugh. 'But no one seemed drunk.'

'Perhaps it wasn't the drink they were interested in.' He balances his mug on his knee. 'I understand you're a teacher at the girls' grammar. Maths, isn't it?'

'That's right,' I reply, wondering where he's going with this.

'Did you know that having an illegal drug – and a class A drug at that – in your house is an offence?'

I stare at them in shock. 'But I didn't know there were any drugs in the house.'

'If we find you turned a blind eye to your son taking or sharing drugs with his friends, you could be charged with possession under the Misuse of Drugs Act. That's not going to go down too well at work, is it?'

For a moment, I can't speak. I take a deep breath, drawing air into my lungs, then address them shakily. 'The first I knew about drugs in the house was when Joe said Annie had taken an E. We don't even know she took it here. She... she could have taken it before she came over.' My shock turns to shame. Victim blaming won't help anyone, least of all poor Annie.

The sound of footsteps on the stairs is a welcome distraction and I force myself to smile, hoping Joe has pulled on a clean T-shirt and hasn't just picked up a dirty one from the floor. 'Here they are. You can ask Joe yourself.'

But the moment Noah walks into the room, I know something's wrong.

'Where's Joe?' I ask him.

Noah's brow knits. 'He's not in his room.'

'What about the bathroom?'

He shakes his head.

'Our en suite?'

'No, Eve, he's not in our en suite. I've checked the rest of the house. He's not here. He's gone.'

8

I have never seen Noah look so agitated. He's one of life's can-do people, positive and upbeat, rarely fazed by anything. He runs his own education recruitment consultancy and is known in the business for being a fixer. If you have a problem, you ask Noah Griffiths. But he looks lost as he hovers in the doorway, his phone clutched in his hand.

'Perhaps you could try calling Joe?' Sergeant Harrington suggests.

'Yes, of course. Good idea.' Noah stares at his phone as if he's forgotten how it works. 'I'll do that, yes.'

The two police officers are silent as Noah retreats to the kitchen. I know exactly what they're thinking: that Joe has fled because he was the one who gave Annie the ecstasy. Well, they're wrong. He would never do that. He's frightened, that's all. He doesn't want to be blamed for something he didn't do.

'When did you last see your son, Mrs Griffiths?' Harrington asks.

'This morning, just before you arrived. Not to talk to: he was still asleep. He probably hasn't seen you're here and has popped out for a run.'

'A run,' Harrington repeats, eyes narrowed. 'Keen runner, is he? Perhaps you could phone me as soon as he comes home from this run of his. We do need to speak to him.' He passes me a card with his number on, then nods to his colleague, and they both get to their feet.

At the front door, the sergeant pauses. 'Rest assured we will find out who gave Annie the ecstasy, Mrs Griffiths. Perhaps you can inform your son that it's in his interests to cooperate with our inquiries in the meantime.'

* * *

I find Noah in the kitchen, staring out of the bifold doors. Outside, a robin pecks about on the patio, its red breast the only colour on this dank February morning.

'His bedroom window was open. He must have climbed onto the garage roof and jumped down from there,' Noah says, not looking at me. 'Where the hell has he gone?'

'In his treehouse, I should think.' When Joe was little he used to hide under his bed when he was worried about something. When he was older he retreated to the treehouse at the bottom of the garden. I'm already reaching for my coat. I shrug it on and slip on the Crocs I use for gardening.

'Look, Eve, I need to pop into the office,' Noah says.

'Now?'

'Something important's cropped up and it can't wait until tomorrow.'

I frown. 'What could possibly be more important than Joe and Annie?'

'Client trouble,' he says, grabbing his car keys from the bowl on the kitchen island.

I shake my head. 'Since when were your clients more important than the kids?'

'They're not, but it's not like there's anything I can do here.

The hospital won't tell us how Annie is, and Joe will come back when he's good and ready. I'll be as quick as I can. Don't speak to the police again until I'm back.'

I swear under my breath and head outside. The robin flies onto the shed roof and watches me as I tramp across the lawn to the oak tree. I can see Joe's footsteps in the dewy grass and there is a certain satisfaction in knowing I was right. By the time I reach the ladder that leads to the treehouse, my socks are soaked.

'Joe,' I call, one foot on the bottom rung. 'It's Mum. Can I come up?'

Not waiting for an answer, I start to climb. We had the treehouse built for Joe's tenth birthday, a wooden eyrie high up in the branches of the huge oak tree that dominates the garden. Joe was beside himself with excitement, and when he abandoned his Nintendo Switch in favour of wholesome activities like bark-rubbing and bird-spotting, I knew the money it cost was worth every penny.

Joe and Annie spent most of that summer in the treehouse, making dens, having picnics, hanging out. They even had a sleepover one sticky night. I didn't sleep a wink, terrified one or both of them would roll over in their sleep and plummet the fifteen feet to the ground below. They hadn't, of course. They'd had the time of their lives.

I reach the top of the ladder and step onto the treehouse deck. The arched door is pulled shut and I tug at the handle and clamber inside. Joe is slumped in the far corner, hugging his knees to his chest.

'Hey,' I say, sitting next to him. 'You OK?'

'What do you think?' he mumbles.

'I know, stupid question. Sorry.' I squeeze his shoulder, trying not to mind when he flinches at my touch.

'Is Annie home yet?'

'She's in intensive care, Joe.'

'Fuck.'

I bite back a rebuke. We have more to worry about than a bit of bad language. 'The police want to speak to you about last night. That's why they were here.'

'I don't want to talk to them.'

'I get that, but you're going to have to, darling. They need to find out who gave Annie the ecstasy. There's an investigation, and it will look better for you if you talk to them voluntarily.'

Joe is silent. I glance around. I haven't been up here for years and had forgotten how the treehouse creaks and shifts with the wind. In the summer, when the oak is in full leaf, it's like being enveloped in a green cocoon, but this time of year, it's another story, and the bare branches resemble bony fingers that clasp us in their grip.

The wind has swept eddies of brittle dead leaves into piles in the corners of the octagonal structure and the Perspex windows are opaque with grime. There's an old wooden box, like a pirate's trunk, on one side of the little room and a couple of stools I picked up from a car boot sale on the other. I need to come back with a broom and a bucket of soapy water. Noah muttered something about putting the treehouse on eBay the other day, saying it had to be worth a few hundred quid, but I expressly forbade him. It's staying put, I told him. For the grandchildren. He looked at me as if I was mad, then shook his head and disappeared into his study.

'Will they talk to the others too?' Joe asks finally.

I nod. Ethan, like Joe, went to South Langley Primary School then onto Elmwood Manor. Unlike Joe, this is not because he failed his eleven-plus. He's scarily bright and is on course for Oxbridge, according to his insufferable mother, Carol, a part-time magistrate.

Lottie, whose parents, Annabel and Ralph Miller, are both human rights barristers, is an up-and-coming event rider whose many successes are often featured in Elmwood Manor's termly newsletter.

Connor and Josh were also in Joe's class at primary school and are now at Nesborough High School. Connor lives with his mum and three sisters in one of the council houses next to the pub. The one with the rusting fridge and decaying mattress in the front garden. Josh's family lives on the small estate of executive homes at the other end of the village, and his dad, Greg, manages the under-18s rugby team for which Joe, Josh and Connor all play. They are cocky boys, the pair of them.

Neither Ethan nor Lottie seem the type to bring a stash of class A drugs to a friend's house party. If anyone gave Annie an ecstasy pill, it's Josh or Connor, I have absolutely no doubt.

Noah might think work's more important, but he's wrong. As far as I'm concerned, Joe always comes first, and there's no way I'm letting the police point the finger of suspicion at our son. No bloody way.

9

I coax Joe back to the house with the promise of a bacon sandwich, and once he's eaten and has disappeared upstairs to shower, I make myself another coffee and sit at the kitchen island to make some calls.

First, I try Lisa, but the phone cuts straight to voicemail. I leave yet another message, then send a text for good measure, asking how Annie is. I stare at the phone for a few moments, willing Lisa to reply, but the text remains unread. Her silence is unbearable; every unanswered message and ignored phone call like a punch to the gut.

Feeling despondent, I ring Sergeant Harrington and offer to take Joe to the police station, grateful it's half-term this week and neither of us will be in school.

'Can you make tomorrow?' he asks.

'Tomorrow's Joe's birthday. How about Tuesday?'

'To be frank with you, Mrs Griffiths, the sooner we speak to your son the better,' Harrington says in a tone that leaves no room for debate. 'I'll see you both at nine o'clock in the morning.'

Finally, I phone Noah, who answers after the fourth ring, sounding irritable.

'Will you be back in time for rugby?' I ask him. Joe's team are sitting second in the league, largely thanks to Joe's skill as a winger. They have an important home match this afternoon and I have no intention of missing it.

'Do you think it's a good idea to go, what with Annie so poorly?' Noah says.

'Don't you think it's important we keep everything as normal as possible? If Joe hides away – if *we* hide away – people might think we've done something wrong.'

Noah exhales. 'It's your call, but we're not going to be flavour of the month. Don't say I didn't warn you.'

* * *

I'm quietly seething as I brush the mud off Joe's rugby boots and fill his water bottles ready for the match. Noah always does this. Lets me make a decision so he can criticise my choice later without being held responsible. I pull Joe's kitbag out from the cupboard under the stairs and pack the boots and bottles, then pop in a couple of the fruit and nut energy bars Joe likes.

I dump the kitbag by the front door and push open the door to Noah's study. He went straight there when he got back from the office, refusing the bacon sandwich I'd kept warm for him.

'We should go or we'll be late,' I say. Noah, hunched over his desk, glances up. His face is drawn, dark shadows ringing his eyes. He looks... haunted. This thing with Annie has hit him hard.

'Is everything all right?'

He rubs his face. 'Yes, sorry. Just tired. And worried about Annie, of course.'

'Of course,' I say, doubt flickering at the edge of my mind.

I'm worried too, but I'm not going to pieces. I have to hold onto the hope that she's going to be OK.

He pushes his chair back. 'I need to get my coat. I'll see you in the car.'

* * *

We drive to the sports field in silence. The small car park next to the clubhouse is already filling up. People stop to watch as Noah crawls past looking for somewhere to park.

'We shouldn't have come,' he says.

'Nonsense,' I reply. 'Look, there's a space.'

Noah pulls in next to Greg Duffy's gleaming white Range Rover Sport. I turn in my seat. Joe is slumped on the back seat, his head resting against the window, his earbuds in and his eyes closed. There's a fuzz of dark hair above his top lip and an angry-looking pimple on his chin, but I can see through them both to the sweet, fresh-faced boy he was not so very long ago.

'Joe, angel, we're here,' I say, as Noah pulls up the hand-brake. His eyes snap open and he grabs his bag and opens the door.

'Good luck, mate,' Noah says, and Joe gives a brief nod and disappears.

'I'll get us a coffee,' I say brightly. A couple of the mums run a stall selling hot drinks and bacon and sausage baps to raise money for the club. 'Want anything to eat?'

Noah shakes his head.

'Are you sure? You didn't have any lunch.'

'Don't fuss. I'm going to watch the warm-up.'

'Suit yourself.' I let myself out of the car and cross the car park to the clubhouse. As I near the tatty prefab building, I become aware that conversations are petering out and heads are swivelling my way. I tighten my grip on the strap of my bag and fix my eyes ahead, trying to ignore every sidelong glance, every whispered comment.

They are talking about Joe, of course. The news about Annie will have spread like wildfire. Kids messaging each other long into the night, feeding titbits to their parents with glee, glad the heat is directed at someone else for a change.

Village gossip with a healthy dose of *Schadenfreude* thrown in for good measure, because who doesn't derive pleasure from someone else's misfortune?

I search the crowd for a friendly face, relieved when I spot Siobhan Murphy with her head in the boot of her car. Shiv's son Ben has been friends with Joe since pre-school and the boys have shared countless playdates over the years, although they drifted apart when Joe started at Elmwood Manor and Ben went to the local boys' grammar.

'Hi, Shiv, how's it going?' I say, forcing myself to sound upbeat.

She straightens her back and turns to face me. Her lips are set in a thin line and her green eyes are cold.

'I can't believe you have the nerve to show your face here today,' she says, her voice loud enough to carry across the entire car park.

I flinch. 'Wh-What d'you mean?'

'You know exactly what I mean,' Shiv hisses. 'Annie's in hospital thanks to your little shit of a son.'

'Joe did nothing wrong,' I say, not dropping my gaze. 'He wasn't the only one at our house last night.'

Shiv gapes. 'You're saying one of the others gave her the ecstasy?'

I stand my ground. 'I'm saying you shouldn't throw allegations around without any proof.'

'You are unbelievable.' She leans in closer. 'How dare you defend your son while Annie's wired up to a life support machine?'

My voice cracks. 'It's terrible what's happened, but I won't let Joe be the scapegoat for something he didn't do.'

She shakes her head. 'You're deluded, Eve, and you're not welcome here. So why don't you all jump back into that Chelsea tractor of yours and piss off? Back to London, preferably,' she adds, before stalking towards the rugby pitch.

'Couldn't have put it better myself if I tried,' another mum says, and a few parents titter.

I stand frozen to the spot, my throat clogged with tears. I can hardly waltz into the pavilion and order two coffees now. Nor can I risk joining Noah on the touchline in case Shiv continues her tirade where she left off. I want to crawl into the car and hide, but Noah has the bloody keys.

I'm still running through my options when Noah and Joe appear from the direction of the pitch. Noah's expression is thunderous. Joe looks dazed. Noah marches up to me and grabs my arm.

'We need to go,' he growls. '*Now.*'

Wordlessly, I follow them through the car park, wondering if this nightmare will ever end.

10

The recriminations begin the moment we're safely inside the car.

'I told you we shouldn't have come,' Noah says, slamming the gearstick into reverse and shooting out of the parking space.

'Why, what happened?'

'Greg practically accused our son of dealing drugs in front of the whole team and half the parents. I have never felt so humiliated in my life. He'd have tarred and feathered us both given half the chance.'

'But Joe's not to blame.'

'Doesn't matter. They've made up their minds. I warned you we'd be *persona non grata*, but you didn't listen. You never bloody listen.'

I let Noah vent, still bruised from the roasting Shiv gave me. When he finally falls silent, I turn to Joe. He's staring moodily out of the window, his hands clenched in his lap. 'I'm sorry, sweetheart. Dad's right. We shouldn't have come. It's my fault. I just wanted to show everyone we had nothing to hide.'

'That's not what they think,' he mutters.

'Who?'

'Greg. The team. The whole village. They think I'm some kind of drug baron, Mum. It's not fair.' His voice thickens and tears prick my eyes. He's right. It isn't fair.

'Look, there's Lisa,' Noah says suddenly.

My stomach plummets as I see Lisa coming out of her cottage with a rucksack. 'Stop the car,' I command, unclipping my seat belt. 'I'm going to talk to her.'

Noah pulls onto the verge and places a warning hand on my knee. 'Do you think that's a good idea?'

'She's my best friend. Annie's my god-daughter. Of course it's a good idea. I'll see you at home.' Without giving him a chance to argue, I jump out of the car and jog across the green towards Lisa's cottage. I catch up with her as she reaches her elderly VW Beetle.

'Lisa,' I call breathlessly. 'How's Annie?'

Lisa's long mane of dark-blonde hair is tangled, and her eyes are red-rimmed and puffy. Compassion for her rips through me. It could so easily have been Joe who took the ecstasy; Joe attached to a life support machine in hospital, me coming home to pick up a bag of his clothes. There but for the grace of God...

Ignoring me, Lisa unlocks the car and chucks a rucksack onto the passenger seat. I dither for a minute, then cry, 'Please, Lisa, talk to me.'

Finally, she looks in my direction. 'What is it, Eve?' she asks tiredly.

'We've been so worried. I've tried phoning the hospital to find out how Annie is, but they won't tell me.'

'I've asked them not to.'

'Why would you do that?' Desperation is creeping into my voice along with the realisation that Lisa has been deliberately stonewalling me. I've never seen this side of her before. We've always shared everything.

'Because it's none of your damn business!'

I gawp at her in shock. This hard-faced, wild-haired woman

is unrecognisable as my funny, kind best friend. Her face starts to work as she tries very hard not to cry, and my shock turns to tenderness.

'You're right. I'm sorry.' I attempt a smile. 'We just want to know how Annie is.'

'She's still in a coma and the doctors can't tell me if she'll ever wake up,' Lisa blurts.

'Oh, Lisa, I'm so sorry. But she'll get better. You know Annie. She's a fighter. You have to hold onto that.'

Lisa shakes her head. I want to fling my arms around her and tell her that she doesn't have to do this on her own because I will always be there for her, but I'm not sure she's ready to hear it. Instead, I stand back as she climbs stiffly into the driver's seat.

'Please let me know if there's any change,' I beg. She doesn't answer, she just stabs the key in the ignition, starts the engine and drives away.

* * *

When I let myself into the house a few minutes later, Joe has slunk back upstairs and Noah is holed up in his study again, hunched over his keyboard.

I take a mug of tea to the front room and start scrolling through the pictures on my phone before I can stop myself.

There are as many photos of Annie as there are of Joe, which doesn't surprise me at all. She's always been naturally photogenic, and while Joe grew camera-phobic when he hit his teens, Annie never minded joining me in a selfie.

It's not long before I've found my favourite photo of the two of us, taken at the village fete last summer. The sky was a startling azure blue and we're each holding a cloud of candyfloss: mine white, Annie's powder-pink. We'd just whipped Noah and Joe's asses at the coconut shy and are laughing our heads off.

I scroll further back through my camera roll. There's Annie competing at the inter-school athletics championships a couple of years ago, as long-legged as a newborn foal. In a bumper car with Joe when the fair came to town. Proudly wearing her Head Girl badge in her final year at primary school.

I stare at the photos until my eyes glaze with tears. It's unthinkable that my vibrant, sparky god-daughter is wired up to a life support machine in hospital. Inconceivable.

I close down my photos and, with nothing else to occupy me, open my laptop and google ecstasy overdoses. I know I shouldn't, but it's like picking a scab. I can't leave it alone.

It doesn't take long for me to discover how many young lives have been needlessly lost to the drug. There are so many stories, so much tragedy. The sixteen-year-old who suffered a fatal cardiac arrest after she and her friends clubbed together to buy ecstasy to celebrate the end of their GCSEs. Another girl, this one just fifteen, who died after taking an ecstasy pill for the first time at a sleepover. I read with growing horror about the promising young footballer who died after his drink was spiked with MDMA at a music festival. The boy whose organs failed after a friend gave him two ecstasy tablets at an under-eighteens disco.

Unlike so many of my peers, I never dabbled in drugs at university, and when I qualified as a teacher, I was too focused on my career for big nights out. Noah and I have always enjoyed a good social life, but when we over-indulge, it's on Prosecco and Shiraz, not cannabis and cocaine. So my knowledge of drugs is hazy, gleaned mainly from the true crime series on Netflix I love to binge.

Other people's kids have drug problems. That's what I've always believed. Not people like us who follow all the rules, who've been to antenatal classes, who feed their privileged offspring organic food and send them to expensive private schools. The more heartbreaking stories I read, the more I begin to wonder if I've been mistaken. Because the teenagers in these stark news reports aren't all from the wrong side of the tracks. They've attended nice village primary schools with outstanding OFSTED reports; they've played football for their county and have been predicted top grades in their GCSEs. They are not lost children. They are regular, well-mannered, middle-class kids like Joe and Annie.

Poor Lisa, I think, as I power down the laptop and make a start on supper. You could do everything right, and it could still go so horribly wrong.

11

Nesborough Police Station is an austere grey cube of a building that wouldn't look out of place in Soviet Russia. Joe lags behind as I march up the disabled ramp to the doors. His face is closed off, almost sulky. I can't really blame him. What kid wants to be dragged out of bed at half past seven on the morning of their sixteenth birthday to attend an interview at their local police station? I'm about to snap at him to get a move on when I stop myself. It won't help his case if we're at loggerheads before we even report to the front desk.

His case.

The words sound official. Serious. But there is no case, I remind myself. We are here simply to answer a few questions about Saturday night. Helping the police with their inquiries, if you like. That's what the newspapers say, isn't it? 'Police investigating an assault say a man is helping them with their inquiries.' An altruistic gesture, because Joe is as much of a victim in all this as Annie.

I have no idea how she is. I tried phoning the hospital again last night but this time the woman on the switchboard wouldn't even put me through to the intensive care unit. All I could do was keep watch on Lisa's cottage from our bedroom window. The house was still in darkness when I finally went to bed just before midnight and her car wasn't there when I peered through the curtains this morning. I can't work out if this is a good sign or not.

I walk up to the counter. A balding man wearing a shirt that strains across his stomach looks up from his computer and smiles.

'How can I help?'

'We're here to see Sergeant Harrington,' I say.

The man glances at Joe, who is staring at his phone, disinterested, and his smile fades.

'Names?'

'Eve and Joe Griffiths.'

He nods and picks up a phone. 'Sarge, your nine o'clock's here.' He pauses. 'Sure, I'll bring them through.'

We sign in and follow him through an internal door and along a corridor to a small square windowless room with scuffed walls and a worn carpet. The only furniture is a rectangular table and three plastic chairs. The air is stale and stuffy. A police interview room, straight from central casting.

'Please take a seat,' the man says. 'Sergeant Harrington won't be long.'

Joe slumps on the furthest chair and I shrug off my jacket and sit next to him. When he reaches for his phone, I shoot him a look and shake my head. He exhales loudly and shoves his hands in his pockets.

'Joe,' I begin, touching his arm. 'It'll be all right. Just tell the police what you know and we can go home.'

He gives a low snort of derision and slides further down his seat. I clasp my hands on the table. Someone has scratched the words 'Fuck the feds' on the Formica surface. I can't help but admire their nerve. The door opens and Sergeant Harrington appears.

'Thanks for coming in this morning,' he says, nodding briskly at me. He introduces himself to Joe and takes a seat. 'This shouldn't take long.'

'How's Annie?' I ask.

His gaze drifts towards the door. 'There's no change, I'm afraid.'

'She's still unconscious?'

'She is.' He fiddles with a tape recorder on the end of the table near the wall.

'You're recording this? I thought you said it was just a chat?' I say, anxiety starting to build in my chest.

'Perhaps I didn't make myself clear. We've asked Joe to attend today for a voluntary police interview.' He addresses Joe. 'While you aren't under arrest, I will be cautioning you as anything you say may be given in evidence if a case is brought to trial. You're free to leave at any time. You are also entitled to free legal advice.'

Legal advice? My alarm is growing, feeding on the undercurrent of suspicion in the room, the insinuation that Joe is somehow at fault. Perhaps I should ask for the duty solicitor, or at least phone Noah to see what he thinks. I steal a glance at Joe. He is pale, expressionless, and my panic gives way to anger. I lift my chin and meet Harrington's eye.

'Why would we need a lawyer when Joe's done nothing wrong?'

'I'm just telling you what he's entitled to.' He sets his pocket notebook on the table, then presses a button on the tape recorder and reels off his name and rank and the date and time. He asks Joe to state his full name and date of birth. 'Also present is Joe's mother, Eve Griffiths. This is a voluntary police interview, conducted under police caution.' He turns back to Joe. 'You do not have to say anything, but it may harm your defence if you don't mention now something which you later rely on in court. And anything you do say may be given in evidence. Do you understand?'

'Yes,' Joe mutters. A muscle is twitching in his jaw.

'Good. As you know, we're investigating an incident at your sixteenth birthday party on Saturday the tenth of February when your friend, Annie Bradstock, collapsed after taking ecstasy. Perhaps you can start by confirming who else was at the party?'

'Connor, Josh, Ethan and Lottie.' Joe's voice is a monotone, devoid of all feeling, and his face is a mask. I silently will him to show some emotion, to *care*. Because Harrington doesn't know Joe like I know him. He sees a sullen, moody teenager with chapped lips and a fresh crop of spots on his forehead. He doesn't see my Joe, the sweet boy who used to nurse injured fledglings in shoe boxes and brought me breakfast in bed every Mother's Day.

'That's Connor Moody, Josh Duffy, Ethan Curtis and Lottie Miller?' Harrington checks, flicking through his notebook.

'Yeah.'

'And what did you do at the party?'

'Played a bit of Xbox. Talked. Listened to music. The usual.'

'Was there any alcohol?'

'A bit, yeah,' Joe says.

'I thought if I provided a few bottles of beer and cider they'd be less likely to sneak spirits in,' I explain again, even though I told Harrington this yesterday.

He nods, then turns to Joe. 'And did anyone sneak in spirits?'

He shrugs. 'Dunno.'

'Did Annie have much to drink?'

'How am I supposed to know? She was talking to Ethan most of the night.'

It's the most animated Joe has been since we arrived. I hope

Harrington hasn't noticed the flush creeping up Joe's neck, but he must have because he asks, 'Did that bother you?'

'No,' Joe retorts. 'Why should it?'

'No reason. I'm just trying to build a picture of what happened before Annie became ill.'

'We were just hanging out, playing *FIFA*,' Joe says. 'No one was drunk.'

'What about drugs?'

He doesn't answer.

'Joe, I asked you a question. Were there, to your knowledge, any drugs at the party?'

He looks up, meeting Harrington's gaze for the first time since the interview began. 'If there were, I didn't know about it.'

'So you didn't see Annie take anything?'

'No, I didn't.'

* * *

I feel a glimmer of relief as I pull out of the police station car park. It has started to rain, a fine drizzle that blurs the windscreen. I flick on the wipers, then glance at Joe, who's staring out of the window, that blank expression still on his face.

'Are you OK?' I ask.

'Am I OK?' he repeats. 'Well, I was woken up at half seven and have spent the morning of my sixteenth birthday being interrogated by the police, who obviously think I forced ecstasy down Annie's throat. What d'you think, Mum? Of course I'm not OK.'

I hold up a placatory hand. 'I'm sorry. Forget I said it. But what's happened isn't your fault. Remember that.'

Joe has been released under investigation.

'We'll be talking to the other people at the party over the next week or so and I'll be in touch if we need to speak to Joe again,' Sergeant Harrington said as he led us back through the station to the front counter.

Although it sounds serious, I'm confident that as soon as he's questioned the others he'll realise how off the mark he was even suggesting Joe was involved.

'Shall we drop by McDonald's on the way home and pick you up some lunch as a birthday treat?' I say, as I negotiate the series of roundabouts on the ring road out of town.

I take his shrug as an affirmative, and turn into the retail park, ordering him a Big Mac and a chocolate milkshake from the drive-thru.

I'm surprised to see Noah's car parked in the driveway when we arrive back at the house. Perhaps he decided to work from home as it's Joe's birthday. I've bought steaks for tonight, not that I feel like eating at the moment. My stomach's in knots.

'What are you going to do this afternoon?' I ask Joe as I pull up the handbrake and unclip my seat belt.

'I might see if anyone wants a kickabout on the rec.'

'Are you sure that's a good idea?'

'As you keep saying, I haven't done anything wrong,' he says wearily, as if we've switched roles and he's the frazzled parent trying to reason with his stroppy teen.

'I know. You're right, you shouldn't have to hide away. But people can be quick to judge. Just be careful. Promise?'

He gives me a small smile. 'Promise.'

I unlock the front door, closing it quietly behind me in case Noah's on a video call. Joe disappears upstairs while I kick off my boots and head along the hallway to Noah's study. The door's ajar and he's talking to someone. I'm about to go in and ask if he wants a coffee when I pause. Noah is animated and chatty when he's talking to clients. Today he sounds... agitated. Curious, I cock my head to listen.

'I can't talk for long,' he says in a low voice. 'Eve's going to be back any minute.'

Frowning, I tiptoe closer to the door, careful not to make a noise.

'I don't think she suspects anything, but you know Eve. She's not stupid. It's only a matter of time before she finds out.'

He is quiet for a moment. I hold my breath. I can't risk him hearing me.

'No, I want to tell her myself. She deserves that, at least.' Another pause. 'OK, I will. Just give me a few more days and I'll do it, I promise.'

A door slams upstairs and I shrink backwards, my heart hammering in my chest.

'They must be back,' Noah says. 'I have to go. I'll call you in the morning, OK?' His voice softens. 'I know you do. Thank you. You too.'

I turn and tiptoe back down the hallway, my mind in overdrive. I can't let Noah know I've been in the house, not until I have processed what I've just heard. So I open the front door and close it with a bang, then call, 'I'm home!' as if absolutely nothing is wrong.

12

Noah appears in the hallway, his hair all mussed up, as if he's been running his hands through it.

'I didn't know you were back,' he says, following me into the kitchen. 'How did it go?'

'Fine.' I march over to the kettle and am about to refill it, but Noah's beside me in a flash, steering me towards the sofa.

'You sit down. I'll make it.'

I do as he says, watching as he busies himself making tea, wondering what he's keeping from me. 'I didn't know you were working from home today,' I say.

'I thought I'd get more done here. I do need to pop in for a couple of hours this afternoon.'

'Hardly seems worth it.'

'There's a meeting I can't miss. But never mind that. I want to hear exactly what happened at the police station.'

He hands me my tea and sits beside me. I bury all thoughts of the phone conversation I've just heard and steer my focus back to Joe, and Noah listens in silence as I describe how the interview went.

'Joe was cautioned even though he hasn't been arrested?' he asks, frowning.

'It's procedure, according to Harrington.'

'And they're going to speak to the other kids at the party?'

I nod. 'The sooner we get this mess sorted out the better.' It sounds simple enough, but I can't help feeling that clearing Joe's name won't be as easy as I hope.

On the sofa between us, Noah's phone chirps with a text. He glances at it but doesn't pick it up.

'Shouldn't you see who that's from?' I ask him.

'What? No, it'll only be Maddy with another daft work query. It can wait.' He takes my mug and sets it on the floor by his feet. 'Listen, we need to talk.'

I stiffen, waiting for him to throw in the grenade that's going to cause our family to fracture. *I don't know how to say this, but I've met someone…*

The same tired cliché so many people have used. Perhaps the same line he trotted out to his first wife, Jenny, just over sixteen years ago. History repeating itself. My friends warned me never to trust a cheater. I should have listened.

I shift in my seat, wishing he'd get on with it. It will be a release, I think. Ever since the day Noah and I walked down the aisle, guilt has hovered in the wings of our marriage like an understudy desperate for his big break. For years I have wondered if the role of 'wronged wife' was one I was destined to play.

It doesn't matter that his marriage was already broken when we met. My fate was sealed the moment we fell in love, and karma is about to have the last laugh. The irony is hard to swallow. I was the other woman then. Am I now the betrayed wife? There is an awful symmetry to it all. The guilt I felt then rears its head again, ugly and unforgiving. It's no use fighting it. I only have myself to blame for trusting Noah in the first place.

I press my lips together, waiting for the grenade to do its worst, but instead, Noah says, 'Where's your iPad?'

'What?'

'Your iPad. I need to show you something.'

Wordlessly, I reach across to the coffee table, extract my iPad from under a pile of maths worksheets I should probably be marking, and hand it to him.

He keys in my passcode, taps away for a moment, then angles the screen towards me. He's on South Langley's Facebook page. It's a place where people go to publicise events and complain about dog poo, where they post pictures of missing cats and moan about the kebab van that visits the village hall car park every Friday night.

'I saw this earlier,' Noah says, pointing to a photograph of a candle, the type people light in churches in memory of loved ones. I quickly scan the post.

All are welcome at a candlelit vigil being held tonight for Annie Bradstock, who is currently fighting for her life in hospital.

Organised by friends of the Bradstock family as a show of support for fifteen-year-old Annie, the vigil is taking place in South Langley Church at 6 p.m.

Everyone attending is urged to wear something yellow as it's Annie's favourite colour.

'I thought people only held vigils when someone died.' I frown. 'I wonder who's organised it.'

'Your friend Siobhan. Well, she's the one who posted this, anyway.'

Glancing back down, I see Noah's right. Siobhan Murphy's name is on the post, and she's a top contributor to the group, apparently. I picture the hatred on her face when she saw me at the rugby match yesterday. Calling Joe a shit and telling us to piss off back to London because we weren't welcome here any more. I understand emotions are running high, but I thought we were friends. I gave her and her son Ben a lift to an away match only last month and we stood on the sidelines putting the world to rights as the boys trounced the opposition 25-3.

'Do you think we should go?' I ask Noah.

'Absolutely not.'

'But if we don't, they'll think we don't care about Annie. Or, worse, they'll assume it's because Joe gave her the ecstasy!'

'You know how emotionally charged these things get. Remember the vigil for those two boys who were stabbed in the park near our old house? The police had to step in when the families started laying into each other. Feelings are running high and the last thing we need to do is inflame the situation.'

'I suppose you're right.' I pause, watching him carefully. 'Is that the only thing you wanted to tell me?'

I'm giving him a chance to come clean about his phone conversation, to tell me to my face that he's having an affair. Because I know what I heard. My heart hardens as I recall his whispered words. The panic in his voice when he realised Joe and I were home, and the way his voice softened as he ended the call to his lover.

'Noah?' I press. 'Is that all?'

A range of emotions cross his face. Indecision. Fear. Guilt. He runs a hand around the collar of his shirt and swallows, his Adam's apple bobbing up and down like a pea in a blowpipe. 'Yes, that's all,' he says.

Even though I know he's lying, I keep my expression neutral, masking my sense of betrayal, my anger. Scratch that. It's fury I feel. A white-hot fury that pulses through my veins and leaves me breathless. I am a volcano, ready to erupt. I rein it in, because I'm not prepared to let another woman waltz into my marriage and help herself to my husband, not while Joe needs us more than ever. I also know that despite my rage, I still love Noah. Whether I can forgive him is another matter, but I want the chance to try.

If I overreact, if I shout and scream and rant and rave, I'll only force him into her arms, and I won't let that happen. We went through too much to be together. I won't let him leave without a fight.

Besides, there's no way I'm allowing history to repeat itself.

13

Noah was married when I met him. There, I've said it. I was the other woman. His 'bit on the side'. A homewrecker. Only it wasn't really like that, because Noah's marriage was already on the rocks the day I walked into his recruitment agency looking for a job.

He and his wife Jenny were childhood sweethearts who grew up in the same Essex town and married in their early twenties. Two years later, their son Billy was born. Jenny left her job in human resources to be a stay-at-home mum while Noah, a former secondary school teacher, worked all hours to build up his education recruitment consultancy.

I was twenty-five and working as a maths teacher in a high school in Camden when, keen to advance my career, I registered with a couple of specialist education recruitment agencies, including Noah's.

The day we met is etched in my memory. One of those ordinary days that starts like any other and ends up changing the course of your life. A friend from uni had recommended the consultancy after Noah helped her secure a head of department role at a prestigious private school.

'It's only a small agency but the guy who runs it knows his stuff,' my friend said, so I refreshed my CV and arranged to attend an informal interview with Noah Griffiths during the Easter break.

The office was tucked down a small side street a short walk from London Fields. I turned up almost fifteen minutes early, but when the receptionist rang through to Noah to tell him I'd arrived, he appeared, shook my hand, and ushered me into his office.

Although it wasn't a formal interview, I'd taken time with my make-up and hair and had planned my outfit carefully, teaming a flattering navy trouser suit with nude stilettos. As I took a seat across the desk from Noah I was glad I'd made an effort, because he may not have been textbook handsome – at a shade under six foot, he was on the lanky side, with dark hair that was already beginning to recede, a square jaw with a hint of five o'clock shadow and grey-green eyes behind wire-rimmed glasses – but there was something about him that made my nerve-endings tingle.

I'd sworn off men after I discovered my last boyfriend had been sending flirty texts to one of my closest friends. I was happily single and sharing a flat with a couple of girlfriends. Yet as Noah ran through my CV, asking about my skills and experience and where I wanted to see myself in five years' time, all I could think about was what it would be like to feel his arms snaking around me, his lips on mine.

The only photo on his desk was of a boy aged five or six sitting on a sandy beach eating an ice cream. There were no happy family selfies, no photos of a wife, and there was nothing about his behaviour towards me that suggested we had anything other than a purely professional relationship.

Later, he told me he'd felt the same spark between us, but it wasn't until he secured me a job in one of Islington's most popular comprehensives that he suggested taking me out for a coffee to celebrate.

'Sod coffee. I want champagne,' I declared, and he'd laughed a deep belly laugh that made my insides turn liquid.

We talked non-stop, and when we finished the first bottle of Moët, Noah raised a hand to summon the waiter, then paused.

'Shall I order another, or will your boyfriend be waiting for you at home?'

'What boyfriend?'

He smiled. 'In that case...'

'Order away,' I agreed, then waited a beat, my heart thudding in my chest. 'Unless your wife is expecting you back?' I was fishing for information, because I still wasn't sure if he was married. He didn't wear a wedding ring, which was interesting but not conclusive.

'Jenny? No, she won't be,' he said, and my heart plummeted. Noah had a wife, and I needed to back off, because this could never be anything more than a celebratory drink between friends. I fiddled with the stem of my glass, not realising he was still talking.

'Jenny won't be expecting me back because she's not... we're not really...' He sighed. 'It's complicated.'

I reached across the table to touch his hand. 'I'm a good listener.'

It was as if I'd pulled open a door that had been wedged shut for years. Words tumbled out of him, thick and fast. He talked about how he and Jenny had been drifting apart for a long time, only staying together for the sake of their seven-year-old son, Billy. How they led separate lives: Jenny and Billy at home in Essex, and Noah spending the working week in a flat above his office in Hackney, only returning home at the weekend. How they were more like brother and sister than man and wife.

Clichés, every one of them. The kind of lines poor, misunderstood men have been rolling out to gullible women for centuries. Nevertheless, I believed him. Maybe it was the raw grief in his eyes or the catch in his voice that convinced me, but I instinctively knew he was telling the truth. Or so I thought.

'I'm sorry,' I said.

'Don't be. It's not your fault.' He gripped my hand, lacing his fingers in mine. 'Thank you. For listening, I mean. You're the first person I've really talked to about this.'

'You and Jenny haven't—?'

He shook his head. 'Whenever I try to bring up how I'm feeling, she changes the subject. Her parents went through an acrimonious divorce when she was young, so I suppose it's inevitable.' He cleared his throat. 'Sorry, we're supposed to be celebrating your fabulous new job, and here I am wittering on about my problems.'

'I don't mind,' I said, and it was true, I didn't. Married men had always been firmly off-limits, but the more I talked to Noah, the more I felt drawn towards him, like we were meant to be together.

He gave my hand a final squeeze, picked up his glass and tilted it towards mine. 'To Eve, maths teacher extraordinaire, for whom two plus two never equals five.'

We clinked glasses tipsily.

'And to Noah, recruitment guru, building brighter futures, one placement at a time,' I said. 'Cheers.'

The next hour passed in a pleasant alcoholic blur, and when we reached the end of the second bottle of champagne, it was dark outside, and not only was my hand entwined with Noah's, but my stomach was spinning somersaults. I hadn't felt lust like this since the boy I'd had a crush on for almost two years asked me to dance at a school disco when I was seventeen.

'Hey,' Noah said softly. 'D'you want to go on somewhere else?'

I did, but I also didn't want to be one of those women who

wasted the best years of her life waiting for a man who would never leave his wife. I deserved better than that. Reluctantly, I pulled my hand back. 'It would have been nice, but it's late. I should go.'

'Of course. You're right,' he agreed, his face falling. 'Will I see you again?' he asked forlornly, when I hooked my bag over my shoulder and stood to go.

'Absolutely,' I said. 'When I'm next looking for a job, you'll be the first person I call.'

'I didn't mean it like that.'

I gave him a twisted smile. 'I know you didn't.'

I could feel his eyes boring into my back as I walked out of the pub with my head held high. I didn't want the evening to end but I knew I was doing the right thing. He was married; therefore, he was out of bounds.

The next day, Noah sent me a huge bouquet of exquisite blush-pink roses. The day after that, a book of love poems by Elizabeth Barrett Browning arrived. On the third day, Noah turned up on my doorstep with tickets for Vivaldi's 'Four Seasons' at the Royal Albert Hall.

'Will you come?' he asked, so hopefully that all my good intentions crashed and burned.

'Oh, all right then. You only live once.' I grinned. 'Wait there, I'll grab my jacket.'

The concert was sweeping and emotional, and the music was still pounding through me when Noah suggested we grab something to eat.

He took me to a smoky jazz club in Soho where we drank tequila and ate buttery garlic prawns and spicy chicken wings. We fell out of the club just after midnight, and Noah flagged down a black cab.

'Where to?' asked the driver as we tumbled inside. I locked eyes with Noah, seeing my own desire mirrored back at me.

'Eve?' he asked softly. I gave a tiny nod.

'Kingsbridge Terrace, Hackney,' he instructed the driver.

As the cab trundled along the empty London streets towards Noah's flat, I realized with a jolt that I was falling for this cute, clever guy who had opened his heart to me and then swept me off my feet.

Although I never meant to fall in love with someone else's husband, I think I knew even then that he would change my life forever.

14

If the tabloids are to be believed, affairs are always 'grubby', 'sleazy' or 'sordid'. Ours wasn't. Looking back, it was the happiest time of my life, despite the gnawing guilt that never quite left me.

During the week I had Noah all to myself. His tiny, rented flat in Hackney was much closer to my new school than my shared flat in Wood Green, so it made sense for me to move in with him. We quickly settled into a routine, cooking together before snuggling up on the sofa with a bottle of wine and a DVD. It was all too easy to pretend we were like any other married couple, and so I did.

Every night at seven on the dot, Noah phoned Billy, but far from minding, I loved the fact that nothing got in the way of Noah talking to his son. He was a good dad. A good man. He and Jenny rarely spoke – in my presence, at least. When they did, their exchanges were about practical, mundane matters. Had Noah remembered the car's MOT and service were due, and could he ring the plumber because the pilot light on the boiler was playing up again.

On Fridays, Noah would leave London before I was home

from work to avoid the worst of the rush-hour traffic and be back in Essex in time for Billy's bath and bedtime.

Time played tricks on me. Weekdays flashed by as if on fast-forward, but the clocks seemed to stop during the long, lonely weekends when I moped around the flat feeling sorry for myself as I pictured Noah, Jenny and Billy on wholesome country walks, or enjoying cosy pub lunches. I filled the time marking and lesson-planning, but I was always counting down the hours till nine o'clock on a Sunday night, when I would hear Noah's key in the lock and my life would be complete again.

There were times when guilt overwhelmed me and I considered ending our affair. My friends didn't help; they told me I was mad, that Noah would never fully commit to me, and even if he did, how could I ever trust a man with a track record of cheating? Although their warnings left me uneasy about our future, I did nothing. Because I loved Noah and I knew he loved me. We were meant to be together; it was as simple as that.

* * *

We were curled up on the sofa watching *Pride and Prejudice* one Thursday night when the doorbell rang. Assuming it was the takeaway I'd ordered earlier, I hit the pause button on the remote control, picked up my purse and ran downstairs. But the furious-looking woman standing on the doorstep clearly wasn't from the restaurant down the road.

'I knew it,' she hissed. 'Where is he?' Not waiting for an answer, she pushed past me and stomped up the stairs. I stared at her back, fear catching my breath. I'd never met Jenny, never even seen a photo of her, but this woman's hair was the same shade of strawberry blonde as Billy's.

Shit. *Shit.*

For a moment I stood clutching the door handle and gazing

up at the stairwell, wondering what the hell I should do. Stay or go? Face the music, or leave them to it?

'Takeaway for Griffiths?' a voice trilled behind me and I gasped in shock, my hand flying to my chest, but it was only the delivery guy brandishing a white carrier bag containing our dinner. 'Sorry, madam, I didn't mean to make you jump,' he said, his smile replaced by a look of concern.

'It's fine,' I reassured him, taking a twenty-pound note from my purse. 'Please, keep the change.'

He nodded his thanks, turned on his heels and disappeared down the street, and suddenly I was on my own again, the handle of the plastic bag biting into my fingers, and an aromatic, spicy smell wafting through the hallway. Reluctantly, I headed back up the stairs, the sound of raised voices growing louder with every step.

The door to the flat was closed, and for one toe-curling moment, I thought I might have to knock to be let in, but then I remembered I'd left it on the latch and pushed it open. Noah and Jenny were in the living room and even though there was another closed door between us I could hear every word of their argument.

'How *could* you? How could you do this to me... to *Billy*?' Jenny screeched.

Noah's voice was low, measured, like he was trying to talk a suicidal person down from a cliff edge. 'Calm down, Jen. Please.'

'Don't you tell me to calm down, you... you *bastard*! Who is she? How long has it been going on?'

I held my breath, preparing myself for Noah to say, 'It's not what you think. It was a mistake. *She* was a mistake. It's you I love. You and Billy. Of course I'll end it. She means nothing to me.'

But he didn't.

'Her name is Eve. We met through work.'

'When?' The question spat out like a bullet.

'Easter,' Noah said.

'*Easter?*' Jenny spluttered. 'Six months ago? And when exactly were you going to tell me?'

Noah cleared his throat. 'I've been waiting for the right moment.'

'The right moment? Don't make me laugh. You're a walking bloody cliché, Noah Griffiths. You've been caught with your pants down. That's the only reason you're admitting to this... this *affair*.'

'C'mon, Jen, you have to admit things haven't been right between us for a long time.'

'Things haven't been right because you're never at home! But I put up with it because I thought you were building the business for our family.' She gave a short bark of laughter. 'More fool me.'

'I never set out to hurt you, Jen. I'm so sorry you had to find out like this. I should've had the balls to tell you sooner.' Noah paused, and on the other side of the living room door, I held my breath. 'We need to talk about what happens next and how it affects Billy,' he said.

'Don't you dare drag Billy into this! It's going to break his heart. If you think I'm going to give my life up without a fight, you've got another think coming.'

The door crashed open and Jenny stormed out, coming to a stop when she saw me hovering in the hallway. Her face was blotchy, mascara tracking down her cheeks, but as she looked me up and down, her lips curled in a sneer.

'Eve, isn't it?'

I nodded, shame blooming in the pit of my stomach. I'd always managed to justify my relationship with Noah because he'd assured me his marriage was over before we met. I stared at the threadbare carpet, eaten up with remorse. Noah may have thought his marriage was over, but it was clear Jenny didn't agree.

'I hope you're proud of yourself.'

'I... I never wanted to—'

'Cut the crap. I'm not interested,' Jenny snapped. 'I just hope that one day you get to know what betrayal feels like.'

Her words felt like a curse, and the hairs on the back of my neck prickled with unease. I wasn't Jenny, I told myself. Noah would never cheat on me.

Seventeen years later, her words have come back to haunt me.

15

I can't settle to anything. I have a pile of ironing I could be tackling, exam papers I should be marking, but all I can think about is Noah's phone call. It replays over and over in my head.

It's only a matter of time before she finds out... I want to tell her myself... Just give me a few more days...

If I'm right, Noah is planning to leave me. I feel blindsided. It is beyond my comprehension. There have been no unexplained absences, no furtive texting, no whiffs of perfume on his collar. He hasn't joined a gym or started running. He hasn't bought a load of new clothes or been emotionally distant. A couple of weeks ago we were planning an Easter break to the Yorkshire Dales, for God's sake. Yes, he's seemed a bit more stressed about work than usual, but otherwise he's been his normal self, bringing me a cup of tea in the morning and massaging my feet while we watch TV after dinner.

I must have caught the wrong end of the stick. That's the logical explanation. Perhaps Noah was talking about someone he works with. Then I remember him mentioning my name. *Eve's going to be back any minute.* The look of guilt on his face when I asked him if he had anything else he wanted to tell me.

Any hopes I was holding onto that I might have misunderstood fade away.

I long to ring Lisa, to summon her over for an emergency summit to unpick what I've heard, just as I have for every big life event over the last sixteen years. She's been there through thick and thin, commiserating, championing, supporting. She was the one who encouraged me to go for the job at Annie's school and spent money she could ill afford on a bottle of bubbly when I was offered the role. She drove us to accident and emergency when Joe broke his wrist on the trampoline because Noah was away at a conference. She plied me with tea and tissues when I miscarried a couple of months after Joe's fourth birthday.

And it worked both ways. I was there for Lisa when doctors confirmed Craig's cancer had spread to his bones. I helped her organise his funeral and minded Annie when she was at work, plucking turkeys and picking apples.

I can't call Lisa to tell her I think my husband is having an affair because she's at the hospital with Annie, who is in a coma after taking ecstasy in our house.

What a mess.

I sit at the kitchen island, my hands clasped round a cold mug of tea, wondering if four o'clock is too early for a glass of wine. The house is quiet, the only sound the soft hum of the fridge. Joe's still out with his mates and Noah's at the meeting he couldn't possibly miss. *Yeah, right,* I think.

Normally, I love having the house to myself. The empty rooms, the solitary quietude, is the perfect antidote to the hurly-burly of a secondary school where there's never a moment's peace. This afternoon the silence is heavy, almost suffocating. A glimpse into my future, perhaps, when Noah's left me for his mistress and Joe's at university. The thought sends a shiver down my spine.

Wanting a distraction, I grab my phone. I can hardly call

Lisa to share my woes, but I can ask her how Annie is. I let out a sigh of frustration when, yet again, the call goes straight to voicemail.

'Lisa, love. It's me, Eve. I wondered how Annie's doing. The hospital won't tell me because I'm not family, but I *feel* like family.' Aware my voice has started to wobble, I pause, trying to compose myself. Dealing with a hysterical friend is the last thing Lisa needs right now. I clear my throat. 'I'm so worried about her. Call me when you get a chance, please?'

I drum my fingers on the worktop, thinking, then slide off the stool and make my way to Noah's study. He uses a MacBook Air for work but has kept his ancient desktop computer for emergencies. He uses the same password for everything: my name followed by the dates of Joe and Billy's birthdays. I've told him countless times he'll be hacked one day. Today I'm glad my warnings fell on deaf ears.

The computer takes an age to fire up, and when it finally does, I navigate my way to the Google Calendar app.

I click through the last couple of weeks. Nothing sticks out among the various meetings, appraisals and Zoom calls. Then something catches my eye. A whole afternoon has been cleared, with no explanation. I check the date. It was last Monday.

I go back further. Every couple of weeks random afternoons have been blocked out with no reason given. I remember Noah telling me once that everyone in his office had read-only access to his schedule, but only his office manager, Bernice, had access to edit it. My breathing quickens. What exactly was he trying to hide from his team?

I consider calling Bernice to ask if she knows, but I quickly dismiss the idea. In her early sixties, short and dumpy with a helmet of frizzy grey hair, Bernice has never liked me. I'm sure she holds me responsible for breaking up Noah's first marriage.

Instead, I click back to the end of last year. The mystery afternoons appear to start at the beginning of December. I cast my mind back, trying to recall a shift in Noah's demeanour that might suggest he was having an affair, but nothing springs to mind.

Wait, there was one thing. Noah flipped out when I told him I'd bought Joe a new laptop for Christmas. Completely lost it. We didn't speak for almost a week. It was totally out of character – Noah's the most generous person I know – and at the time his reaction baffled me. Now, though, everything is dropping into place. He must have earmarked the money for his new life with his mistress.

The front door slams, making me jump. I click away from Noah's calendar guiltily, like I'm the one who's taken a lover. I dart into the kitchen, grab my mug and jump onto the nearest stool. Moments later, Joe troops in and makes a beeline for the fridge without saying a word. He takes out a carton of milk and pulls a pint glass from a cupboard.

I feel a surge of irritation. What's the point of sending your son to the best school in the county if he can't even grunt a simple greeting? It's like I'm invisible. I think of the brand-new iPhone and the hideously expensive Nike football boots I lovingly gift-wrapped and presented him with before breakfast. The A level papers I'll spend the summer holidays marking to pay for his school trip to China. The three sirloin steaks from the farm shop resting in the fridge that I bought specially for our dinner as they're his favourite. The endless hours I've spent cooking and cleaning and ferrying him around and he can't even say a sodding hello. Something inside me snaps and I set my mug down on the granite work surface with a satisfying thwack.

'Hello, Joe, nice to see you too,' I say, my voice oozing sarcasm.

He stops halfway through pouring milk into the glass and looks up, confused. 'What?'

'A "Hi, Mum, how're you doing?" would be nice every now and then,' I gripe.

He looks a little sheepish. 'Sorry, I was in my own little world. How *are* you doing?' he asks with the impish grin he's been employing to win me over since he was about three.

Half of me wants to tell him the truth, to put the cat well and truly among the pigeons. 'Well, it looks like your father's taken a lover and is probably planning our divorce as we speak. Bet you wished you'd never asked.' But the other half, the half that has been hardwired to protect Joe from all life's woes from the day he was born, stops me.

'I'm fine,' I say eventually. 'Worried about Annie, of course, but otherwise fine.'

Joe smiles uncertainly and looks down at his hand, which is still mid-air. He waves the milk carton at my mug. 'Would you like another cup of tea?'

'I would, thank you, darling,' I say, my earlier irritation fading like old newsprint left out in the sun. Perhaps Elmwood Manor is worth the money after all. I watch Joe as he refills the kettle and pops a teabag into a clean mug. He's already taller than Noah by an inch. He's broader too, his jaw squarer and his eyes greener. He has my full lips and twenty-twenty vision. No glasses for Joe. It's as if he has inherited the best bits of us both. A happy marriage of genes. I let out a long sigh.

'What's up?' Joe asks. It appears he's switched from total indifference to an almost forensic interest in my feelings, and for a minute, I'm thrown. Teenagers are like that, I think. A mass of contradictions. One minute they're announcing they're their own person; the next, they're bowing to peer pressure. Craving independence while relying on their parents for everything. Playing the class clown in front of their friends while battling insecurity behind closed doors. Demanding to be treated as adults, while acting out like toddlers.

They think they know everything, when actually they know nothing.

I force myself to smile. It's best all round that Joe continues to know nothing. 'Oh, I'm fine, honestly. Did you have a good game?'

'Nah. No one was about.'

'So how have you been spending your birthday?' I ask, puzzled. It's almost five now and he's been gone since lunchtime.

'I caught the bus into Nesborough.'

'I'd have given you a lift if you'd asked.'

'I didn't need a lift. I caught the bus,' he says patiently.

'That's nice,' I say, when what I really want to ask is, 'What exactly were you doing in Nesborough all afternoon?'

When I was sixteen and went into town with my mates, we trailed around H&M, Miss Selfridge and Topshop, splurging our allowances on tight skirts and tiny tops, before hanging around outside McDonald's checking out the local talent. I don't think Joe has a girlfriend – or boyfriend, for that matter – and he hates clothes shopping with a passion, preferring to order stuff online.

Today he is dressed in his normal black tee, dark-grey hoodie and black baggy cargo trousers. All the boys look the same; the streetwear they favour almost a uniform, which is disconcerting because they could just as easily be Benedict from Elmwood Manor, or Jayden from Nesborough Comp. It's only by their accents that you can tell them apart. That and their shoes. Noah says it's like the law of diminishing returns – the poorer you are, the more expensive your trainers.

Without thinking, I glance down at Joe's feet. I don't recognise the black, red and white trainers he's wearing.

'New shoes?' I ask.

He fishes the teabag out of my mug, his back turned towards

me. 'Um, yeah, I bought them this afternoon, actually. Used the rest of my allowance and the birthday money Gran gave me.'

'Very swish,' I say, then grimace, because no sixteen-year-old wants to be told their new trainers are 'swish'. It's far too cringe.

'Thanks,' Joe says, handing me my tea. 'What time's dinner?'

'About seven.'

He nods, takes his pint of milk and four chocolate digestives and heads upstairs, leaving me alone with my thoughts once again.

16

I'm chopping cherry tomatoes for a salad, a third of the way down my second glass of wine, when I hear music coming from the churchyard next to the house. For a moment, it throws me. We sometimes catch strains of choral music but choir practice is on a Thursday night. This, if I'm not mistaken, isn't 'Abide with Me'; it's 'Fix You' by Coldplay.

When my mother first saw The Old Vicarage she'd actually shuddered. 'You're so close to the church!'

'The clue's in the name,' I replied, through gritted teeth. The ivy-clad house was a Victorian dream with light, spacious rooms, ornate fireplaces, elegant tiled floors and a large, mature garden. Yes, it cost a king's ransom to heat, and we probably didn't need five bedrooms, but we'd fallen in love with it the moment we saw it. Noah's father had recently died, and as Noah was an only child and his mum had passed away a decade earlier, he inherited the family home in Epping. By selling that and using the proceeds from our two-bed terrace in London as a sizeable deposit, we were able to buy The Old Vicarage.

'I don't think I could live so near all those dead people,' my mother added, peering over the thick stone wall at the far end of the garden into the churchyard beyond.

'At least we know the neighbours are quiet,' Noah had joked, while I quietly raged. My mother was the type to be impressed by characterless new-builds with triple glazing and built-in wardrobes. It shouldn't have come as a surprise.

The Old Vicarage was cold and draughty, and everything needed ripping out and replacing, from the kitchen to all three bathrooms. It was, as my father helpfully pointed out, a complete money pit. But I loved the fact that I could see the church tower from the kitchen window. Being woken by the church bells at eight o'clock on a Sunday morning was a small price to pay.

Breathing life back into The Old Vicarage was a labour of love, but sixteen years on, we have the house exactly as we want it. It is my forever home.

I drop the knife onto the chopping board and cross the room to the patio doors, pull them open an inch and listen. Yes, it's definitely Coldplay. I slip on my Crocs and step outside. The chill of the evening catches me by surprise and I wrap my cardigan tightly around me. The music sounds tinny, as if it's being played on an old transistor radio, and an octave below Chris Martin's familiar baritone is the low murmur of voices. I reach the wall and gaze through the gloom into the churchyard, wondering what's going on. It's not until I see the line of flickering flames snaking along the path that leads to the church that the penny drops. It must be Annie's vigil.

'Fix You' draws to a close. Someone coughs. A wood pigeon coos. Then a voice I recognise begins to speak. Siobhan. She must have organised the vigil, which is ironic, because although I've always got on with her, Lisa thinks she's an insufferable gossip.

I crane my neck but can only catch the odd word from this

distance. A need to know exactly what she's saying is too irre-sistible to ignore. Noah may have warned me not to go anywhere near the vigil in case my presence inflamed the situa-tion, but he is a liar and a cheat, and he can go to hell. Besides, if Lisa is there, I might be able to find out how Annie is. I slither over the wall, landing silently on the soft ground on the other side, and pick my way through the moss-covered gravestones, drawn like a moth to the lights of the candles.

Around thirty people have gathered around a headstone east of the nave. Craig's headstone, I realise with a jolt. I scan the crowd quickly, looking for my best friend, but I can't see her. I recognise half a dozen mums from Joe's primary school and a handful of older villagers. The vicar is there, which is also ironic, as Lisa isn't the least bit religious. The only reason Craig had a church funeral was because his elderly parents were members of the congregation. The rest are teenagers Joe and Annie's age. I've known these kids since they were chubby-faced toddlers, tottering out of pre-school clutching finger puppets and bubble paintings. Now the boys have flat-tops and bum-fluff, the girls fake eyelashes and attitude.

'Thank you, everyone, for coming here this evening to show your love and support for Annie Bradstock at this difficult time,' Siobhan is saying, her voice ringing with sincerity. 'As you all know, Annie is fighting for her life in hospital with her mum Lisa by her side...'

Craig's headstone still looks obscenely pristine, the cream Portland stone yet to be softened by a green wash of lichen. It's almost ten years since we buried his cancer-ravaged body. Ten years since Lisa had to become both mother and father to Annie. Her future was ripped from her then, and now it is happening again. I'm hit by a wave of compassion for my friend, coupled with a feeling of helplessness, because there is nothing I can do to make things better.

'... and now I will hand over to the Reverend Patsy Dutton to say a few words,' Siobhan says solemnly.

The Reverend Dutton is a buxom, rosy-cheeked woman who looks more like a farmer's wife than a vicar. This evening her face is pale and careworn.

'I'm sure you'll all want to join me in sending our love and prayers to Annie and wishing her a speedy recovery,' she begins, and I want to step out of the shadows and ask her how she can begin to justify what's happened to Annie as God's will, because what kind of god allows such bad things to happen to good people?

It seems as though I'm not the only one to think this, because as she urges everyone to join her in the Lord's Prayer, it's clear the teenagers are getting bored. A couple even pull out their phones and start scrolling.

The vicar pauses until she has everyone's attention, a trick I learnt in my first term as a newly-qualified teacher, then she holds her candle aloft. 'Let each flame we have lit tonight represent a beacon of hope and healing for Annie. Together, may our lights shine brightly and lead her back to us. Amen.'

As everyone mutters 'Amen', my eyes sting with tears. The sentiment feels clichéd, but is this the reality for Annie, lying unconscious in intensive care? Does she feel as though she's trapped in a darkened room, unable to find her way out until someone opens the door?

The vigil is drawing to a close. The vicar thanks everyone for coming, then the opening chords of 'Angels' by Robbie Williams waft through the air. This... this... ritual, for want of a better word, may have zero impact on Annie's recovery, but at least the people here care, and that has to count for something.

The song ends. The vicar announces that the church will be open for the rest of the evening for prayer and contemplation, before disappearing through the huge oak doors. It's a cue to leave, and people start to wander out of the churchyard.

That's the moment my phone rings, the theme tune to *Mission Impossible* slicing through the dark night like a newly sharpened carving knife. My face burns with shame as the toe-curling horror of my situation sinks in.

Everyone is going to know I'm here.

17

I pull my phone from my back pocket and fumble with the volume, but it's too late.

'Look,' a girl cries, pointing at me. 'Isn't that Joe Griffiths's mum?'

'What the hell's she doing here?' a woman says.

I sense rather than see people turning towards me. Shit. *Shit.*

'Oi,' says a boy I recognise. It's Connor Moody, one of the kids at Joe's party. 'You 'eard the lady. What d'you think you're doin' 'ere?'

My throat is threatening to close over but I force myself to speak. 'I've come to pay my respects, just like the rest of you.'

'"Pay your respects"?' he repeats. 'Why? Annie 'ain't *dead.*' He glances behind him, like he's seeking approval from the others. A woman nods.

'I mean to show my support,' I say, but it's too late. The mood has shifted from curiosity to suspicion and a couple of the teenage boys inch closer.

'That's rich,' the woman says. 'If it wasn't for you and your son we wouldn't be here at all.' She is in her forties and overweight, her greasy hair scraped back in a ponytail. She's dressed in a baggy grey sweatshirt and skin-pink leggings that on first glance give the impression she is wearing nothing from the waist down. I rack my brain, trying to place her. Then I remember. Of course, she's Connor's mother, Lorraine. She used to stand outside the school gates at pick-up because she couldn't smoke on school property.

'I don't think that's fair—' I begin, but she cuts across me.

'You're right, it's not fair,' she says, taking a step forward. She's so close I can smell the vinegar on her breath. I notice she's clutching a small teddy to her breast. Was she planning to leave it on Craig's grave? 'Annie's a lovely girl. She used to babysit for our Bobbi-Jo. Now she's on life support, thanks to your son.'

I glance around, looking for a friendly face, a voice of reason. They can't all blame Joe for what happened. He didn't give Annie the ecstasy, so why's it suddenly his fault? Unless... unless one of the other kids at the party is spreading rumours to deflect the heat from themselves. It would make sense, though right now my main concern isn't who's behind the rumours, it's the mob of scowling faces in front of me.

I need to de-escalate this, and fast. I take a deep breath. 'I get that if Joe hadn't had a party none of this would have happened, but you really can't go around saying it's his fault. He hasn't done anything wrong.'

Lorraine looks to her son for help. 'He told you that, did he?' Connor scoffs.

'He's a lying twat,' someone else says. A couple of the girls snigger. My chest tightens. I feel trapped, pinned against a wall by their contempt, even though logically I know I can turn around and walk out of the churchyard whenever I choose.

I search the faces for Siobhan. She is standing to the right of the group, her arms crossed. Is that a trace of a smile on her face? I send her a pleading look, which she ignores.

Lorraine, it appears, is just getting warmed up. 'I think you should leave. We don't want you here.' There are grunts of approval. I swear I hear one of the older women mutter, 'Bloody Londoners.'

'I understand you're upset, but comments like that won't help anyone, certainly not Annie,' I say. I've slipped into full-on teacher mode, talking with precision as if I'm explaining a basic equation to a witless twelve-year-old. It will probably antagonise them, but, frankly, I'm past caring. 'I have as much right to be here as you. Like it or not, I live here. Have done for the last sixteen years, in fact.'

'Is she for real?' a girl with bleached-blonde hair asks, to more laughter. They have formed a semicircle in front of me now, their faces lit by the candles they're holding, the shadowy church towering behind them. It's like a scene from a low-budget horror film. Vampiric villagers turning on the newcomer. The candles are those fake LED ones with the imitation flames. A fitting metaphor for this whole ridiculous pantomime.

I'm sure these people, with their candles and their teddies and their earnest expressions, think they care. They don't, not really. They are here for their own benefit, not Lisa's, not even Annie's. Saccharine speeches and sappy songs won't pull Annie from her coma, nor will they help Lisa pay her rent.

I used to listen to Connor read when he was in Year 3. He had a slight stutter and was always so eager to please. Now he looks like the kind of sallow-faced youth you'd cross the street to avoid. If anyone knew how to get their hands on a stash of Es, it would be Connor, not Joe. Why's no one pointing the finger of suspicion at him? Or any of the other teenagers?

A man breaks rank. Late forties, a determined chin and wide-set grey eyes. Greg Duffy, the manager of Joe's rugby team. 'Come on, folks,' he says with a quiet authority that grabs everyone's attention. 'Let's not let this get out of hand. We're all here for Annie at the end of the day. Am I right?'

A couple of villagers murmur their assent. It seems to be a cue to leave as they begin to drift towards the road until it's just Greg and me left.

'Thank you,' I say.

'Anytime.' His mouth twitches. 'I could tell a few of them were getting restless.' Like us, Greg and his wife Chrissy are viewed as newcomers, having moved to the biggest house on South Langley's small estate of executive homes about ten years ago. Greg runs his own plumbing firm and does very nicely out of it, judging by the family's designer clothes, holidays to Cancun and Dubai and the Range Rover Sport and Mini Cooper on the driveway.

'It's my own fault. Noah warned me not to come.'

He stuffs his hands into the pockets of his box-fresh navy Musto padded jacket. 'I probably owe Noah an apology. I gave him a hard time at rugby yesterday.'

'He told me.'

'I was upset. We all were. Annie's a good kid.'

'You don't have to tell me that,' I reply hotly. 'That's what makes me so angry.' I point at the last few stragglers filing out of the churchyard. 'This lot have the nerve to ask what I'm doing here, but they hardly know her! I held her in my arms when she was a few hours old.' I pause, trying to collect myself. 'I looked after her when Lisa was at the hospice with Craig. I love her like my own daughter. I would never, *ever*, let her come to harm.'

'And yet she did,' Greg points out.

I flush. He's right. I had a duty of care to make sure everyone was safe under our roof, and I failed. But that doesn't make Joe or me culpable. I have to hang on to that.

'It could have been any one of those kids who gave Annie

the E,' I say, momentarily forgetting Greg's own son, Josh, was at the party.

His face tightens, a muscle pulsing in his jaw, and I feel a prickle of disquiet. Greg's a big guy and his bulk looms over me in the empty churchyard. I'm about to make my excuses and head for home when his lips stretch into a sympathetic smile.

'You're right,' he says. 'We shouldn't jump to conclusions before we have all the facts.' He pauses. 'I hear the police questioned Joe this morning.'

'They didn't question him. It was a voluntary interview. They want to talk to everyone at the party. Who told you?'

'Josh heard it from Lottie. Joe must have told her. You know these kids. Never off their damn phones.' Greg jiggles some keys in his pocket. 'I'll see you home.'

His presumptuous tone raises my hackles. 'Thanks.' I force a smile. 'But I'll be fine.'

He shrugs. 'It's your funeral.'

I glare at his retreating back, stunned by his inappropriate remark. I wait until I hear the deep growl of his car's engine before heading home, unsettled by the encounter. Greg's shift from friendly to combative is yet another thing to add to my growing pile of worries. I'm uncertain about so much right now, but two things are clear: we will always bear the blame for what happened to Annie, and we are no longer welcome in this village.

18

Noah still isn't home when I let myself in the front door. It's only as I'm fishing my phone from my pocket that I remember the missed call in the churchyard. I'd been so focused on turning the damn thing off that I hadn't seen who was calling.

I'm assuming it was Noah feeding me some excuse as to why he's so late, so I'm surprised to see it was my mother.

'Everything all right?' I ask when I phone her back.

'Of course everything's all right. Why wouldn't it be?'

'Because you don't normally phone me on my mobile.'

'Well, no one was answering the house phone,' she says peevishly. I glance across to the answerphone. The little red light is flashing.

'Sorry, I popped out, and Joe can't have heard it ringing.'

'I wanted to wish him a happy birthday. Did he get my card? I sent it first class, but that's no guarantee these days.' She tuts.

The knots in my neck ease a fraction. It's a relief to be thinking about birthdays and the vagaries of the postal system. Normal, routine things.

'It arrived yesterday. He bought himself some fancy trainers with the money you gave him,' I tell her as I head up the stairs to Joe's bedroom at the back of the house.

'I'd like to have given him more, but everything's so expensive these days.'

'Don't be silly. You're always very generous.' I knock gently on Joe's door and let myself into his room. He's ensconced in his gaming chair playing *Grand Theft Auto* on his Xbox, headphones on. I walk in front of the monitor and wave the phone at him. He pauses the game and takes off his headphones, colour draining from his face.

'Is it Lisa?' he mumbles.

'No, it's Gran. She wants to wish you a happy birthday.' I hand him the phone, mouthing, 'Don't forget to thank her for the birthday money,' and leave him to it.

Back downstairs, I pour myself another glass of wine and busy myself laying the table and switching the oven on for the chips. Most evenings, we eat on our laps in front of the TV, but birthdays are special and we always eat at the table.

The front door clicks open, and there's a clatter as Noah drops his car keys onto the walnut console table in the hallway.

'I'm sorry I'm late,' he calls. The door to the cupboard under the stairs opens and closes. 'The meeting ran over, then I had a couple of CVs I had to prep for the morning.' I steel myself as he appears, his tie in one hand and his laptop bag in the other. He dumps them both on the kitchen island, then picks up the wine bottle and raises an eyebrow. 'Started without me, I see.'

How dare he judge me for having a couple of glasses of wine with everything that's going on?

'I had no idea when you'd be home,' I say defensively.

He holds up a hand. 'No need to jump down my throat. I was joking.' He reaches into the fridge for a bottle of beer, unscrews the top and takes a long draught. 'Where's the birthday boy?'

'Upstairs, talking to his grandmother.'

Noah nods. I take a bag of chips out of the freezer and arrange them on a baking sheet.

'Want me to do the steaks?' he asks. It's been his job ever since I nuked two Wagyu sirloin steaks the first time I cooked for him.

'Please,' I say.

He takes the steaks out of their greaseproof wrapper and seasons them while I finish making the salad I abandoned earlier. It's a dance, I think, as we move around the kitchen in sync, our choreography perfected over almost two decades of married life. It's comfortable and familiar. Instinctive. Would Noah risk this easy intimacy for a bit on the side? And if so, who will cook the steaks when he has gone?

'I went to the vigil,' I say.

He looks up from the skillet, his expression wary.

'Before you say anything, I'm glad I did. I spoke to Greg Duffy. He feels bad about the way he spoke to you on Sunday.'

'I should bloody well think so. He was totally out of order.' Noah drops the steaks onto the skillet and it hisses angrily. 'Was Lisa there?'

'No.'

'Have you heard how Annie's doing?'

I shake my head. 'Lisa's still not returning my calls.' Being ghosted by my best friend is almost as hard to stomach as the probability my husband is having an affair. When Joe and Annie were small, Lisa and I were inseparable. Even when I went back to work full time we were always texting or sending silly memes or voice notes to each other. This wall of silence breaks my heart.

Noah flips the steaks and I check on the chips and carry the salad over to the table. Joe appears and hands me my phone. I look to see if Lisa has called. She hasn't. Joe pours himself a Coke.

'How long's tea?'

'Five minutes,' Noah says. 'If you can wait that long.' He reaches out to ruffle Joe's hair.

'Oi, gerroff, old man!' Joe ducks out of the way, laughing.

'Less of the old, thank you,' Noah retorts, holding his fists up, boxer-style. 'I could bring you down any day of the week.'

'You reckon?' Joe says, mirroring him. They dance around each other like two heavyweights in the ring. Normally I'd be smiling indulgently at their antics, but tonight it feels forced, as though they're putting on a show. How can they be larking about when our life is unravelling?

'Shall we eat?' I snap, and they exchange a look, and I can see what they're thinking – *who's rattled her cage?* – and it only adds to my irritation.

I know I'm putting a damper on Joe's birthday but I have neither the energy nor the inclination for small talk, so I eat in silence as they chat about the latest upset in the Premier League and England's much-anticipated match in the Six Nations Cup this weekend. Noah has cooked the steaks to perfection and my knife slides through mine like butter, but I'm so wound up that it tastes like cardboard. I take a perverse pleasure in leaving half of it untouched at the side of my plate.

'Don't you want that?' Joe asks.

'You can have it,' I tell him, and he whoops with delight, just as he used to do when he was little and I saved the last roast potato for him.

I push back my chair and begin to clear the table.

'Is it time for cake?' he asks hopefully, setting his knife and fork on his plate.

I've made a cake for Joe's birthday every year since he was born. A huge, five-egg chocolate sponge covered in chocolate fudge icing. I have all the ingredients in our walk-in larder. This year, I even ordered personalised bunting to put on top of the cake. 'Happy Birthday Joe' in blue and silver to match the balloons. In all the stress of the last few days, I have completely forgotten to make the damn thing.

'God, Joe, I'm so sorry, but I haven't had time to make one. I'll do it tomorrow, I promise.'

'It's OK, Mum, you don't need to apologise. I saw some ice cream in the freezer. Anyone else want some?'

He stands, piles my plate on top of his and carries them to the dishwasher. He is a walking dichotomy, I think, watching his biceps flex as he stacks the plates. One minute as excited as a five-year-old at the thought of chocolate cake, the next displaying a maturity beyond his years.

I should be charmed by this flip-flopping between child and adult, but I am not. I find it deeply unsettling. It makes me think I don't know him at all, which tears me apart. If my son is a stranger and my husband is a liar, where does that leave me?

19

When I wake the next morning, the first thing I do is reach for my phone to see if Lisa has made contact. There's no text, no WhatsApp message, no voice note. Nothing.

Noah's side of the bed is empty again, and when I cross the room to the window and check the driveway, I'm unsurprised to see his car has already gone. Has he left early so he can visit his lover before work? The possibility sends a bolt of pain through my heart. I suppose I should confront him, but with everything going on, I just don't have it in me. Instead, I slump on the end of the bed with my head in my hands waiting for the feeling to subside. When it eventually does, I'm left with an aching emptiness.

'Oh, Noah,' I whisper to the silent room. 'Wasn't I enough for you?'

After I've forced myself to shower and dress, I poke my head around Joe's bedroom door. He's lying on his front, his face squashed against his pillow and one leg dangling over the side of his bed, fast asleep. I pick up a dirty T-shirt and a couple of pairs of pants from the floor and close the door softly behind me.

Downstairs, I make coffee and nibble on a piece of toast as I check my emails. One from my boss, Emma Bradley, catches my eye and when I see the header my stomach lurches.

Urgent: Annie Bradstock

My fingers trembling, I start to read.

Eve,

It has come to my attention that one of our Year 11 students, Annie Bradstock, has been admitted to hospital following a suspected ecstasy overdose after attending a house party at your home on Saturday night.

I have spoken to both Annie's mother and the police, and although I am assured a police investigation is underway to establish the circumstances of the incident, it would be most helpful if we could meet as soon as possible to discuss what happened.

It goes without saying that Annie's health and well-being are my priority, and I am fully committed to supporting Annie and her mother through this difficult time, but I must also address the potential impact this incident may have on the school's reputation. I am sure you will agree that it is imperative we handle the situation with the utmost sensitivity and transparency.

To that end, I am in the process of putting together a statement for the media which acknowledges what has happened – and actions we are taking as a result – while emphasising our commitment to the safety and welfare of our students.

I understand that this is a distressing time for everyone
involved, but I cannot stress enough the reputational damage
this incident could inflict on the school if not handled
correctly.

Please let me know at your earliest convenience when we
can arrange a meeting to discuss this matter further.

Best,

Emma
Ms E. Bradley
Headteacher
Nesborough Grammar School for Girls

My phone slides out of my hands and hits the granite coun-
tertop with a clunk. The email is Emma Bradley all over.
Perfectly courteous on the surface, but read between the lines
and it's obvious she's pulling no punches.

The first time I met her, at my interview six years ago, my
initial impression was of a slightly chaotic but kindly head, who
cared deeply about the school and its students. It was a few
months before I understood that underneath that smiling,
bumbling exterior lay a core of steel. Emma is an old-school
authoritarian who expects one hundred and ten per cent
commitment, not just from her students but from her staff too.
She runs a tight ship and woe betide anyone who veers off
course.

Yes, she cares about the children and staff, but she cares
about the reputation of her school more.

I picture her reaction when she was informed one of her
star pupils was in intensive care following a drug overdose.
Then, to discover this whole sorry business happened at the
home of her Head of Maths. She would have been apoplectic.

Sergeant Harrington must have told her about Annie, presumably with Lisa's blessing. I grab my phone and read the email again, allowing the words to sink in. I pause three paragraphs from the end, blood pounding in my ears as I fix on a line I didn't fully take in the first time round.

...actions we are taking as a result...

What does she mean by this? That I'm to be held accountable for the whole sorry incident? Dismissed for gross misconduct, a sacrificial lamb offered to the media on a plate in a cynical attempt to mitigate the fallout?

Maybe I'd do the same if I were in her shoes.

I consider the ramifications. If I lost my job we'd have to pull Joe out of Elmwood Manor, because there's no way we could afford the fees without my salary. He'd have to move to the high school, where he'd probably be bullied for his posh accent. All this just a few months before his exams.

I could look for another job, but according to Harrington, I could be charged with possession if the police think I turned a blind eye to drug use in our house. What if I was convicted and jailed? My teaching career would be over, for a start. How would I, a middle-aged, middle-class white woman, survive prison?

I weigh my phone in the palm of my hand, wondering what to do. Clearly, the sensible course of action would be to reply to Emma and tell her I'm willing to meet at her convenience. Knowing her, she'll have her read receipt enabled and will see I've opened her email. Ignoring it will only inflame the situation.

I could phone Noah and talk it through with him before I respond. He's good in situations like these. I have a tendency to go in all guns blazing whereas he's so skilled at resolving conflict he should be working for the United Nations. A deputy head in a boys' school in Enfield before he started his recruitment agency, he also understands how schools work. He's dealt with head teachers far more terrifying than Emma Bradley.

But I can't summon the energy to reply to Emma right now, and I don't want to ask my husband for help because I'm not sure he's got my back any more.

I make up my mind. I'm not going to reply to the email just yet. I'll go and see Annie instead.

20

I pull into the visitors' car park at Nesborough Hospital, trying to ignore the nerves that flutter like a cloud of agitated bees in the pit of my stomach. The hospital holds mixed emotions for me. The best and the worst of times. The last time I was here was the winter before last when Joe suffered a concussion playing rugby. The first time was when Joe was born. Sixteen years ago, yet it seems like yesterday.

I park the car and sit for a moment, memories of Joe's birth flooding back. Noah was by my side throughout the exhausting and emotional twelve-hour labour. He helped me breathe through the contractions and instinctively knew when I needed a sip of water or my back massaged. When Joe was finally born, red-faced and wailing, it was Noah who cried tears of joy. I was just glad it was over.

It wasn't his first rodeo, of course. Billy had been born by C-section at a big teaching hospital in Essex seven years previously, and Noah looked after him more or less single-handedly while Jenny recovered from the Caesarean. He was just as hands-on with Joe. He may be a crap husband, but he has always been a good dad.

I scoop up the punnet of plump red grapes and the copy of *Hello!* I bought in the supermarket on the way over and head for the main entrance. I know Annie's not in any shape to eat grapes or read a celebrity magazine, but I didn't want to come empty-handed.

The intensive care unit is on the second floor of the sprawling modular building. I take the stairs and follow the signs down a brightly lit corridor with windows that look out onto an overgrown courtyard with a faded mural of a desert island on one wall and a small leafless tree in the centre.

The double doors to the unit are closed. I give them a tentative push, but they don't swing open. There's a buzzer and intercom on the wall to the right. I hesitate. If I press the buzzer and announce I'm here to visit Annie, they'll check with Lisa and probably won't let me in. Maybe I should wait here until Lisa comes out for a coffee or to visit the loo. I'm sure that if I could just talk to her I could make her see I'm here to help.

Just as I'm deliberating what to do, the doors crash open and a woman and man stumble out. She is crying, her eyes slits, tears streaming down her cheeks. His expression is glazed, as if he's just been given the worst news possible. Perhaps he has.

I seize the opportunity and dart through the doors before they swing closed. It's quiet in the unit, the hushed reverence reminding me of a church. The only sounds are the constant bleeps and hums of the machines keeping the sick alive.

I scan the ward looking for Lisa, but she isn't here. Then, in a side room just before the nurses' station, I spot Annie's golden hair fanned on a pillow like she's sleeping on a slice of the sun. I slip in, unnoticed.

'Annie, sweetheart, it's me, Eve,' I whisper, unable to tear my gaze away from her face, which is the same chalky white as the starched sheets.

She is hooked up to monitors and ventilators and heaven knows what else. I pull up the chair beside her bed and take her hand. Her fingers feel cool to the touch. I give them a squeeze, hoping for a response, but there is nothing.

I think of all the times over the years I've felt Annie's small hands in mine. Crossing the road between our house and hers, walking across the wobble boards at the playground on the rec, skipping beside me on the walk home from school on the afternoons Lisa was working. So many precious memories. Annie was the daughter I'd always wanted but never had. A shudder passes through me. Being back in this hospital, the smell of antiseptic and desperation, reminds me of the miscarriage. I have always known in my gut the baby we lost at eleven weeks was a girl, but having Annie in my life eased my grief.

Lacing my fingers with hers, I smooth her hair away from her face with my other hand. I should talk to her, I think. People in comas can often hear, even if they can't see or speak. I clear my throat, feeling a little self-conscious, but it's just the two of us in this small side room. Just us and the bleeping and whirring of the machines.

'I'm so sorry, Annie. So very sorry. I'd do anything to make you better, to turn back the clock. But that's the one thing I can't do, isn't it?' I rub my thumb in circles on the inside of her wrist where the skin is so pale her veins are clearly visible, like rivers on a map.

'If only you could talk to me, tell me what happened.' I picture Annie when I last saw her. No, not when I last saw her, because then she was prone on our kitchen floor, stiff-limbed and shaking. That's an image I would erase from my memory if I could. No, at the beginning of the evening, when she'd skipped out of Lisa's cottage in the green velvet dress she'd made herself, her hair in a plait and a smile on her beautiful, beautiful face.

To think I'd been worried about vomit in the pot plants and beer stains on the sofa. It all seems so trivial now. Perhaps I knew on some subconscious level that something catastrophic was about to happen. Even if I did, I could never in my worst nightmares have imagined something as terrible as this.

I'm so caught up in my thoughts, in the feel of Annie's baby-soft skin against my thumb as it traces round and round, that I don't pay any heed to the squeak of shoes on the lino floor until I sense a shadow looming over me.

I give a start and jerk round. Lisa is standing in the doorway, her eyes flashing with fury. I blanch in the heat of her gaze, dropping Annie's hand onto the bed where it lays as lifeless as a mannequin's.

'Fuck's sake, Eve,' Lisa hisses. 'What the hell are you doing here?'

21

The air between us fizzes with tension. I swallow, smile nervously.

'I just wanted to see her, Lisa.'

'You have no right.' She scoots to the other side of the bed, cups Annie's face in her hand and drops the lightest of kisses on her forehead. 'I'm here, darling. Mummy's here.' She turns back to me, shooting daggers. 'I don't want you here. *We* don't want you here.'

I glance down at Annie. We both know she's in no fit state to have a view on anything, but if Lisa wants to keep up the pretence that she does, I'm not about to argue with her.

'Look, can we go outside and talk?' I say.

Lisa doesn't answer. She's too busy fussing over Annie's sheets even though they're already perfectly straight.

'Lisa, please. Just ten minutes is all I ask.'

Finally, she looks up at me. Purple shadows ring her eyes and her face is gaunt.

'All right,' she says, gruffly. 'Ten minutes.'

We take the lift down to the Costa on the ground floor, and Lisa finds a seat while I take my place in the queue. There are half a dozen people ahead of me: elderly women clutching purses, a young man in a wheelchair with his leg in plaster, a couple of doctors in scrubs. The baristas rattle through the orders, and before long, I'm asking for two flat whites and a couple of slices of lemon drizzle cake because we could probably both do with the sugar hit.

Lisa has found a free table in the furthest corner of the café. It's sticky with coffee rings and spilt sugar, and I place the tray on my chair and wipe it down with a paper napkin before I set out our drinks.

Once I've sat down, I look her in the eye. 'Thank you.'

'For what?'

'For talking to me. I've been so worried. We all have. How is she doing? Do they know how long she's going to be in a coma?' The questions pour out of me like water from a gushing tap.

Lisa shakes her head. 'I'm still waiting to hear from Dr Connolly, her consultant.' She fiddles with her necklace. Craig bought it for her after Annie was born. Three silver hearts on a slender silver chain, one heart for each of them. I've never seen Lisa take it off in all the years I've known her.

'You remember how much she used to love *Sleeping Beauty*?' she says.

'I do,' I say, nodding. 'More than *Frozen* or *Tangled*. Even though it's over sixty years old.'

'She was Annie's age,' Lisa says, and for a moment I wonder who she's talking about. 'Princess Aurora,' she clarifies. 'She pricked her finger on the spindle of a spinning wheel on the day of her sixteenth birthday.'

'You're right, she did.'

'When I was packing Annie's things to bring here, I automatically picked up the book on her bedside table and put it in her bag. *To Kill a Mockingbird*. It's one of the texts she's doing for English literature.' Lisa's voice trembles and she pauses, gathers herself. 'Who was I kidding? She probably can't even breathe for herself. How's she supposed to pick up a book and carry on reading where she left off, let alone sit an English exam?'

'Come on, you mustn't think like that. You've got to stay strong.'

'But what if the doctors say she's brain dead? What then? I can't lose her as well, Eve. I just can't.'

I reach out and take her hand. 'Don't get ahead of yourself. We'll cross that bridge when – *if* – we come to it. Together. You are not on your own.'

She gives me the smallest of smiles. 'Thank you.'

'Don't be silly. Here, have some of this. It'll do you good.' I push the cake towards her but she makes no move to eat it.

'I'm sorry I was such a bitch. I was lashing out.'

'You don't need to apologise.'

'I was so angry. Then Greg said Joe—' She stops, stares into her coffee cup.

'Greg Duffy? What did he say?'

She bites her bottom lip, unable to meet my eye.

'Lisa,' I press. 'What did Greg say about Joe?'

She sighs. 'He texted me the day after the party to say Joe was the one who had the Es. That's why I saw red.'

I stare at her in shock. 'Greg told you Joe gave Annie the ecstasy?'

'Not that he gave it to her, just that he brought some to his party.'

I can feel the anger vibrating inside me, but I try to keep my voice level. 'Why would he say that?'

'I don't know, Eve.' Lisa's voice is weary. 'I'm just telling you what he told me. I didn't want to believe it either, if you must know.' She doesn't have to say it: Joe's like a brother to Annie. When they were little, they were practically joined at the hip. A memory comes to me. A sunny afternoon at the small playground on the rec. Annie and Joe were taking turns whizzing down the slide when a bigger boy pushed Annie out of the way. Before I could stop him, Joe roared in anger and thumped the kid, not caring he was twice Joe's size. When I relayed the incident to Lisa later that day, she high-fived Joe and told him he was a legend.

'Joe's a good kid, Lisa,' I say, a catch in my voice.

'I know.' This time she reaches across and squeezes my hand, and we sit in silence as visitors and hospital staff scurry past.

Eventually, I pick up my coffee and take a sip. 'You know Josh was at our house the night of the party too?'

Her eyes widen a fraction before she says, 'You think Greg's blaming Joe to protect Josh?'

'Makes sense, doesn't it? You've seen the way Josh struts around the village as if he owns the place, just like his father. Wasn't there talk that he started the fire in the bus shelter?'

The small blaze had been spotted by a shift worker returning home in the early hours a couple of weeks before Christmas. Firefighters said if she hadn't called it in, the whole thing would have burnt to a crisp. The subsequent discovery of a dozen metal nitrous oxide canisters scattered on the ground inside the shelter sent the parish council into freefall, and drug use among young people in the village was top of the agenda at the council's first meeting of the new year.

'We should tell the police,' Lisa says. 'There's an officer I've been speaking to. Harrison, I think his name is. I have his card somewhere.'

'Sergeant Dan Harrington,' I tell her. 'He took a statement from Joe at the police station yesterday. He's talking to all the kids.'

'Except Annie,' she says.

I dip my head in acknowledgement. 'I'm sure he'll get to the bottom of it and whoever gave Annie the E will get what they deserve.'

'You really think so?'

'I do.' Harrington doesn't strike me as the type to give up easily. If he doesn't find out who brought class A drugs to Joe's party, I'll make damn sure I do. I owe it to Annie to find out what really happened at our house that night. One thing's for sure, I'm not prepared to sit back and do nothing while the culprit gets away scot-free.

22

I offer to keep Lisa company for a couple of hours and she smiles at me gratefully.

'I'd appreciate that. It can get a bit soul-destroying in here on your own, you know?'

She takes up her position on the chair by Annie's bed, and I find a second chair by the nurses' station and place it on the other side, careful not to disturb any of the machines.

To fill the silence, I tell Lisa about the vigil, describing the candles and the teddies, the music, and the lovely tributes to Annie. I don't mention the way the villagers turned on me, nor how Greg Duffy intervened.

'Did Noah go with you?'

My lips thin. 'He was at work.'

Because Lisa knows me so well, perhaps better than I know myself, she narrows her eyes. 'What's wrong?'

'Nothing.'

'Come on, Eve, you can't fool me. What is it?'

'Really, you've got enough on your plate. You don't need to hear my woes.'

She raises one eyebrow. A silent signal. *Just tell me.*

I swallow hard. I've been desperate to get my suspicions off my chest ever since I overheard Noah's snatched phone call. Who knows, it might even take Lisa's mind off Annie for a while.

'I think Noah's having an affair,' I blurt.

Two things happen. Lisa's neck flushes bright red and one of the nurses gives a polite cough and appears at the end of Annie's bed.

'Lisa,' the nurse says. 'I'm glad to catch you. Dr Connolly is wondering if he could have a word?'

'Why, has something happened?' Lisa squeaks, dropping Annie's hand and jumping to her feet.

'I think it's best if you speak to him.' The nurse glances over her shoulder. 'Ah, here he is now. I'll leave you to it.'

'Do you want me to go?' I ask Lisa.

She shakes her head as a tall man in his early fifties strides into the room.

'Mrs Bradstock,' he says, 'I wanted to give you an update on Annie.' He glances my way as if unsure whether to continue in front of me.

'It's OK,' Lisa says. 'Eve is Annie's godmother. But is there somewhere else we can talk?' The inference is clear. Lisa doesn't want Annie hearing what the consultant has to say.

'Actually—' Dr Connolly stops himself, then opens his arms wide. 'Of course. There's a small visitors' room just along the corridor. We'll go there.'

The visitors' room is sparsely furnished. Just four easy chairs, with wooden frames upholstered in a hard-wearing blue fabric, arranged around a coffee table, on which is a box of tissues. There's a cupboard in the corner with a sink and a kettle, a mug tree and a jar of Nescafé. Someone has hung a series of prints by Claude Monet on the walls and placed a vase of artificial flowers on a shelf above the radiator, but the room still has about as much soul as a dentist's waiting room.

Dr Connolly waits until we've both taken our seats before he settles into his own. Lisa perches on the edge of her chair, her posture tense, as if she might bolt at any moment. I cross my legs and clasp my hands in my lap, attempting to project an air of calm, despite the crashing of my heart and the trickle of sweat sliding slowly down my back.

'As you know, Annie was admitted on Saturday night suffering from the effects of MDMA, or ecstasy,' the consultant begins. 'For people who are admitted with opioid overdoses, such as heroin, methadone or fentanyl, we can give a drug called naloxone, which can reverse an overdose and save someone's life if administered early enough.'

I sense a "but", and it's not long in coming.

'Unfortunately, there are no drugs that reverse the effects of MDMA.'

Lisa is silent.

'So there was nothing you could have given Annie that would have helped?' I ask.

Dr Connolly shakes his head. 'I'm afraid not.' He steeples his fingers. 'I don't know if you are aware, but ecstasy affects the body's temperature control, and when you have ingested the drug, there is a very real danger of overheating or dehydration. That's why people in nightclubs are told to stay hydrated. What is less well known is that drinking too much to mitigate this, whether it's soft drinks or water, can be just as dangerous. You see, ecstasy causes the body to produce a hormone that retains water, and drinking excessive amounts of water dilutes the level of sodium to such a degree that the brain swells, which can put pressure on the brain stem and lead to a coma.'

'Are you saying the reason Annie's in a coma is because she drank too much *water*?' Lisa cries.

Dr Connolly nods. 'That is what I'm saying, yes. I know it's hard to take in, but, essentially, Annie probably thought she was doing the right thing by drinking plenty of fluids after she'd taken the ecstasy.'

I remember the upturned pint glass and puddle of water on the floor by Annie's head. Sweet, sensible Annie had made one bad decision and, in her attempt to rectify it, had ended up in a coma.

'But she's going to be OK, once she comes out of the coma?' Lisa asks.

'I'm afraid only time will tell. Further down the line we will carry out a series of tests to gauge Annie's brain stem functions, but for the moment our priority is to keep her stable and see if the swelling goes down on its own.'

'You mean there's still a chance she'll get better?' I ask.

Dr Connolly nods, his face grave. 'A chance, yes.'

I glance at Lisa, whose face has filled with hope. But, as the consultant sweeps from the room, I can't help wondering what he really thinks her chances are. If the swelling on Annie's brain will leave lasting damage. Whether she will wake up at all.

23

I spend the following morning marking exam papers, but when Joe slouches into the kitchen just after eleven, I jump down from my stool and make him some toast, glad of the distraction.

'How did you sleep?' I ask, handing him a glass of orange juice.

'OK.' He nods his thanks and takes a slurp, wiping his mouth with the back of his hand.

'What are you up to today?'

'Dunno.'

'You could make a start on your revision timetable. I can help if you like.'

'Mum! It's February, and exams aren't till May. I've got three months to do a revision timetable.'

'They'll be here before you know it,' I tell him. 'Some of the girls in my Year 11 maths set started revising in the Christmas holidays.' Including Annie, I remember with a gut-wrenching pang. Annie, who was predicted straight A's in her exams but might never get to sit them because she's lying in a coma in hospital, attached to machines keeping her alive.

Joe scowls. 'I don't care what the girls in your maths set are doing. I'm not starting a revision timetable today. I'm on holiday.' He attacks his toast as if he hasn't eaten for a week, then jumps down from the stool. 'Actually, I think I'm going to head into town.'

'Please yourself,' I say, my lips pursed. He drops his plate in the sink and stalks out of the kitchen as if he can't stand to be in the same room as me for a moment longer.

The front door slams a few minutes later, and I push the exam papers to one side and reach for my laptop, scanning the dozen or so new emails in my inbox. A second missive from Emma Bradley catches my eye, and with a sense of trepidation, I click on it. This one is short and to the point.

Eve,

I need to speak to you ASAP. Call me, please.

Emma

It's no good. I can't avoid her any longer. I pick up my phone and ring her mobile.

'Emma,' I say when she answers. 'What can I do for you?'

'You haven't seen my emails?'

'I... um...'

'I assume you know Annie Bradstock is still in a coma?'

'I went to see her in hospital yesterday,' I say, my voice wobbling.

'After suffering a drug overdose following a party at your house on Saturday evening,' she continues as if she hasn't heard me.

'Actually, her consultant says the coma was caused by her drinking too much water...' I begin.

'That's neither here nor there. The fact is, she took a class A drug, and she took it under your roof. I've just come out of an emergency call with the governors.' My blood runs cold. She sucks in a breath then exhales loudly. 'I'm afraid we have no option but to suspend you.'

'*Suspend me?* But I haven't done anything wrong!'

'I understand there's to be a full police investigation, during which your part in this dreadful business will no doubt become apparent—'

'I had no part in anything!'

'In the meantime, we have the school's reputation to think about, Eve. Having illegal drugs in your house is an offence. You could be charged with possession under the Misuse of Drugs Act.'

She's been talking to Sergeant Harrington, I think, silently raging at the injustice of it all. What the hell happened to 'innocent until proven guilty'?

'I've already had an enquiry from a freelance reporter asking me to confirm one of our pupils is in hospital.'

'They know about Annie?'

'Evidently, yes. I suspect he heard there had been a vigil and took a punt.'

'What are you going to say to him?' I ask, though the question's redundant, because I know exactly what she's going to say, because she told me in her first email. She's going to acknowledge what happened and explain 'the actions the school is taking as a result'. You don't need to be a rocket scientist to work out that that includes giving me the heave-ho.

'Don't bother answering that,' I say. 'You're going to hang me out to dry, aren't you? That's why you're suspending me now. So you can issue a statement saying you've dealt with the incident. Nothing to see here.' I give a slightly hysterical laugh. 'God forbid anything damages the school's reputation. Well, thanks for nothing.'

Again, it's as if I haven't spoken.

'Your suspension will, of course, be on full pay,' Emma Bradley says smoothly. 'You can expect a letter in a day or so outlining today's conversation. In the meantime, I suggest you help the police with their inquiries. The sooner we can put this whole sordid incident behind us, the better.'

* * *

I decide to go for a run. Anything to get out of the house. I used to run five times a week, regular as clockwork, before work gobbled up all my spare time. I'll have time to train for a marathon now I've been suspended.

As I leave the house I see Ethan Curtis's mum, Carol, walking her Bichon Frise across the green towards me. I'm about to wave a greeting when she scowls and drags the dog in the opposite direction.

What's her problem? If I'm honest, I've never warmed to Carol. She moved to the village about twelve years ago when her GP husband Simon joined our local doctor's surgery. It wasn't long before she began inveigling her way into every group and onto every committee in South Langley. They'd lived here barely a year before she was voted chairman of the PTA. She became co-ordinator of Neighbourhood Watch and secretary of the Gardeners' Society. She volunteered with the food bank and organised litter-picks. When Ethan started at Elmwood Manor, she set her sights higher and, following a stint as chairman of the parish council, is now a part-time magistrate, a fact she is very happy to share should you ever have the misfortune to bump into her at the village shop.

Simon's OK, I suppose. A bit hen-pecked, but nice enough. One of those grey, unremarkable men you'd struggle to pick out in a police line-up. Not that you'd ever need to: like Carol, Simon is a pillar of the community. Ethan takes after his father.

Quiet and unprepossessing. At primary school he was painfully shy. A geeky kid with round glasses and a claret-coloured birthmark that covered half his neck. It made him an easy target for the class bullies.

Once, when Joe was about nine, he came home from school with a grazed cheek and a ripped shirt. When I tackled him about it, he admitted getting into a fight with two other boys.

'Why, Joe? You know better than that.'

'They were being mean.'

I felt a stab of outrage. How dare two little oiks from the village bully my son? 'Don't worry,' I soothed. 'I'll have a word with Mrs Davison and make sure it never happens again. Who was picking on you?'

'Connor and Josh, but it wasn't me they were picking on,' Joe said. 'It was Ethan.'

'Ethan Curtis?'

Joe nodded. 'They were calling him Freaky Four-Eyes and Red Neck in a silly American accent. Because of his birthmark.' Joe touched his own neck. 'Then they took his school bag from the cloakroom and tipped it into the sand pit. I told Ethan he should tell on them, but he said it would be worse if he snitched, so I sorted it out for him.'

'What did you do?' I asked, half horrified, half in awe of my son for standing up to the bullies.

'I told them I had some Match Attax cards I didn't want any more, and if they wanted them, they had to meet me under the conker tree after lunch. When they came, I said they had to stop being mean to Ethan, or else. They just laughed, so I punched them.'

'Both of them?' I asked faintly.

'Yup.' There was a glimmer of pride in his voice. I knew I shouldn't condone what he'd done, that I should drill into him the importance of telling a teacher if Ethan was ever bullied again, but I couldn't bring myself to. I was secretly impressed he'd stuck up for his friend.

'I'm sorry I ripped my shirt, Mum,' he said.

I gave him a hug, crushing his slight frame against my chest and breathing in the heady boy-smell of grass, sweat and plimsolls. 'Don't worry. It's nothing a needle and thread can't fix.' I ruffled his hair, and as he scampered upstairs to change into his Cristiano Ronaldo football shirt, I was glad he'd given Josh and Connor a taste of their own medicine.

Is it a coincidence that all three boys were at our house the night of Joe's party?

* * *

The run clears my head and I'm feeling a satisfying buzz of endorphins when I reach the church. I break into a walk and spend a few minutes stretching my hamstrings and quads before turning into our drive.

The curtains in the sitting room are billowing out of the open window, which doesn't make sense, because I know the window was closed when I left.

Oh God. Are burglars ransacking the house while I hover in the gateway, dread glueing my feet to the ground? I reach in my pocket for my phone, cursing under my breath when I remember leaving it on the kitchen table. I could knock on someone's door, but it's four o'clock on a Wednesday afternoon and all our immediate neighbours will be at work. I run onto the road and look around desperately, hoping to see a dog walker or passing motorist, but the village is deserted. Typical.

I creep up the driveway, wincing every time the gravel crackles under my feet and wishing Noah had got round to installing the burglar alarm he bought before Christmas, which is still sitting in its box in the garage, no use to anyone.

When I reach the front door, I cock my head and listen, my hands balled into fists by my side. The house is in silence. I glance across to the sitting room window, my eyes widening when I see a ring of jagged glass. Holding my breath, I peer through the gap.

24

The sitting room is exactly how I left it, not even a cushion out of place, which is weird, because any self-respecting burglar would have made a beeline for Noah's fancy sound system or my iPad, which I left on the arm of the sofa.

But something *is* out of place. A brick is lying on the rug in front of the woodburner, a piece of paper tied to it with orange baler twine.

'What the hell?' I cry, reaching for the front door key zipped into the pocket of my running shorts. I let myself into the house before I can talk myself out of it and sprint into the sitting room, grabbing the brick and ripping off the sheet of paper. I smooth the paper out, holding my breath. A message has been scrawled on it in thick black marker pen.

WATCH YOUR BACK.

My running shoes crunch over shards of broken glass as I cross the room to the window, but whoever did this has long gone.

I tramp into the kitchen in search of a dustpan and brush, wondering whether I ought to report the incident to the police. I can't imagine Sergeant Harrington or his colleagues being particularly sympathetic. Someone in the village clearly blames us for what happened to Annie, and Joe's an easy scapegoat. I decide to save myself the bother.

Instead, I look up the number of an emergency glazier who arrives a couple of hours later and boards up the window, promising to return in a couple of days to replace the shattered panes of glass.

At six, the door clicks open, and Noah appears, clutching a bag of groceries, a frown on his face.

'How many times have I told Joe not to kick his football so near the bloody house?' he grouses.

'It wasn't Joe.' I show him the brick and the crumpled note that was tied around it. The blood drains from his face.

'Have you called the police?'

'What's the point? They won't do anything. Anyway, whoever did this wants us to react. It's classic bullying behaviour. They're bound to lose interest if we sit tight and ignore them.'

Noah's gaze slides from the brick to the note in my hand. 'And what if they don't?'

I exhale slowly. 'If they don't, we'll just have to deal with it.' I peer into the grocery bag Noah dumped on the kitchen island when he came in, raising an eyebrow at the scallops, salmon, sticky toffee pudding and bottle of Prosecco inside. 'What's all this in aid of?'

'Valentine's Day.' Noah rubs the back of his neck. 'I thought you deserved a treat after the week you've had. I bought a pizza for Joe.'

'Joe's out. Gone into town again,' I say, unpacking the shopping while Noah puts the Prosecco in the freezer to chill.

'How's your day been?' he asks.

I should tell him I've been suspended from work, but as he lights candles and turns on side lights, I decide against it. He's making an effort. I'm a long way from trusting him, but I'm not about to confront him tonight, not with everything else going on.

We sit down to eat at seven. Joe's still not home and after we've finished our scallops I text him.

Dad's bought your favourite pizza so get your skates on and come home! X

'Joe?' Noah asks, inclining his head towards my phone.

'Yes. I thought he'd be back by now. He can't still be in town.'

'Look on Find My iPhone.'

I give a hollow laugh. 'He kicked me off that months ago.' I check my phone again, but although my text has been delivered, it's still marked as unread.

Noah does his best to keep the conversation going while we eat, though I'm not much company. When we've finished, I stand to clear the plates, but he waves his hand at me. 'You stay put. I'll do it.'

'Thanks.' I tip the last of the Prosecco into our glasses and rest my chin on my hands as I watch him stack our plates in the dishwasher and slide the sticky toffee pudding into the oven. His dark hair is flecked with grey these days, and when he smiles, the laughter lines form deep grooves, but he's as slim as ever, that square jaw as chiselled as it was the day we met. He will be fifty next year, something I sense he is dreading. Is that why he's having an affair? One last chance to prove his virility before he sinks into middle age?

I remember the day I found out I was pregnant with Joe. Noah's face split into the biggest of grins before he lifted me up and spun me around the room, whooping with joy. I felt like the luckiest woman alive. Now, the fear of losing everything leaves me hollow.

'It'll be ten minutes,' he says, sitting back down.

'I'm in no hurry.'

'Good.' He picks up his glass and rolls the stem between his thumb and forefinger. 'Because there's something I need to talk to you about.'

I tense up, my stomach clenching. Is this the moment he tells me our marriage is over? And if it is, how will I react? Silently, I make a pact with myself. However bad it is, I will be calm, measured. I will focus on the practicalities. I will not allow myself to be swept away by my emotions. I will not rant and rave. I will not be Jenny.

Noah fixes his gaze on me. His eyes are glassy. 'I've stuffed up, Eve.'

So here it is, his admission of guilt. My heart is crashing in my ribcage as I wait for him to deliver the fatal blow to our marriage. He drags his hands down his face. 'Christ, this is hard,' he mutters.

'Just spit it out, Noah.'

'Yes... I will... I am. I just can't believe I'm doing this to you now of all times, when Annie...' He shakes his head. 'But I need to tell you myself before you find out from someone else. Six months ago, I—'

The front door crashes open and we both jump out of our skin.

'What the—?' Noah cries, leaping to his feet. He eyes the brick on the worktop fearfully, then bounds out of the room. I push my chair back and follow.

A figure is curled up in a ball on the hallway floor. It's the shoes I notice first. Black, red and white trainers with Balenciaga written on the side in white.

'Joe?' I say, dropping to my knees. His whole body is trembling, his hands covering his face. Gently, I peel his fingers away, gasping in shock as I register his swollen eyes and split lip, the dried blood and scraped knuckles. 'Oh my God, Joe. Who did this to you?'

But I don't need to ask him, because I already know.

25

Noah helps Joe into the kitchen and settles him on a chair while I fetch the first aid kit and a couple of clean towels. I run a bowl of tepid water and tear open a pack of sterile dressings, taking one and dipping it in the water.

'Can you turn the main light on?' I ask Noah. He nods, and flicks on the three pendant lights suspended above the island.

Joe's injuries look even worse under the glare of the lights. His bottom lip is split in two places and has ballooned to twice its normal size. There's a cut above his right eye, the kind Sylvester Stallone used to get in the *Rocky* films, and a line of dried blood trails from his left nostril to his swollen top lip. I clean the wounds as best I can, but the cut above his eye is bothering me. It's deep, probably needs stitches, but Noah and I have both drunk too much to drive.

'Can you phone for a taxi?' I ask Noah.

'Wha' for?' Joe mumbles.

'We need to get you to minor injuries to get this cut looked at,' I tell him.

Joe shakes his head, then winces.

'C'mon, mate,' Noah says. 'Mum's right. You don't want to end up scarring that pretty little face of yours, do you?' he jokes.

'I said no. I'm not going.'

'But, Joe—'

Joe jumps to his feet, knocking the clean dressing I'm holding onto the floor. 'Are you deaf?' he yells in my face. 'I am not going to minor injuries, OK?'

The raw fury in his voice leaves me reeling. I look at Noah for reassurance, but his face is mired in confusion, and I know he is thinking what I'm thinking. Who is this angry young man, because he doesn't look or sound like our son?

'All right, mate,' Noah says finally, his palms out and his voice quiet, as if he's approaching a wild mustang. 'We won't go. Eve, I think there are some Steri-Strips in the first aid kit. They'll have to do.'

I find an unopened packet of Steri-Strips and tear it open. Noah ushers Joe back to the chair, pats his skin dry and gently pushes the two sides of the cut together so I can fix the Steri-Strips in place. I have no idea if it'll do the trick, but at least the wound has stopped bleeding.

Joe slumps with his head bowed. All that anger, that rage, seems to have disappeared as quickly as it arrived. I check the rest of him over. There is blood on his white T-shirt and his jeans are ripped at the pocket. I lift the hem of his T-shirt, gasping when I see the red marks on his ribcage.

'Jesus,' Noah says when I show him. 'Who did this to you?'

'No one,' he mumbles. 'I... I fell over.'

Noah opens his mouth to speak, but I shoot him a look. It's clear Joe is too terrified to name his attackers. There's no point pushing it, at least not tonight. I crouch down in front of him and take his hands in mine. 'It's all right. You don't want to tell us. I get it. Just remember we're on your side. We won't tell the police if you don't want us to.'

The mention of the police seems to galvanise Joe and he

jumps out of the chair again, pushing it so forcibly it clatters to the ground, jarring my already frazzled nerves.

'Where are you going?' I cry as he hobbles out of the kitchen.

'To take a shower.'

'I'll come up and find you a clean towel.'

He stops in the doorway and grips the frame, his back to us and the red of his scraped knuckles stark against his clenched white fists. 'I can find a towel, Mum. Don't fuss.'

The minute he's gone, Noah pulls his phone from his pocket.

'What are you doing?'

'Calling the police, of course.'

'You can't.'

Noah's eyes flash. 'I get why you don't want to report the broken window, but our son has been beaten to a pulp by some mindless thug. What the fuck, Eve?'

'You saw him. He's terrified. Can we at least wait until the morning and see what he says?'

Noah stares at his phone for a beat, his finger hovering over the screen, then shakes his head. 'I think you're making a big mistake. Random psychos cannot be allowed to wander the streets beating the shit out of people. What if this maniac had been carrying a knife? We wouldn't be sticking Steri-Strips on our son's face. We'd be standing in a morgue identifying his body.'

As soon as he says this, I'm picturing myself in that morgue, waiting for a mortuary assistant to unzip a body bag and ask me to identify Joe's wax-like face. The image is so real I can almost smell the sharp tang of formaldehyde and feel the chill of the refrigerated air. I shiver. 'It wasn't a random psycho.'

Noah's eyes narrow at the conviction in my voice. 'Then who was it?'

'Someone at the party. It's obvious, isn't it? Joe knows who gave Annie the ecstasy and this is a warning.'

'What, keep quiet or I'll fuck you over?'

'Exactly that.'

'They're kids, Eve. Joe's friends. Lads from his rugby team and that swotty boy from his school. They wouldn't hurt him, certainly not like that. They wouldn't have it in them.'

'Have you seen Josh Duffy recently? He's built like a tank, and I'm not exaggerating. Connor Moody's dad's serving six years for bottling a man over a spilt pint, for God's sake. OK, so maybe you're right about Ethan,' I admit. To be honest, I can't picture the nerdy son of our GP and local magistrate roughing anyone up either, least of all our sporty son who can hold his own in a rugby scrum. 'But,' I continue, 'you're naive to think Josh and Connor aren't capable of assaulting Joe.'

'So why are you letting them get away with it?'

'I'm not,' I tell him. 'I'm going to make sure they live to regret it.'

26

'Knock knock,' I say as I ease open Joe's bedroom door the next morning. 'Are you awake? I've brought you breakfast.'

'Mmmm,' comes his reply, and I let myself into his room. It smells fusty, a faint odour of sweaty trainers and unwashed hair and something else I can't quite identify. I pop the toast and tea on his bedside table and cross to the window, pulling open the curtains and opening the sash window a couple of inches.

'How are you feeling? Did you sleep OK?'

'Yeah, not too bad,' Joe says, pulling himself up onto his elbows. I force myself not to flinch. He looks like he's done twelve rounds with Tyson Fury. The bruises on his face are beginning to blacken and his right eye is still half-closed, but at least the swelling in his lip is going down and the cut above his eye seems to be healing.

I sit on the end of his bed and watch him demolish his breakfast.

'Thanks, Mum,' he says, handing me the plate. 'I needed that.'

'Well, you missed out on your pizza last night, didn't you?'

Joe didn't come back downstairs after his shower. Noah

busied himself packing the first aid kit away while I rescued the sticky toffee pudding from the oven and wondered how to continue the conversation Joe had interrupted. The one in which my husband was about to tell me exactly how he'd stuffed up six months ago. Before I had the chance, he disappeared from the room, muttering about needing an early night. He's been avoiding me ever since.

'Listen,' I say to Joe. 'I know you don't want to go to minor injuries, but what if I sweet-talked the receptionist at the surgery into giving you an appointment with Ethan's dad this morning, just to make sure you don't need a couple of stitches in that cut.'

His face tightens. 'I don't need to see Ethan's dad. I'm fine.'

'What about the police, then? I could call that nice sergeant we saw at the station.' I'm being disingenuous because we both know Sergeant Harrington wasn't nice. In fact, I would go so far as to say he was unsympathetic, verging on confrontational.

'Mum! Which bit of "I'm not going to the police" don't you understand?'

'Don't you want to know who did this to you?'

'No one did this to me. I told you, I tripped and hit my head on the kerb.'

'And grazed your knuckles in the process?' I look pointedly at the scuffed skin on the back of his hands. 'C'mon, Joe, I wasn't born yesterday. It was Connor and Josh, wasn't it? Were they trying to warn you against reporting them to the police for bringing drugs to the party?'

'What?'

'I know they're your friends, but they don't deserve your protection.' I reach out to smooth his fringe from his forehead, but he jerks his head away.

'I'm just worried about you, sweetheart,' I say, ducking down to pick up the torn jeans he wore yesterday, which are lying in a crumpled heap on the floor. Noah's always telling me

I do too much for Joe, and he's probably right. It's what mums do, isn't it? If I didn't pick up his dirty clothes and put them through the wash, who else would? Who would restock the fridge and remember to pick up the honeycomb ice cream he loves if I didn't do it? Who would clean his rugby boots and check if he's handed in his graphic design coursework on time? At sixteen I had a part-time job in a tea room two bus rides from home and was still expected to pull my weight with household chores. Joe gets a monthly allowance of sixty pounds and I wait on him hand and foot. I know he's more than capable of taking care of himself, yet I can't shift that instinct to nurture him.

There are girls at school who seem incapable of even the most basic of life skills, the kids who can't manage their time or don't know their home phone numbers. One sixth-former asked me not that long ago where on an envelope she should stick a stamp. Each time I come up against these clueless kids, I blame their helicopter parents. The irony isn't lost on me. You know what they say about people in glass houses.

'I told you, I'm fine,' Joe snaps. 'Well, I would be if you stopped badgering me.'

Sod it, I think, dropping his jeans back on the floor and marching out of the room. It's about time my son worked out for himself where the laundry basket is.

* * *

I'm still smarting from Joe's curt dismissal when I leave the house a little while later, headed for the Duffys'. Their house is the biggest property on the exclusive Langley Fields estate, a development of twelve executive homes on the far western fringes of South Langley. The homes, built just a decade ago, have block-paved drives and bifold doors, en-suite bathrooms and professionally designed kitchens with induction hobs and sleek, handleless cupboards.

They are the kind of off-the-peg new-builds that leave me cold. The type of houses where period features have been added purely to entice potential buyers looking for character and charm rather than because they have any actual use.

The houses are surrounded by rolling parkland that used to be part of the Langley Manor estate. The once-grand manor house, built by the Baker family in the sixteenth century, is a ruin now, gutted by fire over a century ago. Just the shell remains: four walls and a small vaulted area at the back. Hidden by beech trees on the top of a hill overlooking the Langley valley, the manor house, nicknamed Old Langley by locals, would probably have been swallowed up by undergrowth and long forgotten if it wasn't for a track that leads right past it. Lisa and I often used to walk up there when the children were small. This time of year the woods are dank and dark, but in spring they're a sea of blue, the scent from the bluebells as heady as any designer perfume. In the summer we'd pack a picnic and sit and chat under the shade of the trees while Joe and Annie played among the crumbling walls, but my favourite time to visit has always been autumn, when the leaves turn copper and set the woods ablaze.

Recently, though, Old Langley has become a haunt for local teens, attracted by its relative isolation. Graffiti covers the remaining walls and the ground is littered with bottles, cans and patches of scorched ground encircled with stones where kids have lit campfires.

An investment company owns the parkland now, and when it sold the Langley Fields site to developers about twelve years ago, there was uproar. Although the village was dead set against new housing, the developers wooed the district council into granting planning permission with the promise that a percentage of the homes would be social housing for local people. Somewhere along the way, the two and three-bedroom starter homes disappeared and it became clear that the greenfield site had been sacrificed for a development of huge detached four and five-bedroom homes, like the Duffys' mini-mansion, that the locals hadn't a cat's chance in hell of affording.

After Greg's abrupt shift from genial to belligerent at Annie's vigil, he's the last person I want to see, but to my relief, Chrissy's red Mini is the only car parked on their drive.

Ringing the doorbell sets off a cacophony of barking. I forgot the Duffys have two Dobermanns, which are hurling themselves against the front door by the sound of it. Instinctively, I take a step back.

'Max, Roxy, back to your beds. Now!' a woman yells, and moments later the door opens.

I smile. 'Hello, Chrissy. Do you have a minute?'

For the briefest moment I get the feeling she's about to slam the door in my face, but then she gathers herself. 'Oh, hello, Eve. Of course. Come in.'

Whether it's the baying dogs or Chrissy's frosty welcome, I'm not sure, but I feel a chill of unease as I step into the house.

27

I follow Chrissy through the generous hallway to the back of the house, the two Dobermanns on my heels. I've been here a handful of times over the years, generally when I've dropped Joe off before a rugby match and Chrissy's invited me in for coffee. Even though it's ten years old, the place still looks like a show home, with feature walls, thick pile carpets and perfectly plumped cushions. I could have sworn the huge open-plan living space was shades of coffee and cream last time I was here. Now the walls and sofas are a rich teal. It must have cost a fortune to re-decorate.

We reach the vast kitchen. 'Peppermint tea?' Chrissy asks reluctantly. She's wearing a black cashmere turtleneck jumper and skinny jeans, her honey-blonde hair falling in loose curls around her shoulders and her face expertly made up. Her fore-head is a little too smooth and her lips a little too full for someone in her early forties. An attractive woman who wishes she was twenty years younger.

'Only if you have time,' I say.

She motions me to sit at the breakfast bar then flicks on the kettle. The dogs sit too, watching my every move. Am I imagining it, or is the atmosphere strained? No, I'm being dramatic. Chrissy was probably in the middle of something when I rang the bell but felt obliged to invite me in. She pops teabags into two mugs.

'How's Annie?' she asks, her back to me.

'No change.' I shift on the bar stool. 'They're doing tests in the next couple of days to see where she's at.'

'It's so hard for the kids,' she says, bringing my tea over.

There it is, my chance to probe deeper. I lean in slightly. 'How's Josh taking the news?'

'He's a sixteen-year-old boy. The only time he talks to me is to ask what's for dinner.'

'Joe's the same. Does he seem upset?' I press. 'After all, he was at ours when Annie fell ill. Seeing her like that can't have been easy.' As I reach for my mug, one of the Dobermanns growls at me, its hackles raised.

'Max!' Chrissy says sharply. 'In your bed. Sorry about him,' she says as the dog slinks out of the room. 'He's fine with most people, but sometimes he takes a dislike to someone for no apparent reason.'

I force a laugh. 'I won't take it personally. You were saying about Josh...'

'Here he is. You can ask him yourself.'

I turn to see Josh loping into the room. He's slightly shorter than Joe but much broader. A formidable prop on the rugby field, he's wearing his navy South Langley Rugby Football Club hoodie and trackie bottoms. He stops when he sees me and his gaze shifts to his mother.

'Hello, Josh,' I say, a little too heartily. 'How's it going?'

'Fine,' he mumbles. 'Mum, can you lend me a tenner?'

Chrissy jumps up and roots around in her bag for her purse. She hands Josh a twenty-pound note, and as he pockets it, I notice the suggestion of a graze across the knuckles of his right hand. Seeing the frown on my face, he turns for the door like he can't get away fast enough.

'We were just talking about Annie,' I say a little desperately. 'About where she might have got the ecstasy from.'

Chrissy's eyes widen, her gaze tracking between me and her son. I know what she's thinking: we were talking about nothing of the sort, but I need to know who brought the Es into my house.

For a moment I think Josh is going to ignore me completely, but he stops and turns slowly, locking eyes with me. 'Haven't a clue,' he says with a smirk, before sauntering out of the room. Moments later, the front door slams. Chrissy makes a show of looking at her watch.

'Gosh, is that the time?' She shoots me an apologetic look. 'I'd better make a move. I have a hair appointment in town in half an hour and you know what parking's like on market day.'

'Of course,' I say. She's a terrible liar, but I can hardly refuse to leave. I pat the pocket of my jeans, checking for my keys and phone, and retrace my steps to the front door, the dogs watching my every move with wary, unblinking eyes.

I replay the encounter on the walk home. Chrissy was guarded, almost apprehensive, while Josh's insolence was unsettling. As for the grazes on his knuckles... It's feasible he picked them up on the rugby pitch, but what if he didn't?

What if he grazed his knuckles beating Joe to a pulp?

28

On Saturday morning, I wake early, filled with determination to find out exactly what happened at the party. But first I text Lisa to see how Annie's doing.

No real change, Lisa texts back. *The nurses seem to think it's still early days, so fingers crossed.*

Relieved we're talking again, I tell her to give my god-daughter a kiss from me, then take my coffee over to the sofa with a pen and the pad I use to jot down my shopping lists.

I begin by listing everyone at our house the night of Joe's party. Even though I know it's possible Annie brought the ecstasy herself, I find it hard to believe she did. Far more likely someone gave it to her here.

I stare at the list of names: Joe, Ethan, Connor, Josh and Lottie. Joe has given me his word he knew nothing about the drugs, and I believe him. It has to be one of the others. I drain my coffee and slip the piece of paper into my back pocket. I will start with Ethan.

* * *

The Curtis family live on the far side of South Langley, and their large, detached villa used to be the last house in the village until the Langley Fields estate was built ten years ago. Carol Curtis was instrumental in setting up the Save South Langley pressure group to fight the development, whipping up a storm of protest against the plans, but, despite her meticulously orchestrated campaign, the district council gave the houses the green light.

How that must have rankled, I think, as I walk up the block-paved drive to the Curtis house. Their view of rolling parkland has been totally obliterated by the estate, and the nearest new-build looms over their front garden, casting a gloomy shadow over Carol's immaculately tended herbaceous borders.

After a bit of detective work before I left the house, I'm confident I'll find Ethan home alone. His dad, our village GP, holds a Saturday morning surgery and, according to the parish magazine, the South Langley Historical Society, of which Carol is chair, meets in the village hall on the third Saturday of the month.

A dog starts yapping when I ring the bell, and when the door opens, a little white ball of fluff bowls out, its plumy tail wagging nineteen to the dozen. I bend down to stroke the dog, then look up to see Ethan holding onto the door jamb and watching me guardedly.

'Hello, Ethan. I wondered if you had a minute to talk?'

He stiffens and it's obvious he's about to make some excuse and close the door on me, but I don't give him the chance, smiling at him as I walk right past him into the house. 'Don't worry, it won't take long.'

I've been here once before, when the boys were both in their last year at primary school and Carol hosted a cheese and wine party to raise funds for the PTA. The living room, I remember, is at the back of the house and I march along the hallway towards it, Ethan and their little puffball of a dog close behind me.

I take a seat and gesture Ethan to do the same. He's wearing skinny jeans and a faded black Nirvana T-shirt, which strikes me as slightly ridiculous, as Kurt Cobain died more than a decade before he was even born. He still wears glasses, but the claret birthmark that crept halfway up his neck has almost disappeared. He must have had it lasered.

'I know you've spoken to the police already but I just wanted to get a picture of what happened the night of Joe's party,' I begin.

He glances at the ceiling, then addresses my feet. 'We, um, played *FIFA* for a bit. Talked. Listened to some music.'

It's exactly the same answer Joe gave Sergeant Harrington when I took him to the police station for his voluntary interview. Is this because it's the line the kids have agreed to stick to, or because it's what actually happened? Perhaps I should give them the benefit of the doubt, but how can I when Annie is on a life support machine in intensive care? Either someone is lying... or they all are.

I remember another thing Joe mentioned during the police interview. 'Joe said you spent a lot of the evening talking to Annie.'

The port wine stain may have been lasered away but nothing can stop a dull red flush colouring his cheeks. 'We were catching up,' he says. 'I hadn't seen her in a while.'

'And how did she seem to you?'

'Fine. Good. We were talking about our A level options.'

'What about the others?'

Ethan closes his eyes, as if he's picturing the scene. 'Joe was on his Xbox. Josh was trying to chat Lottie up, not that she was taking much notice.' He gives me a sideways look. 'She spent most of the evening texting her boyfriend.'

'What about Connor?'

'Connor?' Something in his expression shifts, the slightest narrowing of his eyes. I nod, leaning forwards, my elbows on my knees. 'Connor was acting a bit weird, actually.'

'What do you mean by weird?'

Ethan folds his arms across his chest, tucking his hands under his armpits. 'I think... I think he might have taken something.'

I feel a tingle of anticipation. Now we're getting somewhere. 'Ecstasy, like Annie?'

He shakes his head. 'Not ecstasy, no. He was being an annoying twat. I think he'd probably had some coke.'

'*Cocaine?*' I can't hide my shock. The boy's sixteen, for God's sake. And under our roof! I drag my hands down my face. Can this get any worse? 'Where the hell did he get cocaine from?' I demand.

Ethan's demeanour shifts, as if he knows he's said too much, and the shutters come down. With a casual shrug, he gives me the classic teenage catch-all: 'Dunno.'

I swallow down my frustration and head home, my mind spinning. I may be no closer to finding out who gave Annie the ecstasy, but at least Ethan's revelation that she wasn't the only one taking drugs at Joe's party feels like progress. Surely every nugget of information I can prise out of these teenagers will bring me a step closer to the truth?

The wind has whipped up, and I'm glad of my coat as I cross the exposed village green. I'm halfway across when I get the feeling I'm not alone. I glance over my shoulder, but my imagination must be playing tricks on me because there's no one there.

Giving my head a little shake, I set off again. It's that bloody brick, making me paranoid. Perhaps Noah's right and I should have reported it to the police. They might have been able to test it for fingerprints. Not now – I left it on the patio outside the back door, and any prints would have been washed away by last night's rain.

The feeling I'm being watched won't go away. This time I stop and turn slowly, my eyes scanning the green. It's large, pan-flat and roughly the size of a football pitch. Houses line two sides; the main road through the village stretches along another. The fourth side is edged by a scrubby belt of birch and beech trees that separates the green from the recreation ground beyond it. A path with a dog waste bin at each end links the two.

From this distance, it's almost impossible to distinguish one tree from another, and I'm about to give up and go home when I catch a movement in my peripheral vision. I squint, and my stomach flips. A figure is standing stock-still in the trees, watching me.

29

I'm gripped with indecision, unsure if I should run home or march up to the figure in the woods and ask what the hell they think they're doing. Curiosity wins out, and I stride towards the trees, my heart thudding in my chest.

As I draw closer, the figure begins to take shape. It's a man; I can tell by the bulk of his shoulders and the way he's standing with his hands thrust deep into the pockets of a navy padded jacket. My eyes widen in recognition, but it doesn't make sense. Why would Greg Duffy be following me?

'Greg,' I say when I reach him. 'Did you want something?'

Frowning, he takes his hands out of his pockets and folds them across his chest. 'You came to my house.'

'I popped round for a chat with Chrissy the other day, if that's what you mean.' I smile pleasantly.

'She said you were asking questions about the party.' He scowls. 'About Josh.'

'Just passing the time of day.'

'You need to stay the fuck away from my family.'

I flinch. 'I don't know what you're—'

He laughs, the sound as jarring as a volley of gunfire. 'Cut the crap. I know you're planning to stitch up my son.' He takes a step towards me. 'Let me make myself very clear. If you even think about blaming Josh for what happened to Annie, I'll be all over you like a ton of bricks. Understand?'

A reply is forming in my head, but before I have a chance to say a word, he turns on his heels and disappears through the trees.

* * *

I let myself into the house, Greg's warning still ringing in my ears, when Noah calls from his study, 'Eve, is that you?'

I unzip my boots and poke my head round the door. 'I've just seen Greg Duffy. You won't believe what he said.'

But Noah isn't listening, and it soon becomes apparent why.

'When were you going to tell me you'd lost your job?'

My heart sinks. 'I've been trying to find the right time.'

He raises an eyebrow.

'Well, you're never here,' I retort hotly. 'And when you are you shut yourself in your study. We barely see you.'

'So, it's my fault you haven't had a chance to tell me you've been suspended? Don't you think that's something that, on a need-to-know basis, I *needed to know*?'

'Don't overreact. I'm trying to find out what happened here the night of the party so I can exonerate Joe and show Emma bloody Bradley I had nothing to do with what happened to Annie.' I narrow my eyes. 'How do you know, anyway?'

'Your school bursar phoned me this morning asking if I had any maths teachers on my books because their head of maths had been suspended after an incident involving one of their pupils. Pretty indiscreet of him, but I gather he's new in post. Which is why he had no idea we were married, I suppose.'

'He only started in September,' I agree. 'He's a bit of a twat.'

'Don't change the subject,' Noah says officiously.

'And don't take that tone with me.' My voice rises. 'I don't work for you, remember.'

'You don't work for *anyone*, apparently.'

'I'll get my job back once I can prove Joe had nothing to do with Annie's overdose. That's why I went round to talk to Ethan Curtis this morning. D'you know what he told me? Connor Moody was coked up to the eyeballs the night of Joe's party.'

'What?'

'Connor bought class A drugs to our house, Noah. I just need evidence he gave Annie the E before I talk to Harrington.'

'No,' Noah says, shaking his head. 'You need to stay well out of it. Leave it to the police, for Christ's sake.'

'I need to find out who did this to her.'

'No one did this to her. You told me yourself. Annie's in a coma because she drank too much water. It was an accident.'

I stare at my husband in disbelief. 'How can you say that? It wouldn't have happened if someone hadn't given her ecstasy! Besides, don't you want everyone to know Joe had nothing to do with it?'

He drags his hands down his face. 'Of course I do, but it's the police's job to prove it, not yours. What if Connor Moody takes exception to you poking around in his business? You said yourself his dad's in prison. He probably mixes in some pretty unpleasant circles. Christ knows how he might retaliate. We've already had a brick through the window. What next?'

I don't mention Greg Duffy's warning to stay away because Noah will only have a meltdown. The list of people baying for our blood is getting longer by the day.

'I can handle Connor Moody, don't you worry,' I reassure him. 'As for leaving it to the police, they've been completely useless.' I flop onto the faded leather armchair next to Noah's desk. I bought it for him for his birthday, knowing it would suit the clubby vibe of his book-lined study perfectly. 'I'm sorry I didn't tell you I'd been suspended. As soon as I can prove Connor's responsible, I'll be back to work. I'm still getting paid, if that's what you're worried about.'

'Of course I'm worried about the money. How the hell are we going to pay Joe's school fees if you lose your job?' He shakes his head. 'Since when did we keep secrets from each other, Eve?'

That's rich, coming from him. I let out a bark of laughter. I can't help myself. 'Why should you be different? Everyone's keeping secrets from *me*,' I say.

His gaze drops to his desk and he picks up his pen and examines it. It's an elegant black Waterman fountain pen with a gold-plated nib. He refuses to write with anything else. It's an affectation I used to find endearing but now irritates the hell out of me. What's wrong with a Biro, for heaven's sake?

At that moment his mobile rings, and his eyes dart nervously to the screen. I strain my neck hoping to see who's calling him but, frustratingly, I'm too far away. He gestures to the phone. 'I need to get this.'

Sighing loudly, I push myself out of the chair and stalk out of the room as Noah mutters, 'Hi, Bernice. Thanks for calling back. I'm sorry to trouble you on a Saturday, but I need to talk to you about the Southlands account.' Noah follows me to the door and shuts it behind me. I can't tell if I'm relieved or furious that the conversation we so clearly need to have has been interrupted yet again.

* * *

I spend the next hour mulling over what to do. Is Noah right? Should I leave it to the police, or should I carry on digging myself so I can go to them with enough evidence to exonerate Joe once and for all? It would help if the police were keeping us updated about the investigation, but I haven't heard a peep for ages. On a whim, I find the card Sergeant Harrington gave me and dial his number. If he isn't working today, I'll leave a message asking him to phone me as soon as he's back on duty. I'm rehearsing what to say when he picks up.

I clear my throat. 'It's Eve Griffiths, Joe Griffiths's mum. I'm phoning for an update on the investigation.'

'I believe I said we'd be in touch if we had anything to report, Mrs Griffiths.'

'You did, but it's been a week since the party. You must have made some progress.'

'Well, we've spoken to everyone who attended. We're also working closely with our Operation Kestrel colleagues to try to understand where the ecstasy came from.'

'Operation what?'

'Operation Kestrel. Their remit is to disrupt and dismantle county lines operating in the area.'

'County lines?' My grip on the phone tightens. A Police Community Support Officer from Nesborough Police Station came into school a year or so ago to give an assembly on the London gangs who recruit children to supply drugs in rural areas, using a mobile phone network – the county line – to distribute the drugs. 'You're saying the ecstasy Annie took is linked to *county lines*?'

'At present, we're keeping an open mind.'

'What happens next?'

'I'm afraid I'm not at liberty to share our investigation strategy with you. Or anyone, for that matter,' the sergeant says.

I exhale. 'I appreciate you're probably understaffed and overworked, but we're in limbo here. Joe's living under a cloud of suspicion and I've been suspended from my job pending the outcome of your investigation, even though there isn't a single shred of evidence that Joe had anything to do with the drugs.' I consider telling him about Connor Moody and the cocaine when I stop myself. I need something more concrete than the word of a sixteen-year-old boy if Harrington is going to believe me. Instead, I plead, 'You must see the effect this is having on my family? And what about Lisa? She deserves to know what happened to Annie.'

'We are where we are,' he trots out blithely.

We are where we are. What the hell's that supposed to mean? It's one of Emma Bradley's favourite expressions, which basically translates as we're in the shit but we've just got to deal with it.

'Please be assured you'll be the first to know if we have any news. In the meantime, if that's all...?'

I'm fuming as he ends the call. What a pointless waste of time. It's clear I can't rely on the police to get us out of this mess. I will have to do it myself.

30

The sulphurous smell of blocked drains hits me as I walk up the pitted, uneven path to Connor Moody's shabby front door that afternoon. Everything about the place screams neglect, from the rusty pink kid's bike abandoned by the overflowing wheelie bins to the overgrown lawn and the filthy windows.

Nerves are bubbling in the pit of my stomach because, if I'm honest, I'm not sure what kind of reception I'm going to get. Connor and his mother, Lorraine, weren't exactly friendly towards me at Annie's vigil. They're not going to welcome me with open arms.

I take a deep breath to steady my nerves and rap the door knocker. After a moment the door swings open to reveal a skinny-limbed girl with white-blonde hair tied back in a high ponytail. She's dressed in a crop top and leggings despite the chill February wind, and I'm not surprised to see goosebumps puckering her skin.

I dimly remember Lorraine with a grubby-looking toddler at Joe and Annie's primary school leavers' service five years ago. This girl must be Connor's younger sister, the one Annie used to babysit.

'Hello,' I say with a reassuring smile.

She doesn't reply, just regards me with deep mistrust, her big blue eyes wide.

'You must be Bobbi-Jo.'

'Are you from social services?'

'What? Oh, no. I'm a teacher, actually.'

'Not at my school, you're not.'

'No. I'm at the girls' grammar in Nesborough. I was wondering if—?'

'Mum's not here,' she says before I can finish.

'Actually, it was Connor I was hoping to speak to. Is he at home?'

Her eyes dart towards the ceiling, then back at me.

'He's not in any trouble,' I tell her. 'He's friends with my son, Joe.'

Her eyes light up. 'Joe Griffiths?'

'You know him?'

'He's nice, Joe is.' She turns and yells up the stairs, 'Connor! Joe's mum's here!' When there's no answer, she says, ''Spect he's got his headphones on. I'll fetch him for you.' She takes the stairs two at a time, her earlier wariness gone. I wait on the doorstep, hoping Lorraine doesn't make an appearance before I speak to Connor, because I have a feeling she wouldn't take kindly to me turning up out of the blue to quiz her son without her knowledge.

Eventually, Connor clumps down the stairs, closely followed by his sister. He looks at me with bloodshot eyes. 'What are you doing here?'

I dredge up another smile. 'I just wanted a quick chat. It won't take a minute.'

' S'pose you'd better come in.'

I follow him into the front room, which is dominated by a huge television on the wall above an electric fire. A black and white cat with a distended stomach basks in a shaft of sunlight on the threadbare carpet.

'Maisie's having kittens soon,' Bobbi-Jo says, skipping over to the cat and chucking her under the chin.

'Mum'll have kittens if she finds out you've been here,' Connor mutters. The bravado he wore like a suit of armour at the vigil has disappeared now he doesn't have an audience, and I'm reminded of the little boy who used to try so hard with his reading when he was Bobbi-Jo's age.

'I won't be long,' I say again. I sit at one end of the tatty leather sofa. 'I used to come into school to listen to you read, do you remember?'

He nods. 'I was in your group on the school trip to London, an' all.'

'That's right! I had you, Joe, Josh and Ethan. That was a fun day.' I turn to Bobbi-Jo. 'We went to Madame Tussauds, the Tower of London and the London Aquarium. I expect you'll go too when you're in Year 6.' I turn back to Connor. 'It's so nice that you've all stayed such good friends. Especially at the moment...' I trail off, glancing at Bobbi-Jo, who's still crouched on the carpet flicking a length of baler twine for the cat, who bats at it half-heartedly.

'It's all right, she knows what's happened to Annie,' Connor says.

'I like Annie,' Bobbi-Jo pipes up solemnly. 'She used to babysit me sometimes when I was little. She's really kind.'

Unexpectedly, my eyes fill with tears. 'She is,' I agree. 'That's why I want to find out what happened to her the night of Joe's party.'

Connor wipes his nose on the back of his hand. I surreptitiously inspect his nostrils for traces of fine white powder, feeling like a detective in a crummy television crime drama. I can't see any.

'No point asking me,' he says, unaware he's being scrutinised. 'I was on *FIFA* all night.'

'Connor loves Manchester United,' Bobbi-Jo says. 'Josh likes Liverpool, and Joe likes Chelsea.' Her face clouds over. 'I don't know who Ethan likes. He never comes round to ours.'

Bobbi-Jo may be young, but it's clear she's one smart cookie. It occurs to me that she probably knows more about my own son than I do these days.

I want to ask Connor whether he knew there were drugs at the party, not because I think he'll tell me but so I can gauge his reaction, but I can't bring myself to in front of his sister. Instead, I say, 'I saw Ethan this morning.'

He stiffens. 'Ethan?'

I nod. 'He said he spent most of Joe's party chatting to Annie.'

Bobbi-Jo looks up from the cat. 'Did he want Annie to be his girlfriend?'

Connor lets out a derisory laugh. 'Ethan doesn't like girls, if you know what I mean.'

She clearly doesn't and returns her attention to the cat, which has sat up and is washing its face fastidiously. Meanwhile, my mind is spinning. *Ethan doesn't like girls*. This is news to me, and I wonder idly if Carol and Simon Curtis know their only son is gay. Not that it matters in the least, but it's yet another secret these teenagers are keeping.

'Ethan also told me Josh was talking to Lottie all night,' I say.

'The silly twat thinks he stands a chance with her, but I could've told him he's flogging a dead horse.' He sniggers at his own joke. 'Get it? Because Lottie's into her horses, yeah?'

'That's funny, that is,' Bobbi-Jo says.

I smile weakly. 'You mean Lottie isn't interested in Josh?'

'Course not. She thinks he's a knob.'

'That means willy,' Bobbi-Jo informs the cat.

'I suppose she's too focused on her riding to have time for boyfriends,' I say.

'Nah, that 'ain't it. Ethan let it slip that she's been seeing someone, but she's keeping it on the down-low.'

'You mean she's keeping it secret?'

He nods.

'Why?'

'Dunno. Think it's because he's, like, well older than her.'

'Did Ethan say who he was?'

'Nope. All I know is he told me the shit would hit the fan if anyone found out.'

I let this sink in. Sixteen-year-old Lottie is seeing an older man. An older man who should know better than to take advantage of a teenage girl. It is yet another mystery to add to the bubbling cauldron of secrets and lies.

'And what about Joe?' I ask. 'Was he playing *FIFA* with you?'

'Some of the time, yeah. Then he disappeared for a bit.'

The ground shifts under my feet. 'He disappeared? Where?'

'Outside, I think.'

'To do what?'

'Dunno.'

There it is again. *Dunno.* These kids might as well have the word tattooed across their foreheads.

Bobbi-Jo gives her brother a confused look. 'Thought you said he was vaping?'

'Fuck's sake, sis.'

'I'm only saying what you told me.'

'I know, but...'

'Joe vapes?' I ask, shocked.

Connor shrugs. 'Everyone vapes.'

'I don't,' Bobbi-Jo says indignantly. 'It's really bad for you,

Mrs Emerson told me. She's my teacher,' Bobbi-Jo adds for my benefit.

'Right,' I say faintly. 'Bobbi-Jo, I don't suppose I could have a glass of water?'

'Course.' She scrambles up and dashes from the room, leaving Connor and me alone.

'Connor, I'm going to ask you something, and I want to assure you that you won't be in any trouble, whatever you say.' I take a deep breath. 'Did you bring drugs to our house the night of Joe's party?'

He runs a hand over his buzz cut but says nothing.

I glance towards the door. I can hear the tap running in the kitchen. I don't have long. 'Because Ethan told me you took cocaine that night.'

He springs to his feet. 'Ethan is a fucking liar! I might've smoked a bit of weed but I didn't take *cocaine*. I'm not an idiot.'

'I'm only repeating what he said.' I keep my voice neutral. 'Why would he lie to me?'

'As payback, of course,' he snorts.

'Payback for what?'

His expression changes from fury to evasion and he turns away.

'Connor,' I press. 'I promise you this won't go any further.'

He glances at me, uncertain. I can see his agitation in the jerky way he sits back down. He's not sure he can trust me, and he's right, because it's an empty promise. My desire for the truth trumps everything, and I'll say anything to get to it.

'You have my word,' I lie.

He gives the slightest of nods, as if he's reached a decision, but at that moment Bobbi-Jo walks back into the room, holding a glass of water in her outstretched hands like a priest carrying a ceremonial cross to the altar. The tip of her tongue sticks out of the corner of her mouth as she concentrates on not spilling a drop.

'How lovely. Thank you.' I take the glass, and Bobbi-Jo beams. I watch Connor as I sip in silence. His face is inscrutable once again and I know the moment for sharing confidences has passed. I might as well cut my losses and leave.

As I walk back down the crumbling path to the road, I replay everything I have learned from Connor and his little sister. My thoughts linger not with what Connor said, but with everything he didn't say.

It seems that every time I get closer to the truth, I stumble upon another damn secret. Just how many will I have to unravel before I reach the truth?

31

There's a note on the kitchen table when I let myself back into the house. It's from Noah.

Have popped into the office. Should be back before dinner but don't wait for me.

I take great delight in scrunching the note into a ball and lobbing it into the bin. My hands are still clenched as I stalk over to the patio doors and stare out into the garden.

I wish more than anything I could turn back the clock. Not just to the day of Joe's party, but further still. To the time when Lisa and I would sit at the kitchen island drinking coffee and gossiping as we kept half an eye on Joe and Annie playing camp in the treehouse. When I knew what Joe was up to every second of every day. When the worst scrapes he got into were playground tussles, and if there was a problem, he came straight to me.

He used to be one of those children who wore his heart on his sleeve. A single look at his face was enough to assess his mood as accurately as a weathervane gauges the wind direction.

These days he's a closed book. I have no idea what he's thinking, how he's feeling. He is an enigma to me. A puzzle I have little hope of solving. How did I not know my own son vaped, for God's sake? What else is he hiding from me?

With nothing else to do, I busy myself tidying up the kitchen and half-heartedly running the vacuum round the house. Once that's done, I strip our bed and find a clean duvet set in the airing cupboard. Joe's bed needs changing too. I should make him do it, but sometimes it's easier to do it yourself.

I trip over one of his new trainers as I carry clean bedding into his room. I bend down to pick it up, running my finger over the Balenciaga logo. I've never heard of the make before; Joe favours Nike or Adidas. Balenciaga sounds Italian. Curious, I pull my phone from my pocket and type the brand into Google. I was wrong. According to Wikipedia, Balenciaga was Spanish originally, although it's now owned by a French company.

I click through to the website, which looks high-end. A fancy black leather handbag is artistically arranged on the home page. I almost drop my phone in surprise when I see it costs over £3,000. Frowning, I search for men's trainers, or cargo sneakers as they're called on the Balenciaga website. My jaw drops when I see the prices. The cheapest pair I can find is £875 but most are around £1,025. There's a light grey pair dotted with tiny rhinestones that costs nearly two grand. I glance down at Joe's trainers then scroll through until I find them. They're £875.

Exactly how much money did my mother send Joe? I settle on the end of his bed and phone her.

'Strange question,' I say when she picks up. 'How much did you give Joe for his birthday?'

'Fifty pounds. Why?'

'Oh, no reason.'

'He told me he bought some trainers with the money.'

'That's right,' I say, gazing at the designer sneakers that cost nearly eighteen times as much as she'd given him.

'Was there anything else? Only it's my bridge afternoon, and I'm already running late.'

'No, that was all.'

I end the call with a promise to phone for a proper catch-up at the end of the week while wondering how the hell Joe managed to afford a pair of £875 trainers.

Something Sergeant Harrington mentioned when I phoned him for an update comes back to me. He said he was working closely with colleagues from a special unit to find out where the ecstasy came from. I wrack my brain, trying to remember his exact words. Operation Kestrel, that was it. The team tasked with disrupting and dismantling county lines gangs operating in the area. I call to mind the school assembly on gangs given by the Police Community Support Officer from Nesborough Police Station last year. He looked barely out of sixth form himself but had spoken with authority about county lines and the havoc they wreaked.

'People think the gangs only recruit kids from inner city estates, kids who are already known to the police, but it's a dangerous assumption to make. Gangs target children from all walks of life, especially those who've never been in trouble before, because they're less likely to be stopped by the police while they're going about their business.'

Girls listened slack-eyed as the young PCSO listed some of the signs parents and teachers should look out for. Changes in behaviour, such as staying out late or going missing. A decline in school grades or attendance. Withdrawing from family life or becoming angry, anxious or secretive. Coming home with unexplained injuries. Carrying lots of cash or a second phone. Wearing expensive new clothes or trainers they are unable to account for.

I remember all the times Joe has gone out to play football

with his mates recently, the night he turned up on the doorstep beaten black and blue, the way he's so quick to anger if I so much as ask him the time of day.

The bedding forgotten, I search on my phone for people whose children have been caught up in county lines.

Soon I am reading about the woman whose son was being sent messages from a gang on his PlayStation while his oblivious family watched TV downstairs. The mum whose youngest son would disappear for days then return wearing expensive designer clothes.

One woman described how she'd received the dreaded knock on the door from a police officer telling her that her seventeen-year-old had died from multiple stab wounds. Another spoke of how her outgoing, affectionate boy turned into a zombie with dead eyes and a machete in his school bag. I read with growing horror an interview with parents from a sleepy market town not so far from Nesborough whose son was robbed by the same gang that had recruited him, only to be pressured into paying back the money he owed the only way he knew how – by selling more drugs.

Every story is both a statistic and a personal tragedy. Young people's lives ruined by criminals who befriend, groom and ultimately exploit them. They are promised money, power and respect. Instead, they are coerced into a life of drug dealing and violence. A life that must be almost impossible to leave behind.

Fear squeezes my heart, making it difficult to breathe. Is this what Joe is caught up in?

32

I stare at my phone in a daze. The more I think about it, the more convinced I am. Joe has somehow become embroiled in county lines. There's no other explanation. All the signs are there. All those red flags I've either not noticed or subconsciously chosen to ignore. The new trainers. The beating he shrugged off as a fall. His obvious fear of the police.

How could I have missed it?

I jump up from the bed and rummage through his chest of drawers. I'm not sure what I'm looking for. Plastic bags of white powder? A pair of scales? An old Nokia phone? But the most incriminating thing I can find is an unopened packet of water-melon-flavoured vape pods hidden at the back of his sock drawer. To think I'd been shocked when Connor told me Joe vaped. It seems unimportant now.

I turn my attention to Joe's wardrobe, searching through his clothes with an almost manic energy. There's a coat I don't recognise, and I yank it off the hanger and inspect the label. It's a navy Tommy Hilfiger bomber jacket that must have cost well over a hundred pounds. Digging deeper, I find a pair of designer sunglasses and a stack of new Xbox games which must have cost a small fortune. My stomach lurches. There's no way Joe could afford all this on the sixty-pound allowance we give him every month.

My phone rings in my back pocket, making me jump. I pull it out and stare at the screen, surprised to see it's Joe. It's as if he knows I'm in his room, trawling through his things. I answer, my cheeks burning.

'Mum, I meant to tell you at breakfast, but I have a match this afternoon, so I won't be home till late. It's against Bossington.' It's a rival independent school about twenty miles from here. 'They had to rearrange the fixture because the pitch was flooded last time, remember?'

'Do you need Dad or me to pick you up?'

'Nah, it's fine. I'll get the bus.'

'If you're sure?'

'Course. Don't keep me any dinner. I'll grab a Maccy D while I'm in town. Better go, they're all waiting for me. See you later,' he adds, and the line goes dead.

Nothing about this call should ignite my suspicions. Joe has rugby matches at least twice a month this time of year and he often catches the bus home afterwards, mud-covered and ravenous. Before I can stop myself, I scroll through my contacts and phone the school office, glad it's open six days a week.

'Elmwood Manor Independent Day School. How may I help you?' the school secretary asks. Her accent is pure cut-glass, designed, no doubt, to show prospective parents the school's faultless upper-class credentials.

'Oh, er, hello, it's Eve Griffiths, Joe's mum. I just wanted to check what time his rugby match is this afternoon. The Year 11 match against Bossington? My husband and I thought we might come along to watch them play,' I improvise.

'Of course. I'll pop you on hold while I check.'

I head to the window, my gaze drawn to the churchyard at

the end of the garden. My thoughts stray to Annie, as they so often do. I hope she's staying strong.

There's a click in my ear and the secretary is back on the line. 'Mrs Griffiths? I'm afraid there isn't a match against Bossington this afternoon. I managed to get hold of Mr Green and he says the Year 11s aren't playing again until next Thursday when they have a match against Thurley Hall.'

'I'm so sorry. I must have got the wrong day.' I force a laugh. 'Either that or Joe has his dates muddled, which isn't unknown. You know what teenage boys are like.' Aware I'm gabbling, I force myself to shut up.

'Not a problem,' the secretary says. 'If that's all...?'

I tell her it is and thank her again before ending the call and slipping my phone back into my pocket, a feeling of dread settling on my chest like a heavy cold.

I might not have found a stash of drugs or wads of cash in Joe's bedroom, but I have witnessed my son trot out a barefaced lie with no compunction.

And if he can lie about a rugby match as easily as breathing, what else is he lying about?

33

The house phone rings as I head back downstairs. It can't be my mother; she was on her way out to play bridge. It's probably a cold caller, and I'm about to let the answerphone kick in when I remember it could be the police with an update on the investigation.

'Is Noah there?' an imperious voice asks when I pick up, and my spirit plummets. I need an awkward chat with my husband's ex-wife about as much as I need a hole in the head.

'Hello, Jenny. He isn't, I'm afraid. Have you tried his mobile?'

'Of course I've tried his mobile. It went straight through to voicemail.'

'He's at the office. He's probably in a meeting.'

'On a Saturday?' Jenny tuts. 'He never worked weekends when Billy was small.'

'Yes, well, he's very busy at the moment. And Joe's sixteen. He's off doing his own thing half the time.' I fall silent, wondering if Jenny knows about Annie. Then it occurs to me that of course she must. If Noah hasn't told her, Billy will have.

'So I hear,' Jenny says cryptically. 'It's terrible what's happened to that girl. Your friend's daughter. I can't remember her name.'

'Annie,' I say through gritted teeth. 'She's my god-daughter and, yes, it is. We're all still reeling.'

'Billy said she's in a coma. I don't know what her mother must have been thinking, letting her experiment with drugs like that. It was inevitable she'd go off the rails.'

Anger courses through me, but I need to keep a lid on it. I refuse to give Jenny the satisfaction of knowing she's riled me. I close my eyes briefly. 'Annie didn't "go off the rails". It was just one of those stupid, preventable, split-second decisions. A mistake any teenager could make.'

Jenny lets out a disdainful snort. 'She overdosed on ecstasy at a sixteenth birthday party. If that's not going off the rails, I don't know what is.'

I don't bother to explain that Annie is only in a coma because she tried to do the right thing. It's all semantics, anyway. As far as Jenny's concerned, she's practically an addict.

'I suppose I've always been lucky with Billy. He never gave me a moment's worry when he was a teenager.'

I have to bite the inside of my cheek to stop myself from spluttering with disbelief. Billy was always getting into trouble at school. One time, he was suspended for smoking in the boys' toilets. On another occasion, Noah and Jenny were summoned to the head teacher's office after a younger pupil claimed Billy had been bullying him. But as far as Jenny's concerned, the sun shines out of his backside. It always has.

'Well, you're very lucky,' I say.

'Oh, I don't think luck has anything to do with it, do you? It's all about how you parent your child. Boundaries and consequences. Unconditional love and being a good role model through difficult times.'

I'm seething now, my stomach twisting with fury. The "difficult times" she's referring to are the days after she discovered our affair and Noah started divorce proceedings. She made everything as unpleasant as it could possibly be, from challenging the financial settlement to refusing to supply information about her own assets to Noah's solicitor. She hasn't been much better since. I used to feel sorry for her, knowing that although her marriage was already in its death throes when I met Noah, I was the catalyst for her divorce. But she's been so objectionable over the years that any sympathy I had ran out a long time ago.

'Billy's very lucky,' I agree. 'You really do deserve each other.' Fortunately, she's too much of a narcissist to detect the irony dripping from my voice. 'What was it you wanted to talk to Noah about?'

'A nice young man knocked on the door this morning and told me my chimney needed repointing.'

'He knocked on the door to tell you that?'

'He's a roofer, working on an extension round the corner. He was walking to work when he spotted it. He can fit me in on Monday, but it's going to cost eight hundred pounds.'

And you want Noah to pay for it, I think. Noah might have stopped giving Jenny maintenance when Billy turned twenty-one, but he continues to hand over cash whenever she or Billy come cap in hand with a sob story. He still feels guilty for leaving them, even after all this time.

'It sounds like a scam to me,' I say. 'Once he's on the roof he'll spot something else that needs fixing and you'll end up forking out thousands.'

'I'm not naive. I've checked the website on the business card he left me. It looks perfectly legitimate,' she says crisply.

'Anyone can build a website, Jenny.' I sigh. 'But I'll make sure to tell Noah when he's back. Was that it?'

'Well, there was one other thing, but I'm not sure it's my place to say anything,' she begins.

I roll my eyes. Along with pleading poverty, Jenny has a habit of throwing verbal hand grenades into my life and watching with glee as they detonate.

'It's just something Billy let slip the other day,' she continues. 'He wasn't going to tell me, but I could see something was niggling him and I teased it out of him eventually.'

'Go on.'

'He's worried about his dad. The last couple of times Billy has suggested they meet after work for a drink, Noah's stood him up at the last minute, claiming he was too busy. Billy said that when they have met up, Noah has seemed absent, as if his mind's elsewhere.'

'What are you trying to say?'

'That I recognise the signs, and it wouldn't be the first time, if you know what I mean...' Her voice takes on a faux-caring tone. 'I'm only telling you this because I wouldn't want you to have to go through what I did. Is everything all right between you and Noah?'

'Of course it's all right,' I snap, instantly regretting jumping down her throat because I know it won't have gone unnoticed. 'Noah's a bit stressed about work, that's all. Billy's got the wrong end of the stick. We're absolutely fine. So if that's all, I really must go. I have a mountain of marking to get through.'

'Don't let me stand in the way of your marking.' Jenny pauses. 'But if you ever do want to talk, you know where I am.'

I slam the handset on the sideboard and howl with frustration. History may be repeating itself, but Jenny is the last person on earth I'd talk to if Noah was having an affair.

I stomp into the kitchen, my eyes filling with angry tears. I thumb them away and run myself a glass of water. I used to pity Jenny, having to bring up her son on her own because she couldn't hold onto her husband. Now that my own family is splintering, I'm ashamed of my arrogance. Are we so very different?

Yes, I think. *Yes*. Because, unlike Jenny, I love Noah, and I'll do everything in my power to save my family.

34

Joe appears just after six o'clock, in sweatpants and a Nike T-shirt, his kitbag over one shoulder, dressed for the part.

I smile tightly. 'How was the match?'

'Didn't happen. I got the wrong day. It's in a couple of weeks.'

'So where have you been all afternoon?'

He raises an eyebrow.

'It's a simple enough question, Joe. Where were you?'

'In town.' He dumps his kitbag on the floor by the washing machine, as if leaving it in such close proximity will be enough for the bag to magically empty itself and its sweaty contents into the machine and on a cool wash.

'Again?'

Joe glowers. 'You have a go when I never go out, and now you're moaning because I am. I can't win.'

I hate to admit he's right. I'm always nagging him about the hours he spends cooped up in his bedroom on his Xbox. Gaming all day every day isn't good for anyone. Although I'd rather he was getting square eyes and repetitive strain injuries than dabbling with drugs.

'I'm sorry,' I say. 'I'm just interested, that's all.'

He huffs. 'I was helping Billy with his app if you must know.'

Since he dropped out of university a year into his computer science degree, Billy's had more jobs than some people have had hot dinners. He's worked in bars and coffee shops and on petrol station forecourts. He's waited tables, sold houses and laboured on building sites. Six months ago, he turned up on our doorstep, crackling with excitement as he outlined his idea for a tech start-up company inspired by his latest obsession: weightlifting.

'It's a fitness app,' he explained as we sat around the kitchen table. 'It'll allow users to create personalised workout plans tailored to their fitness goals, including strength training routines, cardio workouts and rest days.' He counted them off on his fingers. I'd never seen him so fired up about anything before.

'I've already started filming videos of me doing all the exercises so people can see how they're supposed to be done. They'll be able to track their progress over time, and,' he said, holding up a finger, 'the app will have a built-in nutrition tracker so they can monitor their daily food intake.' He stopped and grinned at us like the cat that got the cream.

'Cool,' Joe said, nodding his approval. 'Can I be in some of your videos?'

'Course you can, little bro.'

'It sounds great, son.' The pride in Noah's voice was unmistakable. He turned to me. 'Doesn't it, Eve?'

'Isn't the fitness app market already saturated?'

'Here we go,' Billy said, shaking his head. 'The wicked stepmother pisses on my dreams yet again.'

'Billy—' Noah warned.

I held up a hand. 'It's all right. I'm playing devil's advocate, Billy. What's going to make your app stand out from the rest? What's your USP?'

The tension in his jaw relaxed. 'Isn't it obvious?' he said, grinning again. 'I'm the USP.'

A week later, Billy asked us to invest £10,000 in his new venture. How could I say no, especially when I wanted him to succeed as much as anyone? I hated the thought that his inability to stick at anything was a direct result of his parents' divorce. Noah took the money out of our savings and transferred it into Billy's account the same day.

'We spent the whole afternoon filming training videos at this cool gym Billy's set up,' Joe says, dragging me back to the present.

'Billy asked you to film him?'

Joe flushes with pleasure. 'No, he was filming me. D'you want to see them?'

'Of course,' I say, and Joe fiddles with his phone, then hands it to me. 'This is the sumo squat.'

I peer at the screen. Joe, dressed in gym shorts and a vest, holds a barbell across his shoulders. He squats down then pushes himself back up, a look of concentration on his face. He takes the phone back and scrolls through his pictures. There are at least a dozen different videos of him demonstrating various exercises, from bench presses and deadlifts to lunges and more squats.

The pride in Joe's voice as he talks me through every video is unmistakable, and a wave of self-doubt washes over me. I've been so worried about Annie I've barely slept for days, and it's taking its toll. What if the lack of sleep is affecting my judgement, making me paranoid? What if I've got it all wrong?

* * *

Noah arrives home soon after Joe, looking tired and slightly dishevelled. When he bends over to peck me on the cheek, I catch a whiff of whisky on his breath.

'I've ordered a takeaway,' I tell him as he shrugs off his jacket and takes a beer from the fridge.

'How much is that going to cost?'

'I don't know. Forty quid?'

'Forty quid?' Noah shakes his head.

'Oh, and your first wife called, on the scrounge as usual. Wants you to phone her.'

'Marvellous.'

I look at him properly. His eyes are bloodshot and puffy and there's a greyish tinge to his skin. 'You look knackered. Why don't you take a shower and I'll open a bottle of wine. The takeaway's not coming till seven.'

He nods and tramps from the room, his shoulders drooping. I don't feel pity, I just feel numb. He's brought it on himself.

We eat the takeaway on our knees in front of the television, and at nine o'clock, I announce I'm going to bed. I know I'm avoiding the conversation we need to have, but I'm too exhausted to go there. By burying my questions, there's a danger they'll burrow under my skin and fester, but I don't care. When Noah comes up an hour later, I deepen my breathing and pretend to be asleep.

35

The next morning I'm up and showered by half past six. Noah's still snoring softly as I leave the bedroom, which is a relief. If I tell him where I'm going he'll only try to talk me out of it.

Downstairs, a coffee in my hand, I double-check the address of Lambhurst Eventing, the competition livery yard where Lottie keeps her two horses, according to a feature I found about her online last night.

'Lottie Miller is one of the South-East's most promising eventing talents and has already competed at international level for her country,' the article gushed. 'While most teenagers are still in bed, Lottie is at the yard by seven every morning, come rain or shine, looking after her two horses, Nexus and True Blue.'

Lambhurst Eventing is only six miles away and it's not long before I'm turning through a pair of stone gateposts into a long gravel drive flanked by fields of grazing horses. I longed for riding lessons when I was a child but my mother thought ballet was more befitting a ten-year-old girl than mucking about with ponies, and so ballet it was.

There's a small parking area before another set of gates, and

I pull in next to a huge steel-grey horse lorry with the Lamb-hurst Eventing logo sign-written on the side. I leave my bag on the passenger seat and head through the gates into the yard.

Even at half seven on a Sunday morning, the place is brimming with activity. Horses watch imperiously over their stable doors as their owners – mainly jodhpur-clad women, as far as I can tell – scurry around pushing wheelbarrows and filling water buckets and haynets. It occurs to me that looking after horses is much like bringing up teenagers – a lot of hard work for very little thanks.

I spot a door marked 'office' on the far side of the yard and march towards it, my head swivelling from side to side as I walk, looking for Lottie. As I'm nearing the office, the door bursts open, and a lean-legged woman about my age strides out. Seeing me, she stops and smiles.

'Can I help?'

'Actually, yes. I wanted to ask about riding lessons.'

'We're a livery yard first and foremost, though I occasionally offer one-to-ones alongside the jumping and dressage clinics.' She cocks her head to one side. 'Would you be bringing your own horse?'

'God, no.' I let out a nervous laugh. 'I'm a complete beginner, I'm afraid. I'd have to borrow one of yours.'

'I see.' The woman's smile fades. 'Then I don't think we'd be the right fit for you. There's a great little riding school on the other side of Nesborough called Greenacre that has adult beginner lessons.'

'Thank you, I'll look it up. I'm sorry for wasting your time. I thought I'd try here first because one of my son's friends keeps her horses here. Lottie Miller?'

The woman's smile is back. 'Ah, Lottie. She's been with us since she was twelve. She's over there if you want to say hello.' She nods towards a huge dappled-grey horse that's tied up outside a stable on the far side of the yard. A slim girl wearing a red bobble hat is running a brush over its flank as it tears hay from a net.

'Thanks. I'd love to.'

The woman nods and disappears. I make my way towards Lottie, hoping she can help me piece together everything that happened the night of Joe's party.

* * *

It is immediately apparent that Lottie Miller is not pleased to see me. The moment she recognises me, a scowl darkens her pretty features.

'Hello, Lottie,' I say brightly. 'This is a nice surprise.'

'What are you doing here?' she asks in her plummy, public-school voice.

'I was enquiring about riding lessons.'

'At half past seven on a Sunday morning? Bullshit,' she mutters.

'OK, so it's not entirely true. I was hoping to speak to you.'

She turns away, ferreting through the plastic grooming box by her feet. It's so I can't see her face, I think. She's hiding something from me and, as a result, is on her guard. I need to tread carefully if I'm to winkle any information out of her. I stroke the horse's neck. 'He's stunning. Have you had him long?'

She glances up at me. 'Nearly a year. I've had Nexus, my other horse,' she says, pointing to the adjacent stable, where a dark-brown horse with limpid eyes is watching us with interest, 'since I was fourteen.'

'You're doing very well with them both. I'm always reading about you in the school newsletter. You'll be winning Badminton before you know it.'

'I don't think so. What did you want to talk to me about?'

'Joe's party.'

She takes what looks like a hairbrush from the grooming box and starts brushing the horse's tail. 'What about it?'

Where to start? I plunge my hands deep into the pockets of my coat. 'Did you know I'm a secondary school teacher?'

She nods. 'At Annie's school.'

'Not any more. I've been suspended.'

Her hazel eyes widen a fraction. 'What for?'

'Bringing the school into disrepute.'

Lottie stops brushing and stares at me. 'What did you do?'

'That's the thing. I haven't actually done anything. I've been suspended because of the police investigation into Annie's overdose. Schools aren't like the British justice system, you see. There's no such thing as innocent until proven guilty. Picture a kangaroo court in a corrupt dictatorship and you'll still be way off the mark. Governing bodies can do what the hell they want, and they want me out of the picture because the fact that Annie's in a coma after taking drugs is a stain on the reputation of their school.'

Lottie is listening to me intently, a pinched expression on her face. Something's going on here. An undercurrent I can't quite decipher. She looks troubled, even frightened. Why would my suspension have such a dramatic impact on her?

Maybe it's guilt. Maybe she was the one who gave Annie the ecstasy and is now having to face up to the ramifications. It would make sense, I suppose.

'I need my job back,' I tell her. 'If I don't work, we can't afford to keep Joe at Elmwood Manor. I can't pull him out just before his GCSEs, it would be disastrous. I need to find out exactly what happened at his party so I can clear our names and get justice for Annie. I've already talked to Josh, Ethan and Connor.'

'Yes, Ethan told me. Now it's my turn.' She starts brushing again. The horse's iron-grey tail resembles fine strands of molten silver in the weak sunshine. 'You're wasting your time,' she adds. 'I've told the police everything I know.'

'I'm sure you have. Humour me, please. If not for me, for Annie.'

She inclines her head, which I read as a signal to carry on.

'Do you know Annie well?'

'Only through Joe and Ethan. Then last year we both joined Nesborough Athletics Club. I only run to keep fit for riding, but Annie's a decent middle-distance runner.'

'She is,' I agree. Annie finds everything easy, always has. 'Had she been drinking that night?'

Lottie shakes her head. 'She had a big race coming up and was doing the whole "my body is a temple" thing.'

'Did you know she'd taken ecstasy?'

'Of course not,' she says with a frown. 'The first thing I knew about it was when she started acting all weird. Pulling faces and stuff. When she started fitting, I screamed at Joe to call an ambulance, but he said you were only over the road, and he phoned you instead. He was shit-scared. I mean, we all were. It was horrible, just horrible.'

I wonder if those few extra minutes would have made a difference. But Annie had already drunk too much water by then. It was already too late to stop her from slipping into a coma. I can't help worrying that the longer she's in that dark place, the less likely she is to wake up.

36

Lottie is silent for a moment, perhaps reliving those last few horrifying seconds as Annie jerked and twitched on the floor. She shakes her head as if chasing the memory away, and I resume my questioning.

'Connor told me you were talking to Josh for most of the night. Are you two an item?' I ask, guilelessly.

She pulls a face. 'God, no. Rugger buggers are so not my type.'

'Who is your type?'

That guilty look again, so fleeting I wonder if I've imagined it.

'No one,' she says. 'I don't have time for relationships. I'm too busy with the horses.' She drops the brush in the grooming box, takes out a hoof pick and picks out the horse's feet, working quietly and efficiently, and it strikes me, not for the first time, how much more mature sixteen-year-old girls are compared to boys their age.

'Very sensible. Men are more trouble than they're worth, if you ask me.'

'I didn't, but whatever.'

'Ethan also said Connor was off his face.'

'He'd had a few beers, but he wasn't wasted.'

'According to Ethan, he'd taken cocaine.'

Lottie lobs the hoof pick in the grooming box and straightens her back. 'That's ridiculous. Connor might smoke the odd joint, but he wouldn't touch coke.'

'Then why would Ethan say he had?'

She considers this for a moment, then shrugs. 'No idea. Though they were really off with each other that night, come to think of it.'

'In what way?'

'Connor was winding Ethan up. Calling him a nancy, stuff like that. When Ethan called him out, Connor said he had the evidence to prove it and started waving his phone around. You could tell Ethan was getting really worked up, but then the stuff with Annie happened, and... well... you know the rest. That's probably why I'd forgotten about it.'

'And you don't know what the "evidence" was?'

She shrugs but doesn't directly answer. 'I guessed Ethan was gay ages ago, and I can't be the only one. I'm pretty sure Annie knew.'

'But he hasn't come out to anyone else?'

She shakes her head. 'I assume that's why he was so mad at Connor. He didn't want him announcing it to everyone.'

'Who do you think gave Annie the ecstasy?'

'Well, it wasn't me... Won't be a sec.' She pats the horse's neck briskly and sets off across the yard, disappearing through a door marked 'tack room'. I'm stroking the horse's velvety nose, wondering if I'm too old to start riding, when a phone buzzes. At first, I think it's mine, but then I realise the buzzing is coming from inside Lottie's grooming box. Glancing over my shoulder to check no one's watching, I stoop down, pick up her phone, and check the screen. There's a WhatsApp message on it. No profile picture, just the initials NG and the first line of a message. *Hey babe.*

Hearing footsteps behind me, I jerk upright and the phone slithers out of my grip and back into the grooming box with a loud clatter. The noise spooks Lottie's horse, and his head flies up, his ears flat.

I hold up my hand to stroke his face, but that only seems to frighten him more. His nostrils flare and he pulls back from the metal ring on the wall he's tied to, the lead rope as taut as a steel cable. I look around helplessly, but the previously bustling yard is suddenly empty. The horse tosses his head again, his flight instinct kicking in. He's going to snap the lead rope at this rate. An image of Lottie's prize eventing horse careering down the drive, through the gates and straight into the path of a speeding car floods my mind. The image is so vivid I can almost hear the sickening sound of splintering bone.

'What on earth is going on?' Lottie cries, appearing by my side. She thrusts a saddle and bridle into my arms and releases the lead rope with a single tug. Running her hand along her horse's neck, she croons, 'Steady, Bluey. It's OK. I'm here.'

It's mesmerising, watching this slight girl calm down a ton of horse with touch and voice alone. Slowly, he settles, and she reties him and takes his saddle from me, her face tight with anger.

'What happened?' she asks as she places the saddle gently on his back.

'It was your phone bleeping.'

She doesn't reply, just busies herself buckling the girth and fiddling with the stirrup leathers. It's only when she holds out her hand for the bridle that I see that all the colour has drained from her face.

'Aren't you going to see who it was?'

She shoots me a filthy look. 'Not right now, no. I have a lesson with Paula in' – she checks her watch – 'three minutes.

So I really need to get going.' I stand back while she finishes tacking up and swaps her bobble hat for a riding helmet. She leads the horse over to a mounting block, jumps on and gathers her reins.

She looks down at me, her composure restored. 'Next time you want to cross-examine me,' she says coolly. 'I'd rather you did it in the presence of my parents.'

With that, she turns her horse and rides towards an outdoor arena where the lean woman I spoke to earlier is waiting.

They exchange a few words, then both look in my direction, but I barely notice. All I can think about is the WhatsApp message on Lottie's phone. There is no doubt in my mind that it's from her boyfriend.

When the wave of dizziness hits, I have to grab hold of the stable door to stop my legs from buckling beneath me.

Lottie's boyfriend is older than her. I'm convinced my husband is having an affair.

The initials NG.

Noah Griffiths.

I want so badly to be wrong, but I know I'm not. My stomach folds in on itself and I grab the only thing to hand. Groaning, I empty the contents of my stomach into Lottie Miller's red bobble hat.

37

My fist curls around the rim of the bobble hat as I walk stiffly to my car. Better for Lottie to think she's lost the hat than to find it's been used as a makeshift sick bag.

I throw open the boot of the car and chuck the hat into a shopping bag, grimacing at the sour smell as I fold the bag over twice. There's a packet of hand wipes in the glove compartment, and I pull a couple out and clean my hands and face as best I can, then scrabble about in my handbag for a packet of mints.

I drive away on autopilot. I don't have the headspace to think of anything other than the WhatsApp message and what it must mean.

Noah, rushing headlong towards his fiftieth birthday and a midlife crisis.

Lottie, young and ridiculously pretty, having a secret affair with an older man.

I want to believe I'm completely overreacting and that Noah would never look at a sixteen-year-old girl, let alone seduce her. Lottie is the same age as our son, for Christ's sake. Just because her boyfriend shares the same initials as Noah doesn't make him guilty of anything.

But a vindictive little voice in my head reminds me that Noah has a track record for cheating. When we jumped into bed, he broke the unspoken rule that you never, ever sleep with a client. Worse, I was seven years younger than him. Jenny's words come back to me. *It wouldn't be the first time.*

I yo-yo back and forth until my head is spinning. Then, suddenly, I'm almost home. South Langley looks picture-perfect in the hazy sunshine. The first of the daffodils are bobbing their yellow heads on the village green, and the hedges are bursting with blackthorn blossom. Normally, the sight would gladden my heart, but not today. Today, my heart is indifferent, empty.

I've been burying my head in the sand for too long, using the fallout from Joe's party as an excuse not to face up to the fact that my marriage is over.

It's time to confront Noah.

* * *

As I pull into our drive, I growl in frustration. Noah's car isn't here. I rack my brains, trying to remember if he mentioned a round of golf or a game of squash, but nothing springs to mind.

I kill the engine and check my phone to see if he's left a message. He hasn't. I text him.

Where are you? We need to talk.

Two blue ticks appear almost instantly, but it's a couple of minutes before he replies.

Had to pop into work. Should be finished by lunchtime. Everything OK?

No, I think. Everything is not OK. In a fit of childish petulance, I don't reply. Let him stew.

I let myself into the house and hang my bag and coat over the newel post. It's only just gone nine o'clock. Joe won't surface for at least another hour. I make myself a cup of tea and march down the hallway to Noah's study, closing the door softly behind me.

I start with the desk drawers, rifling through them to see if I can find concrete evidence of my husband's infidelity. Something more tangible than an overheard conversation, a WhatsApp message and a sick feeling in the pit of my stomach. I don't care if it's a single earring, a hotel receipt or a packet of bloody condoms, I just want to prove beyond doubt that Noah is having an affair, so I know I'm not losing my mind.

The first drawer I pull open is full of junk. Old pens and paperclips, hole punchers and staplers. The ancient Casio calculator with the Space Invaders-style shooting game Noah had at primary school and still occasionally plays. Half-forgotten digital cameras, old pairs of glasses, a handful of charging leads and a roll of sticky tape. I push it closed and move on. The next drawer is filled with stationery. Creamy envelopes and matching writing paper, compliment slips for Noah's recruitment consultancy and brand-new notebooks. There's a box of business cards, and I tip them onto the desk and flick through them, but nothing stands out.

The third drawer is where I find evidence of my husband's deception. I don't know why the three crumpled envelopes catch my attention, but the moment I notice them poking out from behind a bundle of old birthday and Father's Day cards from Joe and Billy, I know they are significant.

I pull them out and, with trembling fingers, open the first.

38

At the top of the sheet of paper is the Elmwood Manor logo, a coat of arms and the school motto, *Integritas et Fidelitas*. Integrity and fidelity.

12 January 2024
Mr and Mrs N. Griffiths
The Old Vicarage
South Langley

Dear Mr and Mrs Griffiths,

Re: Outstanding School Fees for Joe Griffiths

I hope this letter finds you well. I am writing to bring to your attention the outstanding school fees for your son, Joe Griffiths, a Year 11 student at Elmwood Manor.

According to our records, the fees have not been paid since the start of the academic term in January. The balance owed is £9,920.

Timely payment of school fees is crucial to the smooth operation of our school and the provision of high-quality education to all our students. We do, however, under-stand that unforeseen circumstances may arise, and we are happy to discuss payment arrangements if needed.

Please settle the outstanding balance as soon as possible to avoid any disruption to Joe's education. If you require assistance or would like to discuss payment options, please contact me at your earliest convenience.

We greatly appreciate your co-operation in this matter and your continued support of Elmwood Manor.

Yours sincerely,

Andrew Surridge
Bursar

I stare at the letter for a moment, puzzled. We've never been late paying Joe's school fees before. I went back to work specifically so we could afford to send Joe to Elmwood. My wages are paid straight into a separate instant access savings account and Noah transfers the money at the beginning of every term.

Only this time, he was late.

I rip open the next envelope. Mr Surridge is clearly losing patience, talking about the 'significant financial strain' the non-payment of Joe's fees is causing the school, and how it's 'crucial' the matter is addressed at our earliest convenience.

The third and final letter is more strongly worded still. It's the final paragraph that makes my stomach clench.

'Failure to settle the outstanding fees within the next

seven days will regrettably leave us with no option but to
suspend Joe's attendance at Elmwood Manor and to
instruct a professional debt collection agency to recover
the unpaid school fees.'

I glance at the date at the top of the letter. Monday 12 February. Less than a week ago. A term's worth of fees unpaid. The school is threatening to send in the bloody bailiffs. Worse than that, they're about to kick Joe out of school two months before the start of his exams.

I sink back on Noah's swivel chair, the third letter still in my hand. Noah's always meticulous about paying bills. He hates owing people money, has a virtual phobia about it. Once, when we first started seeing each other, I lent him twenty quid for a taxi home because he'd left his wallet at work. The money had been transferred to my account before breakfast the following morning. How has he let things get so bad that Joe's school is on the brink of calling in the debt collectors?

I drop the letter onto the carpet, switch on Noah's computer and log into our bank. The current account is five hundred pounds overdrawn, but to be honest, that's not unusual. It's been an expensive month, what with Joe's birthday and an unexpected garage bill when my car developed a loud clanking noise. I click on the instant access savings account we use for Joe's school fees. There should be around £4,000 in that. My eyes widen when I see the balance: £1.57. I scroll down our accounts, checking the ISA, our holiday fund and the high interest savings account. Empty. Empty. Empty. Even Joe's university fund, which had a little over £6,000 in it when I last looked, has been cleared out.

A balance of £21,543 on a linked account catches my eye. Perhaps Noah's moved all the various pots of money into one account with a higher rate of interest. Just as relief is damping my anxiety, I see the figure is our credit card balance. We owe over twenty thousand pounds.

I push the keyboard away and cradle my head in my hands, trying to think. Then I jump out of the chair and burrow through the bottom drawer, finding more envelopes hidden at the back. Final reminders, every one of them. From the looks of it, we haven't paid the gas or electricity bills for months. We're behind with the council tax and the water bill, and our life assurance has been cancelled as the premiums haven't been paid since August.

None of it makes sense. Noah and I are comfortably off. Although most of my salary is sucked up by Joe's school fees, Noah's recruitment company has provided us with an enviable lifestyle. We can afford a big house, nice cars and far-flung holidays. That's not to say we don't work damn hard for it, because we do. It's just that money isn't something we worry about. Admittedly, we've stayed in and ordered takeaways instead of eating out recently, and I can't remember the last time we had a weekend away, but we haven't had to watch the pennies for years.

So I thought.

I wrack my brains, but I can't work out where all the money's gone. Perhaps Noah's been siphoning it off to fund his new life without me. It makes sense, and going by the dates on some of the final reminders, he must have been planning this for months. The sheer duplicity of his actions rips through my heart.

Then an even worse thought sends me rifling through the pile of letters again until I find one with the familiar green and blue logo of our building society emblazoned on the letterhead. My fears are confirmed. Our mortgage is in arrears and our house, our characterful, elegant home, is about to be taken from us, thanks to my lying husband.

39

I don't know how long I spend slumped in Noah's office chair, my hands bunched into fists in my lap, the letter from the building society on the desk in front of me. Ten minutes? Twenty? Long enough for my back to stiffen and my tea to grow cold. Questions buzz around my head, as insistent as a cloud of midges on a muggy summer's evening. I pick up the letter and reread it carefully. There are options, it seems. We could take a repayment break, switch to an interest-only mortgage or extend the term.

I check the date of the letter, finding more crumbs of comfort in the fact that it's dated January 19, just four weeks ago. Perhaps there is time to sort out this mess before our house is repossessed.

Footsteps thunder down the stairs and the study door swings open. I freeze, but it's only Joe, asking what's for lunch.

I shove the letters back into the drawer and plaster on a smile as I mentally run through the contents of the fridge. 'I can make some leek and potato soup.'

'Sounds good,' he says before disappearing again.

I force myself to my feet and make my way to the kitchen. I

feel as though I've aged ten years in the last few hours. Everywhere I look, there's evidence of the love we have lavished on this house. The stunning tiled floor I discovered in the hallway when I pulled up the hideous floral carpet; the chunky radiators I sourced from a salvage yard because a previous owner had ripped out the originals and replaced them with ugly storage heaters; the stained-glass window in the downstairs loo I had commissioned for Noah's fortieth birthday. I love every inch of the place, from the high ceilings and ornate ceiling roses to the intricately carved oak newel post at the bottom of the stairs.

I pad along the hallway as if in a trance. There are memories in every room. Joe as a baby, lying on his play mat in the living room, gurgling with laughter as he tries to grab his toes. Sitting in his highchair at the kitchen island, smearing spaghetti hoops over his face. Holed up in the snug with Annie watching cartoons while Lisa and I gossip in the kitchen. Family Christmases in the dining room, Easter egg hunts in the garden, cosy winter nights in front of the fire.

How dare Noah risk it all?

Resolve hardens my heart. My marriage might be over, but I will be damned if I lose this house as well.

Noah texts again as I'm ladling soup into two bowls.

> *So sorry. Something's come up that can't wait till tomorrow. Be back by six.*

It's almost seven o'clock before I finally hear his key in the lock. I spent the afternoon in the garden, savagely chopping back shrubs and sweeping the paths and patio, hoping the hard physical work would keep a lid on my simmering anger.

It didn't.

Noah shrugs off his jacket and leans over to drop a kiss on my cheek. Stubble shades his face and he smells very faintly of sweat.

'Sorry I'm late. Bitch of a day.' He pulls a bottle of red from the wine rack and fetches two glasses.

'Not for me,' I tell him. I want to keep a clear head.

He raises an eyebrow, pours himself a glass and takes one sip, then another. 'You OK?' he asks. 'You look a bit... tense.'

I want to scream at him, to ask how the hell he's managed to burn through our entire savings, rack up a twenty-grand credit card debt and risk our home. I want to know if it's all because he's having an affair. It'll have to wait. This is a conversation we need to have later, when Joe is safely out of earshot.

As if on cue, Joe bounds into the kitchen and pours himself a pint of water from the tap. 'TV dinner?' he asks hopefully.

'Sure,' I say. 'Why not?'

I can feel Noah's wary gaze on me as I dish up bowls of spaghetti bolognese. He knows me well enough to recognise something's up.

Joe finds the latest episode of a spy series on Netflix we've been binge-watching, but I can't concentrate on the antics of a group of misfit MI5 agents, not while my life is falling apart. My appetite has deserted me too, and I push the pasta around my plate with little enthusiasm.

When the programme is over, Joe disappears upstairs and Noah follows me into the kitchen, stacking the dishwasher while I wipe down the worktops.

He turns the dishwasher on and then leans against the kitchen island, watching me. 'What's wrong, Eve?'

I drop the sponge into the sink and nod towards the door. He closes it, then takes my elbow and guides me to the sofa. 'Talk to me,' he says. 'Please.'

I lick my lips. Once the accusations are out there I can't take them back. Given oxygen, they will take on a life of their own, become real. We will have to start divorce proceedings, discuss child maintenance, divide our assets. Sell the house. Yet I can't keep up the pretence that everything is fine any longer.

'I know about the affair,' I say finally.

'Affair?' He blinks. Frowns. 'Whose affair?'

'Don't take me for a fool, Noah. *Your* affair. The affair you are having.' I enunciate the words slowly, as if I'm talking to the village idiot.

'But I'm not having an affair,' he says. He appears genuinely bewildered. He could win an award for his performance.

But I'm not buying any of it. It's time for the truth.

40

'I heard you on the phone to your *girlfriend* on Joe's birthday.' I mimic Noah. '"I don't think she suspects anything, but you know Eve. It's only a matter of time before she finds out."' I fold my arms across my chest. 'You said you wanted to tell me yourself. When exactly were you planning to do that?'

Noah jumps to his feet, strides over to the kitchen and returns with two whisky tumblers and the Glenfiddich my mother gave him for Christmas. He pours a generous measure into each and hands one to me. I don't argue; my earlier intentions to keep a clear head are long forgotten. The alcohol burns my throat. I grimace, take another sip and wait for Noah to speak.

'That phone call you heard, it's not what you think. I was talking to Bernice.'

'*Bernice?*' Noah's office manager is the last person on earth I would suspect him of having an affair with, as far removed from Lottie Miller as you could hope to get.

'Bernice,' he says, nodding. 'She was telling me I needed to come clean with you about what I've done. I should have listened to her, but I thought I could fix things before you found out.'

'Found out what? About the money? Before you try to deny it, I found the letters in your drawer this afternoon. The credit card bills, the reminders from Joe's school and the building society. Where has all the money gone, Noah? No, actually, don't tell me, because I can guess. You've siphoned it off so you can start a new life with your mistress. My friends always warned me I couldn't trust you. Once a cheat, always a cheat, isn't that right?'

Noah groans, shaking his head. 'How many times do I have to tell you before you'll listen to me? I am not having an affair. I would never do that to you. You mean everything to me, Eve. Everything. I love you.' He sets his tumbler on the rug and buries his face in his hands. 'It's worse than that.'

Worse than an affair? I rack my brains, wondering what the hell he's done. An unwelcome thought occurs to me. Maybe he's ill and is feeling guilty because he sought medical help too late. I look surreptitiously at him. His face has a grey pallor to it and the skin around his eyes is puffy and dry. He looks like he hasn't had a decent night's sleep in weeks. But that still wouldn't explain where all the money's gone.

'Just tell me,' I plead, and as he nods and takes my hands in his, his grip as tight as a vice, I know that far from hoping for the best, I need to prepare for the worst.

A silence hangs heavily between us, broken only by the soft thrum of the dishwasher and the beating of my own heart.

'NG Recruitment has gone bust,' he says finally, his voice barely a whisper.

This is not what I expected at all. Sure, recruitment is a crowded market, but Noah's agency has always more than held its own. He has a knack for fitting the right people to the right jobs. In the last twenty years he's been a leading player in education recruitment.

'Bust? How?'

'It started going wrong during the pandemic. Placements were falling through left, right and centre. Rocketing salaries and a shortage of trained staff created a perfect storm.' He meets my gaze. 'But you know all this already. I told you at the time.'

'I know things were tough during lockdown, but it picked up, didn't it? You've never been busier. You're always at the bloody office, at any rate.'

He shakes his head. 'People have been applying for positions with higher salaries, knowing full well they have no intention of leaving their old jobs. They just want their bosses to match the new salaries. I'm only paid when a position is filled. No job, no money.' He lets go of my hands and picks up his whisky. Takes a sip. 'I've thrown everything I have at it, but I'm trying to fill a bottomless pit. I called in the liquidators last week. I had no choice.'

'What about Bernice and the others? Do they know?' Noah employs two recruitment consultants alongside his formidable office manager.

'I told them on Friday. It was awful. Maddy's just bought her first house and Tim's wife's expecting their third baby. They... they didn't take it well.'

'It can't have been easy,' I say, although the flash of sympathy I feel is short-lived. We're about to lose everything too.

'It was the worst day of my life.'

'If things were as bad as you say, they must have seen it coming.'

'I haven't wanted to worry them, so I've been pretending everything's fine. They have no idea I've spent the last few months holding regular crisis talks with the bank. Only Bernice knew.'

That would explain the blocked-out afternoons on Noah's calendar app.

'Did you ask the bank for a business loan to tide you over?' I ask. 'You've weathered other storms. Things are bound to pick up sooner or later.'

Noah lowers his gaze to the tumbler in his hands and I know without him telling me that he has already taken out a loan, in fact is probably in hock up to his eyeballs.

'Is that where our money went, to prop up the business?'

'It was only meant to be a short-term loan to tide us over. I had no idea things would get worse, not better.'

'But the agency's a limited company, so we're not personally liable, right?'

'No,' he concedes. 'But it's not just the money I sank into the business—'

His words jar and fear unfurls in the pit of my stomach. 'What do you mean? What else have you done?'

He shifts in his seat. 'You know the ten grand we invested in Billy's app?'

I nod.

'He asked for more.'

I take a slug of whisky and wonder what other secrets my husband has been keeping from me.

41

'More?' My eyes narrow. 'How much more?'

Noah swallows. 'Another fifty thousand.'

'Fifty thousand pounds?' I explode. 'What the hell did Billy need fifty thousand pounds for?'

'Start-up costs. Software development, market research, marketing, office space, that kind of thing.'

'Office space?'

'He's taken on the lease of a unit on the Nesborough Business Park. Then there's all the other costs involved in starting a new business. Internet, data storage, an accounting system, computers...'

He sees my expression and looks at me almost pleadingly. 'I really thought Billy could make a go of his app, and how could I say no, after what we did to him?'

I jump to my feet, anger coursing through me. 'Don't you dare,' I cry, jabbing a finger at him. 'You were the one who was married, not me.' I frown, replaying his words. 'And what d'you mean, you thought he could make a go of it? What's happened to our investment?'

Noah's eyes dart around the room avoiding my gaze, and I

know. 'He's spent it all, hasn't he? And now we're going to lose our home.'

'I'm sure we can—'

I am so angry I could punch Noah square in the jaw. An affair would be easier to stomach. This feels like the ultimate betrayal: Noah has sold our lives down the river for his feckless, self-centred son. How can he not see that Billy has taken him for a fool? I doubt there ever was an app. Maybe there had once been a nebulous idea, but Billy would have soon lost interest, as he always does. Noah was throwing good money after bad.

'Sixty grand,' I hiss. 'Sixty thousand pounds! We could lose our home, Noah! You do realise that, don't you?' Everything is falling into place. He's been acting so weird about money recently. It's why he was muttering about putting Joe's tree-house on eBay, why he was quibbling about last night's take-away. It explains his reaction when he found out I'd been suspended. He's known for months that we're drowning in debt.

'I'm sorry—'

'Not good enough.'

'Look on the bright side.' He tries a tentative smile. 'At least I'm not having an affair.'

'This isn't funny.'

'Who did you think I was having it off with, anyway? Someone young and glamorous, I hope. Like Donna at the pub?'

The Swan's newest barmaid is pretty in an obvious sort of way. You know the type, all tight tops and teased blonde hair, fake eyelashes and duck lips. She's also in her early thirties. If Noah considers she's young...

It hits me with the force of a freight train. I was wrong about Lottie. She might have an older boyfriend with the same initials as Noah, but it isn't him. My husband may be a lot of things, but he is not the type to prey on teenage girls. Something else is clear. I can never let him know I suspected him of seducing her, because he would never forgive me. Our marriage is in enough trouble as it is.

'Something like that,' I agree. 'But don't change the subject. When exactly were you going to tell me about the mess we're in? When the bailiffs rang the doorbell demanding the keys to the house?'

He winces. 'I tried to tell you on Valentine's night, but then Joe turned up on the doorstep covered in blood.' He runs his hands through his hair. His nails are short and ragged. 'I kept thinking something would turn up. A big contract or a new investor. I finally admitted defeat on Friday morning. Twenty years of blood, sweat and tears down the drain.'

He turns away, but not before I see the tears sliding down his cheeks. I take the whisky tumbler from his trembling hands and place it on the floor, then pull him towards me. At first his shoulders are stiff and unyielding, but then he crumples like a deflated balloon. As he crumples, my resolve hardens.

'The money you gave Billy, would it have made a difference to the business?'

'It would have kept the wolf from the door for another few months. Why?'

'What's the address of his unit?'

He pulls away from me. 'No, Eve,' he says, shaking his head.

'I'm just going to talk to him, explain the situation. I'm sure if he knew the trouble we're in he'd understand.' I know nothing of the sort, but I need to convince Noah to give me the address somehow.

Wordlessly, he pushes himself to his feet and leaves the room, returning a few moments later holding a red file. He pulls a sheet of paper out and hands it to me.

I skim-read the closely typed A4 sheet of paper. It's a contract between Noah and a company called Ackman and Son Property Services.

This deed of guarantee is made between the guarantor, Noah Griffiths, and the landlord, Ackman and Son Property Services, and relates to the terms of the tenancy agreement for the property at Unit 5B, Nesborough Business Park. The guarantor agrees to fully cover and compensate the landlord for any loss, damage, costs or other expenses, including any rent arrears...

I stare at Noah. 'Does this mean what I think it means? That you're liable if Billy defaults on his rent?'

He nods.

'How long is the lease?'

'A year.'

'And the rent?'

'Just under a thousand a month.'

'Jesus, Noah. Can this get any worse?'

'How could I say no? He's my son,' Noah says weakly.

'So is Joe!'

He cradles his head in his hands. I want to be sympathetic, but all I feel is a white-hot rage. How can he have gambled everything on Billy's spurious start-up?

'I'll make it right somehow,' he mutters.

I shake my head and leave the room. Perhaps I should be grateful I was wrong about the affair. Perhaps I should feel guilty for ever doubting him. How can I, when he has risked our home, our future, everything?

42

Unit 5B, Nesborough Business Park, is a single-storey concrete building with a flat roof and a large steel roller door. It is one of three identical units close to the entrance to the business park. There is a bodywork repair specialist on one side and a laundry on the other. All three are closed and shuttered, which you'd expect at seven o'clock on a Monday morning.

A single street light casts an orange glow over the small car park in front of the units. I pull up next to the only other car parked there, a white, sporty-looking VW Golf. Yawning, I climb stiffly out of the car. I'm dog-tired. I barely slept again last night, restlessly tossing and turning as Noah's revelations played over and over in my mind. The business going bust. The mortgage arrears. Noah's foolhardy decision to act as guarantor for Billy's lease. My anxiety-fuelled thoughts were in overdrive and switching them off was impossible. It didn't help that, beside me, Noah slept like the dead. At five o'clock I gave up altogether, grabbed some clothes and crept out of the room.

I blip the key fob to lock the car and cross the car park to the unit. Unlike its neighbours, there is no signage outside 5B. It is completely anonymous, the single window as blank-eyed as a corpse, and I give an involuntary shiver. Perhaps I should have come mid-morning when Billy's more likely to be here, but I wanted to see the lay of the land before I tackled him. Fore-warned is forearmed.

I cup my hands round my face and stare through the window, expecting the unit to be in darkness, shocked when it isn't. A six-foot-high partition separates an entrance area from the rest of the building and a light is on behind it.

Without thinking, I rap my knuckles against the door, then peer back through the window. Billy's probably left the light on by accident, something he used to do all the time when he stayed at ours when he was younger. It used to drive me mad.

I'm about to knock again when the light goes out. Either it's on a timer... or someone is inside. I'm debating whether to walk round to the back of the unit to see if there's a fire door when there's the scrape of a bolt being drawn across and the front door opens an inch.

Billy peeks at me through the crack in the door. His face has frozen and his hands are grasping the door jamb so tightly his knuckles are bloodless.

He stares at me in a daze. I am clearly not the person he was expecting to see.

'Whatcha doing here?' he mumbles, his eyes darting over my shoulder to see if anyone's with me.

'Let me in. I need to talk to you, Billy.'

He shakes his head. 'Can't at the moment. Bit tied up.'

I lower my voice to a growl. 'I don't care if you're busy or not. Let me in *now*.'

He exhales loudly, opens the door and stands back to let me in. Once I'm inside, he locks the door and draws a heavy-duty bolt across before disappearing around the side of the partition. Shaking my head, I follow him.

I find myself in a large, airy space. The only light is a dull, blueish glow from a computer monitor to my right.

'Can you please turn a light on so we don't have to stand here in the dark?'

Billy shuffles over to a modern tripod floor lamp and flicks it on. I look around, taking everything in. The high ceilings and concrete floor. The kitchenette next to a door which presumably leads to the toilet. To my left, a home gym has been set up. I correct myself. It's more than a home gym. There's a treadmill and a cross trainer, a spin bike and a rowing machine. A punchbag and boxing gloves, a couple of weight benches and a complicated-looking multi-gym. Not to mention various barbells and dumbbells, medicine balls and gym balls. This stuff must have cost thousands.

I step further into the unit, doing a double take when I spot a pool table in the corner. The computer monitor is one of those curved ones Joe has his heart set on. It's balanced on a packing case, a gaming chair in front of it. The chair is surrounded by empty beer cans, food wrappers and overflowing ashtrays. On the screen flickers the image of a soldier in army fatigues holding a sub-machine gun. In the sky behind him are a couple of weaponised drones. Beyond the gaming chair is a camp bed, on which a sleeping bag and a grubby T-shirt are crumpled. More empty food packets poke out of an overflowing bin. Billy moved from Jenny's place in Essex to a room in a shared house in Nesborough last summer, so why the camp bed?

'Are you sleeping here?' I ask him with a frown.

He grunts in reply.

'What about your house share? Don't tell me they kicked you out?'

'Course not,' he scoffs. 'I needed to keep under the radar for a bit, that's all.'

'Under the radar? Why?' I frown. 'What have you done, Billy?'

'There was a bit of a misunderstanding with one of my suppliers.'

'Of the gym equipment?'

'Something like that,' he says. I regard him properly for the first time. He looks unkempt, as if he's just stumbled out of bed, but although his eyes are bloodshot, his face isn't sleep-creased. His fingers drum against his jeans as he eyeballs the unit's roller doors. He is... twitchy.

'Do you owe them money?'

He makes a non-committal noise, then says, 'Why are you here, anyway?'

'Do you know your dad's business has gone bust?'

His eyes widen, and he gives a small shake of his head.

'No, I didn't think so. And now we're in very real danger of losing our house.' My gaze sweeps across the unit. This isn't the nerve centre of a tech start-up. It's the ultimate man cave. Every teenage boy's wet dream. 'So we need our investment back, I'm afraid.'

'Your investment?'

'Yes,' I say patiently. 'The sixty thousand pounds your father gave you to set up the business. I appreciate you've already spent some of it, but we need the rest back.'

'You can't ask for it back. Dad gave it to me.'

'As a loan, Billy. Not as a gift. Now we're calling it in. You'll have to ask the bank for a loan, like everybody else.' I smile thinly. 'I'm sure if your app is as good as you claim it is, the bank will be falling over itself to lend you the money.'

His tongue darts out between his lips. 'Thing is, I can't pay the money back.'

'Can't?' My eyes narrow. 'Or won't?'

Beads of sweat have broken out across his forehead. 'Can't,' he says.

'Why not?' My stomach swoops as I brace myself for his answer.

'Because it's all gone. Every single penny.'

43

I sit in the car with my head in my hands, wondering if things can get any worse. Though I think I knew the moment I walked into Billy's little kingdom that the money had all gone, that he'd spent every penny indulging himself.

The question is, what do I do about it? Curl up and admit defeat, or come out fighting?

All I want to do is go home and lick my wounds, but I can't. I start up the engine and head to the drive-thru Costa on the edge of town, ordering a flat white, which I nurse as I wait for the eight o'clock pips to sound.

I drain the last of my coffee and call Joe's school.

'Elmwood Manor Independent Day School,' the secretary purrs. 'How may I help you?'

'Can I speak to Andrew Surridge?'

'Certainly. Who shall I say is calling?'

'Eve Griffiths.'

'Mrs Griffiths,' she repeats. Is it my imagination or has her tone cooled? 'Putting you through.'

'Surridge,' Elmwood Manor's bursar booms so loudly I move the phone away from my ear. I've only spoken to Andrew

Surridge a handful of times, but I've never warmed to him. A short man with a weak handshake and a puffed-out chest, he struts around the school grounds like he owns the place.

'Hello, Andrew, it's Eve Griffiths,' I say, attempting to inject warmth into my voice. Much as it pains me to have to ingratiate myself, I need him on side. 'I don't suppose you have a moment to talk about Joe's school fees?'

'I've been trying to talk to your husband about Joe's fees for the last month,' he says piously.

'I know, and I apologise. I know we're in arrears, but I want to assure you that it was merely an oversight on our part and that this term's fees will be with you by end of play today.'

'Today, you say?'

'You have my word.'

'And next term?'

'Next term's fees will be paid in good time,' I reassure him.

'Excellent.' Surridge clears his throat. 'I don't know if you are aware, but we can arrange special repayment terms for parents who need to spread the cost of their fees—'

'That won't be necessary,' I say smoothly. 'Anyway, I won't take up any more of your time.'

Once the call has ended, I tip my head back onto the headrest and close my eyes. Toadying to Andrew Surridge leaves a bitter taste in my mouth, but it's worth it to keep Joe at Elmwood.

I type my next destination into the satnav and pull out of the car park. The jeweller's is on the other side of Nesborough, a fifteen-minute drive away. I made the decision to sell my jewellery in the early hours of this morning. It's the quickest way I can think of to get my hands on enough cash to pay Joe's school fees.

I arrive at the nearest car park half an hour before the jeweller's opens and use the time to call Lisa.

'How's Annie?' I ask when she answers.

She sighs. 'Much the same. I keep telling myself I should be glad she's not deteriorating, but I don't know. She's due to have another scan this morning, and if there's no improvement, her consultant wants to carry out the brain stem function tests.'

'That's good, isn't it?'

'What if they show she's brain dead?' Lisa gulps, and I feel a sharp stab of grief. Billy's failed app, Joe's unpaid school fees and our drowning debt are nothing compared to the ordeal she and Annie are enduring.

'Then we'll deal with it,' I say. I want to reassure her, to tell her Annie is going to pull through, but I can't give her false hope, it would be too cruel. 'I know it's hard, but you must try not to worry.'

'I know.'

'What would Annie say?'

'"Don't be a Negative Nelly, Mum."'

'Exactly. You've got to stay positive.'

'You're right,' she says in a small voice, and I wish yet again that I could turn back the clock to the day of Joe's party and change everything.

'You're doing amazingly, Lisa. Remember that.'

'I guess.' She sighs, then says, 'Oh, I nearly forgot. Sergeant Harrington called yesterday. They've identified the ring-leaders of a London gang they believe has been running drugs into Nesborough. A county line, he called it. They're planning a series of raids in the next couple of weeks and are pretty confident they'll catch whoever supplied the ecstasy Annie took.'

'That's good,' I say, my stomach swooping as I picture Joe's designer trainers.

'I don't suppose you're any closer to finding out what happened that night?' she asks.

'Not yet,' I say. 'I'll keep trying.' I mean it too, because I want to do the right thing by Annie. I owe her that much.

* * *

I've only ever visited the small family jeweller's at the top of Nesborough High Street to buy a new battery for my watch. According to their website, they also buy and sell jewellery, promising realistic, fair and accurate prices for gold, silver and other precious metals. I just hope they'll offer me a fair price for mine.

A bell chimes as I push the door open, and a woman behind the counter looks up and smiles.

'How can I help?'

I reach into my handbag for the black velvet bag I filled earlier and tip its contents onto the glass-topped counter.

'Could you give me a price for this?'

We both inspect the jumble of precious metals and sparkling stones. The diamond earrings I inherited from my grandmother. A solitaire ruby ring left to me by my great-aunt. The pearl bracelet and matching necklace Noah's father gave his mum on their thirtieth wedding anniversary. I have brought along some less expensive pieces too, like the twisted gold necklace my parents gave me for my twenty-first, and the slim gold watch I bought myself with my first pay packet.

I stand back as the woman sifts through the pieces, examining each carefully with an eyepiece. It seems to take an age, and my gaze wanders around the shop, taking in the display cabinets filled with glittering rings, bracelets, necklaces and earrings, silver tankards and glass ornaments. As I edge over to a cabinet displaying Casio watches, I notice the security cameras mounted in each corner of the shop, recording my humiliation.

'I can give you five thousand for the lot,' the woman says.

My attention snaps back to her. 'Five? I was hoping it was worth closer to six.'

'Five and a half, tops. Of course, you might get more online.'

'I don't have time for that.' I smile tightly as I quickly calculate. There's just over £2,500 in the building society account I opened for Joe when he was a baby. It's a passbook account and I'm the only one with access to it, which is why Noah hasn't emptied it already. The term's fees are £9,920, which still leaves me £1,920 short. I drum my fingers on the counter.

The woman points at my engagement ring. 'I could give you a price for that.'

'What? Oh, right, OK.' I pull the ring off and drop it into her outstretched palm.

Noah proposed on the beach at Lyme Regis the day after his decree absolute came through. We'd gone away for the weekend to celebrate his divorce, wandering through the town's pretty streets, eating fish and chips on The Cobb and searching for fossils at Charmouth.

On our last night we took a bottle of champagne onto the beach to watch the sunset. Before Noah opened the champagne, he reached into the pocket of his jeans, pulled out a ring box and asked me to marry him.

'I love you, Eve. You complete me. We are meant to be together, like... like cookies and cream.'

'Or fish and chips,' I joked.

'Bacon and eggs.'

'Gin and tonic!'

'Cheese and crackers.'

'You're crackers,' I said, flinging my arms around him. 'Of course I'll marry you, you silly sod.'

He'd slipped the ring on my finger, and as I'd admired the three perfect diamonds in their contemporary platinum setting, he'd told me the three stones were supposed to represent our past, present and future.

Funny how I should remember that now.

The woman places her eyepiece on the counter. 'I can give you eighteen hundred for it. Cash.'

I hesitate. Selling the ring would leave me £120 short for

Joe's school fees. Noah will be livid, but perhaps it serves him right for giving all our money to Billy.

'Call it two grand and it's a deal,' I say.

She nods and draws a black triplicate receipt book towards her, filling in brief descriptions of every piece of jewellery and the agreed sale price before she asks me to fill in my name and contact details. I tick the box saying the items are my property to sell, and she tips the jewellery back into the velvet bag and disappears through the door to the back of the shop, reappearing a few minutes later with a bundle of fifty-pound notes.

She counts out £7,500 and I stuff the money into the bottom of my bag, knowing it'll be a nerve-wracking walk back to the car.

The sound of the bell above the door ringing jauntily as I leave is at odds with my heavy heart. I have never been a superstitious person, yet I can't help worrying that by selling my engagement ring I'm somehow putting a curse on my marriage.

That, of course, is assuming Noah and I still have a future together. After the events of the last week, I'm not sure we do.

44

Elmwood Manor is an imposing Victorian behemoth of a building that stands proudly at the end of a long, sweeping drive. With a ragstone façade and mullioned windows, it is both gothic and lofty. Probably a bit pretentious, if I'm honest, though it still has the power to intimidate, and I find myself smoothing down my hair and straightening my shoulders as I step through the oak doors into the entrance hall.

Portraits of long-dead head teachers frown down on me as I make my way to the school office. It's half past three, half an hour before the end of the last lesson, and the atmosphere in the entrance hall is hushed, almost expectant, as if the building is holding its breath before an army of chattering children break through its ramparts.

The secretary is on the phone when I arrive, and I hover awkwardly outside her door until she wraps up the call and beckons me in.

My grip tightens on the strap of my bag. 'I've come to settle Joe's fees.'

'There was no need to come in,' she says. 'A bank transfer would have been fine.'

'I was picking Joe up anyway. I'm afraid it's a mixture of cash and a building society cheque. I hope that's all right?'

'Of course, Mrs Griffiths. You'd be surprised the different ways people pay their fees. One parent once offered us a string of polo ponies to settle his account.'

Even so, her eyes widen when I lay £7,420 in cash on her desk, along with the cheque for £2,500. She counts the money three times, then locks it and the cheque in a safe at the back of the room.

'We'll be sending out the next invoice on the fifteenth of April,' she says as she hands me a receipt.

My throat constricts. I might have scraped together enough money to cover this term, but how the hell am I supposed to find another ten grand in the next six weeks, let alone the two years' worth of fees when Joe's in sixth form? I fake a smile. 'No problem.'

* * *

I text Joe, telling him I'll give him a lift home, then wander out to the sports fields. On the nearest all-weather pitch, a girls' hockey lesson is underway, and I lean against the railing to watch. The girls, with their long, lean legs and perky ponytails, look about Joe's age and remind me of Annie so acutely that I find myself welling up.

The blast of a whistle makes me start. It's the PE teacher, an attractive Kiwi in his early twenties called Mr Green, who's been at the school since September. He won Joe's undivided loyalty when he made him captain of Elmwood's first XI rugby team in the first week of term.

'Nice work, ladies,' he calls, as the girls pull out mouth-guards and sling their sticks over their shoulders. They drift back towards the school, chatting as they walk. All except one girl, who hangs back to help the PE teacher collect bibs and training cones from the pitch. Something about her is familiar. I study her closely. It's the way she scoops up the bibs, hooking them over her arm with quick, economical movements. Horses, I think, and then it hits me. It's Lottie Miller, the girl at Joe's party. The girl I thought was having an affair with my husband.

Lottie stops in front of the PE teacher, looking up at him, her head cocked to one side. He is talking. I can't hear what he's saying from this distance, though it's clear Lottie is drinking in every word.

Unaware she is being observed from afar, she touches his arm. He glances towards the school, presumably to check no one is watching, then, for the briefest of moments, laces his hand in hers. It only takes a second for me to understand what I'm seeing. Lottie Miller is in a relationship with her PE teacher, Mr Green. Nick Green.

NG.

It's why she looked so shifty when I told her I'd been suspended for bringing the school into disrepute. I thought it was because she'd given Annie the E, but I was wrong. It's because she knows that if anyone found out Nick Green was in a sexual relationship with a pupil, he wouldn't just be suspended, he'd be sacked on the spot.

More secrets, I think, as I turn and walk back across the immaculately mown grass to the car park. Does everyone have something to hide?

45

I wait for Joe back at the car, and he appears just after four o'clock. He chucks his rucksack onto the back seat and climbs in beside me.

'I could have caught the bus,' he says, fixing his seat belt.

'It's no problem. I was passing.'

'Got anything to eat? I'm starving.' He peers into the glove compartment hopefully, as if he might find a three-course dinner in there.

'I think there are some sweets in my bag.'

'Result!' he crows, bending down to ferret through my handbag. 'Want one?' he asks as he tears a gold wrapper off a toffee and pops it into his mouth.

'I'm fine, thanks.'

I glance at him as I turn on the ignition. His fringe is flopping over his forehead and there's the lightest fuzz of bum fluff on his chin. My heart contracts when I notice the grass stains on his trousers and his mud-encrusted shoes.

Can a boy who still loves toffees and spends his lunchtimes playing football with his mates really be up to no good?

'Joe,' I say, my hands gripping the steering wheel. 'You would tell me if anything was bothering you, wouldn't you?'

He folds the gold sweet wrapper into squares before he answers carefully, 'Like what?'

I hesitate. Play the wrong card now and I could ruin everything. After all, what actual proof do I have that Joe is mixed up in the Nesborough drug scene? Some designer trainers and a gut feeling? It's not enough.

'I know how hard the last week or so has been for you,' I say. 'What with Annie and everything.'

A shadow crosses his face and he turns away from me to look out the window. 'I don't want to talk about Annie.'

'I know, and I get that, but you can't bottle everything up inside, Joe. It's not good for you.'

'I said I don't want to talk about her,' he snaps.

I hold up a hand. 'All right. I'm only trying to help. Grief, it's not linear, it's—' I break off. Joe is ripping the sweet wrapper into tiny pieces, his movements jerky, almost frantic. 'Oh, never mind,' I say with a sigh. 'But if you do want to talk about what happened, you only have to say.'

We drive the rest of the way home in silence.

* * *

For the first time in weeks, Noah's home before me. I walk through the house looking for him, eventually finding him in the garden, where he's taking pictures of Joe's treehouse on his phone.

'What are you doing?' I ask.

'I've just seen one on eBay for three hundred quid. Before you say anything, Joe hasn't used it for years.'

'He does still use it, actually.'

Noah frowns. 'What for?'

'I don't know. Chilling.' Although, thinking about it, he probably escapes up there to vape. Or worse. My chest tightens.

'I'll put a reserve on it, and if it doesn't sell I'll take it off, OK?' Noah says.

'Whatever.' I turn on my heels and stomp back to the house. I know there's no point getting worked up about a treehouse when we're probably going to lose the roof over our heads, but it's yet another kick in the teeth. Another reminder that life as we know it will never be the same again.

I know I should sit down with Noah and work out a plan of action. We're not the first people to end up in debt, and we won't be the last. There are things we could be doing, such as reaching out to the building society and bank and working out a repayment plan with the credit card company, but I don't have the bandwidth. It's as if I'm stuck in a peat bog, and every time I try to move forward I sink even deeper into the bowels of it.

Instead, I shuffle around the kitchen like someone twice my age, preparing a perfunctory supper of baked potatoes with baked beans and cheese. Noah hates baked beans, but I heap them on his plate anyway.

We eat in silence, Joe excusing himself from the table before I've taken my last mouthful, and after Noah has helped me load the dishwasher, he too disappears, as if he can't bear to be in the same room as me. I can't say I blame him. I'm radiating anger, practically throbbing with it.

Noah's already asleep when I finally head up to bed. He's lying on his back with one arm tucked under his pillow, his breathing slow and steady. I undress and slip under the covers knowing that it's pointless, that I'll never sleep. There's too much to think about. Too many worries swirling around my head. Joe's strange behaviour. Noah's gullibility. Billy's total lack of remorse. The police investigation into Annie's overdose. My suspension.

Since Joe's party, everything I took for granted – my son, my marriage, our home, my job – has been under threat. The landscape of my life has changed beyond recognition. On the surface, all these things are unrelated, and yet... and yet I can't help feeling that somehow they are connected, that a malevolent force is playing with me, as a cat plays with a dead shrew, chucking it up in the air, prodding it with a paw, willing it to come back to life just so it can torment the poor thing some more.

My brain spins in circles trying to connect the dots. A psychologist would say I was looking for patterns in an attempt to make sense of everything, but that feeling won't go away; the sense that something – *someone* – is behind this.

Finally, around one in the morning, I fall into a dreamless sleep.

46

I'm contemplating the overflowing washing basket the next morning when my phone chirps with a text. It's Lisa.

They're carrying out the tests today. Will you come? X

Of course, I reply. *Be with you in half an hour.*

Traffic is light, and soon I'm pulling into the hospital car park. It's hard to believe it's only ten days since Annie was rushed here in the back of an ambulance. So much has happened, yet for Lisa, time has stood still as she waits for her daughter to wake up.

I stop in the café to pick up coffees before making my way to the second floor. This time, when I reach the double doors to the intensive care unit, I press the buzzer and tell the nurse I'm here to see Annie. A second later the doors swing open and I am hit once again by the quiet thrum of the ICU.

Lisa jumps up from the chair by Annie's bed when she sees me, and we hug briefly.

'They've done the tests,' she says when we break away. 'I'm just waiting for the results.'

I take my place on Annie's other side, then retrieve some hand cream from my bag and massage first one of Annie's hands, then the other, while Lisa dampens a flannel and gently sponges her face. We are like handmaidens tending to our queen. It is both intimate and absorbing and, for the first time since Joe's party, I feel at peace.

When we have finished, we talk quietly, reminding Annie of the adventures she and Joe have had over the years. The trips to the zoo and the park. The picnics at the beach. The time we caught the train to London to visit the Natural History Museum and Joe was so terrified of the animatronic Tyrannosaurus Rex he had nightmares for weeks.

When we run out of stories, I ask Lisa how she's been.

'Everyone's been so kind. It's true what they say: you know who your friends are at times like these.'

'They'll be dropping round casseroles next,' I say, and she stifles a snort of laughter, because we used to mock the playground mums who bombarded any poor sod going through a bereavement or divorce with home-made lasagnas and hotpots just so they could satisfy their desire for drama or find out all the gossip.

'Not the casseroles,' Lisa splutters. 'Then I really will know we're in trouble.' The smile slips from her face and she grips Annie's hand.

I stiffen at the sound of voices in the corridor. A moment later, Dr Connolly, Annie's consultant, appears in the doorway.

'Mrs Bradstock,' he says solemnly. 'Do you have a moment?'

Lisa pales, shooting me a desperate look as she scrambles to her feet.

'Want me to stay with Annie?' I ask her.

She shakes her head. 'Come with me?'

'Of course.' I drop a kiss on my god-daughter's smooth forehead and follow Lisa and the consultant down the corridor and into the visitors' room.

We perch on the same seats as before and wait for Dr Connolly to speak. Just when I think I can't bear the silence a moment longer, he clears his throat.

'As you know, we carried out brain stem function tests on Annie this morning.'

Lisa nods.

'I am very sorry to tell you that she didn't respond to any of the tests.'

There is a ringing in my ears. This can only mean one thing. I look at Lisa in horror. She is bent forwards at the waist, her arms wrapped around herself, her chin tucked into her chest as if she would fold herself up and disappear altogether if she could.

'I'm afraid Annie is brain dead.'

'No, no, that can't be true.' Lisa looks up, her eyes like hollow sockets. 'I want a second opinion.'

Dr Connolly adjusts his tie. 'The diagnosis of brain death has to be confirmed by two doctors to ensure there is no room for error. In Annie's case, both a senior registrar and I carried out the tests twice.'

'But she's still breathing,' Lisa wails.

'The ventilator is blowing air into her lungs, yes, but without it, Annie would not be able to breathe.'

Lisa starts to weep, and my own heart breaks, because I can't see how the world can keep turning without Annie in it. Time slows to a crawl. Dr Connolly leaves, and a nurse bustles in with a new box of tissues and two glasses of water. Still, Lisa keens, the low, anguished sound echoing around this small, soulless room, causing the hairs on the back of my neck to stiffen. It is a lament, I think, as I rise from my chair and envelop her in my arms. A lament for the dead.

47

The afternoon passes in a blur. Dr Connolly introduces us to the specialist nurse for organ donation; a plump-faced woman called Maggie, who asks if Lisa has had a chance to consider whether she would like to donate Annie's organs. Lisa, white-faced, barely holding it together, tells her it is too soon. Maggie pats her on the arm and says she'll come back later. I make Lisa a tea, which sits untouched on the cabinet beside Annie's bed. We keep watch over our Sleeping Beauty, overwhelmed by grief, because we know that nothing can wake her now.

At six o'clock, I heave myself out of my chair, and tramp, stiff-limbed, into the corridor to update Noah. I texted him not long after the consultant left to tell him the results of Annie's brain stem tests, and his phone barely rings before he picks up.

'How's Lisa?' he asks. He sounds as dazed as I feel.

'She's... she's...' I break off. 'Not good,' I say finally.

'I still can't believe it. Poor Annie. Poor Lisa. Have they—?'

'Tomorrow morning, they said. They want to talk to her about organ donation again.'

'Organ donation? Oh, Christ, no.' Noah's voice cracks. 'I

should come. I want to come. If I leave now I can be there in twenty minutes.'

'No, Noah.'

'But I want to be there with you all!'

'They only allow two visitors at a time. I'll tell Lisa you send your love. Look, I need to get back to them. There's some bolognese sauce in the freezer. Second drawer down, I think. Don't save me any. I'm not sure when I'll be home.' I pause. 'Have you told Joe?'

'Joe?' Noah asks, as if he can't place the name.

'Have you told Joe about Annie?' I repeat, swallowing my irritation.

'He's out.'

'Again? Where?'

'I don't know, I'm not his bloody keeper. Hanging about at the rec with his mates, I should think.'

'OK. Look, I'd better go. I'll talk to you later.'

* * *

At eight o'clock, Lisa sends me home.

'But—' I begin.

'No, Eve. Mum's going to be here soon.'

Lisa's mum, Jackie, was on a trans-Atlantic cruise when Annie went into hospital and has only now been able to get back. Just in time, as it turns out.

'If you're sure.' I hug her tightly, shocked at how thin she feels, how insubstantial. 'Ring me if you need anything, promise?'

'Promise.' She looks from me to Annie. 'I'll give you a moment.'

I nod, my eyes welling with tears. Understandably, Lisa wants it to be just her and her mum when they switch off

Annie's ventilator tomorrow. Which means... which means the time has come for me to say goodbye.

Once Lisa has gone, I take Annie's hand. Beneath the sheet, I watch her chest rise and fall. She looks so peaceful it's impossible to believe that the only thing keeping her alive is the ventilator.

As I drop a kiss onto her forehead, a fat tear splashes onto her cheek. More are threatening, and I press my thumbs into my eyes to curb the flow.

'I will find out who did this to you,' I say fiercely. 'I will find out who did this, and I will make them pay.'

48

The house is in darkness when I pull into the drive half an hour later. I find Noah hunched on the sofa in the kitchen, several empty bottles of beer on the floor beside him. He heaves himself up to his feet when he sees me and I go straight to him, desperate to be held, to be told everything is going to be all right.

Brain dead. The words are so bloody callous, so... *final*. I shiver, and Noah rubs my arms, as if he can warm the ice crystallising inside me by touch alone.

Eventually, he holds me by my shoulders and studies me. 'You OK?'

It's like looking in a mirror. His face is as ravaged as mine.

'Not really,' I say flatly. 'You?'

'Same.'

I pour myself a glass of water. There are two dirty pasta bowls on the draining board. The bolognese sauce has congealed like smears of dried blood. I turn back to Noah. 'We should tell Joe.'

'Now?'

I nod. 'I don't want him hearing it from someone else.'

Joe is on his Xbox. Today it's *FIFA*, Real Madrid versus Manchester City. Real are winning two-nil. Joe pauses the game and pulls his headphones off when he sees us.

'Uh-oh. This looks serious,' he jokes. 'What have I done wrong now?'

He must register our distress because the grin slips from his face and his brow wrinkles.

I take a deep breath. 'Joe, there's no easy way to say this. Annie, she's... The doctors say she... she won't ever come out of the coma. They're going to... they're going to turn off her life support machine in the morning.'

Joe's eyes widen and he turns away, a hand covering his mouth. Noah reaches out and touches his shoulder, but Joe shrugs his hand away almost angrily.

'Can I see her?' he mumbles. 'Before they—'

'I'm sorry, Joe, but you can't. Lisa just wants it to be her and Annie's gran tomorrow.'

He makes a strange gulping sound, his broad shoulders shuddering. He is crying. Choking, gut-wrenching tears wracking his boy-man body. I am across the room in a heartbeat, cradling him in my arms as if he's six and has fallen and grazed his knee, as if a kiss will make it all better.

'Oh, Joe, I'm so sorry.'

'It's my fault,' he sobs. 'All my fault.'

'Of course it's not your fault, sweetheart,' I soothe, feeling his grief as if it's my own. Which, of course, it is. What mother doesn't absorb their child's heartache, their pain? It doesn't stop the day their voice breaks or when they start to shave; not even when they marry and have kids of their own. It's for life, this need to smooth over the cracks, to make things better. 'You weren't to know this would happen. The chances are...' I think about maths, the comforting predictability of it. The patterns and structure. 'Infinitesimal,' I say finally.

'But it should never have happened.'

'What do you mean, Joe?' Noah asks. I glare at him, warning him to back off. Now is not the right time. Can't he see our son is in bits?

Joe hiccups a couple of times and wipes his nose on the sleeve of his hoodie. He stares at his feet, his shoulders hunched. There's a hole in his sock, and I make a mental note to buy him some new ones, then shake my head. What does it matter that Joe has a hole in his bloody sock? Annie's life support machine is being switched off in the morning. That is the only thing that matters.

'Joe?' Noah asks again. 'What d'you mean it should never have happened?'

Finally, Joe looks up, his eyes puffy and his voice ragged. 'If I hadn't had the party she would still be here.'

He's right, I think. Though Noah and I are just as culpable. We could have both said no. Despite my instincts screaming that a party was a bad idea, I still let Noah talk me into it. Joe isn't to blame. We all are.

49

I can't eat. I can't sleep. I spend the night tossing and turning, going over the events of the last few days until my head threatens to burst. I torture myself imagining what will happen in that little side room in the intensive care unit in the morning. Will the hospital chaplain visit? Will they take out Annie's drips and lines first? How do they turn the ventilator off? Is it a case of simply switching off the power at the mains, like turning off a side lamp?

I wonder if Lisa has decided whether to donate Annie's organs. I have been on the organ donor register ever since a woman I did my teacher training with was able to stop dialysis after a successful kidney transplant. As far as I'm concerned, the doctors can help themselves once I'm dead. If, God forbid, something should happen to Joe, I know the decision wouldn't be so clearcut.

At 5 a.m. I give up all attempts at sleep and head downstairs. The house is chilly, the heating yet to fire up, and I'm glad of my dressing gown as I steal through the silent hallway to the kitchen. I make tea and drink it in the dark, the only light the glow of my phone as I scroll mindlessly through Facebook and Instagram.

It's a window on another world, a world where people are still going about their daily business, eating in restaurants and taking their kids to the park or for walks in the country, celebrating birthdays and posting photos of their pets. How is the world still turning when ours is in stasis?

At 6 a.m. I do what I promised myself I wouldn't and text Lisa.

Hey, honey. Just checking in. Did your mum arrive? How are you both bearing up? Eve xx

I can tell by the two blue ticks that she's seen my text, but it's another ten minutes or so before she replies.

Mum arrived not long after you left. The doctor is coming at 8 a.m.

The phone trembles in my hand. Eight o'clock. In two hours' time my precious god-daughter will be gone. It is too much to take in. I bury my head in my hands and weep.

Two hours. That's all Lisa has left before her world shatters. No longer clinging to hope by Annie's bedside, but organising her funeral. I ache for my friend, and my tears wet the screen of my phone as I type out a reply.

I am so, so sorry. Please let me know if there's anything I can do. Xx

I reread the message. It seems trite. Inadequate. Because there is nothing I can do. Nothing at all.

* * *

Noah appears at half seven, showered and dressed.

'You're not going into work today?' I ask, aghast.

'I have to, Eve.'

'But today's the day—'

'I know what today is,' he says wearily. 'But I have too much on.'

'Couldn't you at least work from home?'

He shakes his head. 'There's a meeting I can't miss.'

'There's always a bloody meeting,' I mutter.

He makes himself toast and eats it leaning against the island, then picks up his laptop bag and phone and gives me a quick kiss. 'I don't know what time I'll be home,' he says as he heads for the door. Over the chimney breast, our vintage clock ticks away, edging closer to eight o'clock with every damn second.

The front door slams, leaving the house cloaked in a suffocating silence. I stare at the spot on the kitchen floor where we found Annie, stiff-limbed and unconscious, the night of Joe's party. Tick, tick, tick goes the clock. It's now a quarter to eight. I cannot be in this house, the house where Annie overdosed, when she dies, I just cannot.

Reaching a decision, I bolt up the stairs and change into my running gear, leaving the house minutes later. I don't bother to warm up, I just start running, through the village and along the Langley valley, my eyes fixed on the horizon.

After a couple of miles, I veer left into the woods and run up the rutted track towards the ruins of Langley Manor, pushing the memories of winter walks and summer picnics from my mind.

I run until my thighs burn and my lungs scream in protest, and only then do I slow to a walk. As I gulp in air, I glance at my watch. It is nine o'clock. Annie has gone.

* * *

Once my heart rate has returned to normal, I jog slowly home. I came out without my keys or phone and have to feel under the flowerpot behind the back door for the spare key before I can let myself in.

My phone is on the kitchen island where I left it. I should text Lisa and see how she is, but I'm not sure I can find the words. What do you say to a mother who has just watched her daughter's life support switched off? She'll phone when she's ready. Instead, I heel off my running shoes and head upstairs to take a shower.

The doorbell rings as I'm towel-drying my hair. I peer out of the window and my stomach churns. A police patrol car is parked on the drive next to my car.

50

This time, Sergeant Dan Harrington has sent his sidekick, the fresh-faced PC Marcus Anderson.

'Mrs Griffiths,' he says when I answer the door. 'Would it be possible to have a quick word? With Joe too, if he's in.'

'Of course.' I muster a smile and lead him into the living room. 'Won't be a sec. I'll fetch him.'

Joe is still asleep. I shake his shoulder gently and tell him he needs to get up.

He groans and turns over, pulling his duvet over his head and muttering, 'Too early.'

'The police are here again, sweetheart. They want to talk to you.'

It takes a second before my words sink in, but when they do, it's like I've plugged Joe into the mains. He throws his duvet off and bolts upright, his gaze sliding first to the door and then to the window, as if he's weighing up his escape routes.

I open and close a couple of drawers and fling underwear, a pair of jeans and a T-shirt onto his bed. 'It'll be routine questions,' I reassure him. 'Nothing to worry about.'

He dresses silently and slouches down the stairs, his hands

rammed in his pockets and his expression surly. I know that beneath the hard exterior is the old Joe, the Joe who cried when his pet rabbit Buster died, the Joe who was still letting Annie paint his nails when he was eleven. The Joe who used to follow his half-brother Billy around like a shadow. The same Joe who beamed with pride when he was made a Sixer in his Cub pack and was prepared to take on the school bullies to protect his friend. I want to shake him by the shoulders to see if the old Joe falls out of this toughened shell. Instead, I troop down the stairs after him and wish Noah was at home, so I didn't have to face this on my own.

Joe and I take opposite ends of the sofa, facing Anderson.

'I'm afraid I have some bad news,' he says. 'Sadly, Annie Bradstock passed away this morning.'

Joe's eyes bulge for the briefest of moments and it's all I can do not to leap to my feet and wrap my arms around him.

Anderson looks at me, then frowns. 'You don't seem surprised.'

'I was with Lisa, Annie's mum, at the hospital yesterday,' I explain. 'We knew they were withdrawing life support this morning.'

He nods briefly and turns to Joe. 'As we're now having to prepare a report for the coroner, I wanted to see if you remembered anything else about the night of your party, Joe.'

The subtext is clear. He doesn't believe Joe's claims that he knew nothing about the ecstasy. Before Joe has a chance to answer, I ask, 'Have you spoken to the other kids again?'

'We have, and, like Joe here, they say they aren't aware of anyone bringing ecstasy – or any other drugs, for that matter – to your house.'

'Annie could have taken something before she arrived,' Joe says.

'Joe!' I cry, shocked. 'I don't think she had.'

'You saw her beforehand?' Anderson asks.

'She was leaving her house as we arrived.'

'What time would that have been?'

I think back. 'Just after half past six.'

'She didn't appear to be under the influence of drink or drugs then?'

A lump forms in my throat as I recall Annie that last time. Eyes sparkling as she twirled in her green dress. 'Absolutely not,' I tell him.

'She could have brought it with her,' Joe says.

'More likely Connor or Josh gave it to her when she arrived,' I say hotly. I want to tell Anderson what I know about the kids who came to Joe's party. The secrets and the lies. But I decide to hold the cards close to my chest... for now.

'At this stage we're keeping an open mind,' he says, addressing Joe. 'That's why it's imperative that you tell us if you remember anything.'

He nods, and asks, 'Can I go now?'

'Of course.'

Once Joe has disappeared upstairs, I turn to Anderson. 'Annie's death has hit him hard.'

'I can imagine. We all think we're invincible at his age.'

This is a bit rich as he looks barely old enough to shave. I show him to the door, and I'm about to close it when he stops on the doorstep, jingles his car keys and says, 'We'll be in touch.'

As he drives away, I can't help thinking his parting words sound a little like a threat.

51

Later, I'm upstairs sorting through laundry when I spot Lisa's car parked on the verge outside her home. I poke my head around Joe's door.

'I'm popping over to Lisa's.'

He grunts, and I hurry downstairs, grab a coat and cross the green to Lisa's cottage. Jackie, Lisa's mum, opens the door, and when she sees me, she gives me a watery smile and ushers me in.

'She's in the garden,' Jackie says. 'I keep telling her she'll catch her death, but she isn't taking any notice.'

'How's she doing?' I ask quietly as we walk through the house.

Jackie shakes her head. 'Not good. It's a terrible business. I just can't understand it. Annie's not the type to touch a drop of drink, let alone drugs.'

It breaks my heart that she's still talking about her grand-daughter in the present tense, and I try to swallow the lump that seems permanently wedged in my throat.

'Lisa,' Jackie calls when we reach the back door. 'Eve's here to see you.' She turns to me. 'Go and sit with her. I'll bring you both out a cuppa.'

Lisa's garden is narrow but over 120 ft long. I spot her at the far end, sitting on the old swing seat overlooking the wildlife pond Craig dug the summer before his cancer diagnosis.

'Hey,' I say. 'OK if I join you?'

She nods. I sit next to her and take her hand.

'You're freezing,' I scold. It's little wonder. She's not even wearing a coat.

'I'm fine.'

We are silent for a bit, watching a wren hopping along the fence on the far side of the pond before it flits into the garden next door.

'How was it?' I ask eventually.

'Peaceful, I suppose. Everyone in ITU was very kind. Mum was in bits.' She sounds spaced out, almost robotic. It's the shock, I think. 'I need to organise the funeral but I have to wait for the post-mortem before they'll release Annie.'

I squeeze her hand. 'There's no rush.'

'Will you help me choose the music and readings? I can't think at the moment.'

'Of course.'

Jackie appears carrying two mugs of tea and a packet of digestives on a tray. 'Someone's just dropped off a chicken casserole,' she says.

'It was only a matter of time.' I glance at Lisa, but it's as if she hasn't heard me. She's shivering, and I set the tray on the grass by our feet, slip off my coat and drape it over her shoulders. She's always been slim, but she seems to have lost half a stone over the last few days.

'Are you eating properly?' I ask gently.

She looks at me with a puzzled frown.

'Oh, Lisa, love, you need to look after yourself.'

She doesn't answer, just stares vacantly at the floating crocodile head Annie bought her as a joke last Christmas. I want more than anything to ease her pain, and the only way I'll do that is by finding out who killed Annie. There were six people at Joe's party. Annie is dead and Joe is innocent. That leaves four: Connor Moody, Josh Duffy, Ethan Curtis and Lottie Miller.

One of them gave Annie the drugs that killed her. I just need to work out who.

52

For the next two weeks, I throw myself into helping Lisa and her mum organise Annie's funeral.

'It's not as though I have anything else to do,' I remind them the morning I drive them to Nesborough to visit the funeral directors for the first time. 'And, besides, I want to help.'

Outwardly, Lisa is coping. Only someone who knows her well would see that she is on autopilot, going through the motions because she has no other choice. It's as if her spirit, the spark that makes her who she is, has been snuffed out, leaving darkness in its place.

There are so many things to think about: the order of service, the hymns, the flowers, the wake. It's like organising a wedding, only we're marking an ending not a beginning.

Sometimes, when I suggest a reading or a piece of music, I worry I'm interfering, but Jackie is always assuring me I'm anything but.

'We're both so grateful, Eve. I don't think we could do it without you.'

When the day of Annie's funeral finally arrives, it is raining. Not spitting, not even drizzling, but lashing down in torrents, as if a rain cloud has burst directly over South Langley. Water runs in rivulets down the bay window in our bedroom as I shrug on the jacket of my black trouser suit and run a brush through my hair.

Automatically, I step in front of the full-length mirror in the corner of the room and check my reflection. I am pale, my eyes puffy and tinged with pink. For the last two weeks, I've kept myself busy, trying to keep my heartache, like a hungry wolf, at bay. Now, all at once, it breaks through my barricades and hits me with a force that knocks the wind out of me.

I was naive to think I could insulate myself from the pain, but I'm realising you can't run away from grief. You have to endure it, like shingles or toothache. You have to live with the throbbing agony every single day until one morning you wake up and the pain is a dull ache, still there – always there – but tolerable.

A tear trickles down my cheek and I brush it away with an impatient hand. Every atom of my being wants to hunker down in bed and weep until there are no tears left, but I can't. I have to pull myself together for Lisa. For Annie.

I take a couple of calming breaths, smooth down my jacket, and leave Noah scrabbling through his drawers in search of a black tie while I check if Joe's ready.

When I push open his bedroom door, he's playing *Fast and Furious* in trackies and a grubby white T-shirt. His black trousers, ironed shirt and dark-grey lambswool sweater are still hanging from the wardrobe door where I left them last night.

I try to hide my frustration. 'Joe, we need to leave in ten minutes.'

He bobs in his gaming chair as he swerves to overtake a car. His bruises have faded and the cut above his eye is now a thin white line. Noah thinks he'll have the scar for life.

'I'm not going.'

'Don't be silly. Of course you're going. Jump in the shower

while I find your shoes.' When he makes no move to leave, I cross the room and unplug his Xbox at the socket. The screen turns satisfyingly black.

'Hey, what d'you do that for?' he bellyaches.

'I mean it, Joe. I'll let you off the wake, but you're coming to Annie's funeral. End of. Get ready now before I see what your father has to say on the matter.'

Shooting me a filthy look, Joe tosses his controller on the floor and stalks out of the room. Moments later the shower begins to gurgle. Noah pokes his head round the door and points to the bathroom.

'He's cutting it fine, isn't he?'

I pull a face. 'He doesn't want to go.'

'It's not up to him.'

'I know, though I do get it. I don't much want to go either, to be honest. It's going to be awful.' My throat tightens again, the tears threatening to make a comeback, and I swallow hard.

'We're not doing it for our sakes though, are we?' Noah says. 'We're doing it for Lisa and Annie.'

I sigh. 'You're right.'

Joe reappears, his hair damp and a towel wrapped around his waist. Noah claps him on the back. 'Quick as you can, mate. We don't want to be late.'

I'm applying lipstick in the downstairs cloakroom when there's a loud rap at the door. Wondering if it's Lisa, I dart out and yank the door open, surprised to see my stepson standing on the doorstep, stony-faced, his hands in his pockets.

'Billy.' I take in his black jeans and polished shoes, the black V-neck jumper over a white shirt, the clumsily knotted black tie. The last time I saw him was at his lock-up over two weeks ago when he announced without a hint of remorse that he'd spent every penny of the money Noah had loaned him. 'I didn't know you were coming to the funeral.'

His eyes flash. 'Why shouldn't I come? I've known Annie just as long as the rest of you.'

'Of course you have. We weren't expecting you, that's all.' My smile is tight-lipped. 'You'd better come in.'

'Noah!' I yell up the stairs. 'Billy's here.'

Noah looks as surprised as I was to see his eldest son, but he disguises it far better, pulling Billy into a bear hug.

'You're soaked,' he chides. 'Let me find you a coat.'

I leave them to it, heading upstairs to chivvy Joe up. He brightens when I tell him Billy's here, which rankles. Am I the only one who can see Billy for what he really is?

* * *

The church is packed, as I knew it would be. Every pew heaving with bodies, a low murmur of voices like the babble of a brook as we step through the huge oak doors. Lisa promised to keep a row at the front of the church free for us, and I take a deep breath and walk up the aisle, trying not to mind that the voices fall silent as we pass.

We take our seats and I avert my gaze from the wicker coffin on a stand in the nave, focusing instead on the faded red hymn book and the order of service on the narrow shelf in front of me. There's a photo of Annie on the front of the order of service. She is tanned and laughing, her sparkling green eyes full of merriment. I remember the day Lisa took the picture. It was the summer before last and we'd caught the train down to Brighton: me, Joe, Lisa and Annie. We'd done all the touristy things – wandering The Lanes, exploring the Royal Pavilion, eating ice creams on the beach and playing arcade games on the pier. A happy day.

A hush falls over the congregation and I glance over my shoulder to see Lisa approach, closely followed by her mum and her uncle Pete. Lisa's face is pale but composed as she slips into her seat. I lean forwards and squeeze her shoulder, and she turns and gives me a watery smile.

The vicar takes her place at the pulpit and begins her eulogy. I tune out, knowing that if I listen to the portrait she is painting of my beloved god-daughter, I risk falling to pieces, and I can't allow that, not here. It wouldn't be fair to Lisa. This is not about me.

We sing a hymn, and then Lisa walks calmly up to the pulpit. She unfolds a sheet of paper, looks down at the mourners, clears her throat and begins.

'What can I say about Annie that hasn't already been said? She was both funny and kind, smart and sassy; she had big ambitions and even bigger dreams. She was five when she told me she wanted to be a princess when she grew up...' Lisa's voice is steady as she shares a couple of anecdotes from Annie's childhood, even managing to raise a gentle laugh or two. Not from me. My throat is a hard ball of grief. I doubt I could utter a sound if I tried.

Next to me, Joe's shoulders are shaking. I reach over and take his hand, half expecting him to shrug me off, but he grips me like a vice, his breathing coming in short, sharp puffs as he fights tears. The sound breaks my heart.

To distract myself, I glance around the church, shocked to see Josh Duffy slouched between his parents on the opposite aisle. Greg looks awkward in a black pinstriped suit, the jacket straining across his broad chest. Chrissy is wearing a full-length black wool coat with a faux-fur trim and a small black feather fascinator in her honey-blonde hair. She is dabbing at her perfectly made-up face with a handkerchief. As if he senses my gaze, Josh looks up. His body language screams indifference, but a flicker in his jaw gives him away.

Three rows behind Josh, Connor Moody sits with his mother Lorraine and sister Bobbi-Jo. Mother and daughter are openly crying, their faces red and blotchy. Connor looks as shell-shocked as a young infantryman encountering the bloody battlefields of the Somme for the first time.

I scan the nave, looking for Ethan Curtis and Lottie Miller. I'm beginning to think they haven't come when I spot them sitting together at the back of the church. Lottie is clutching a sodden tissue. Ethan, pale-faced and sombre, is fiddling with the order of service. Both are wearing their Elmwood Manor uniforms.

Five friends, bound by Annie's death. Is one of them hiding the truth, or are they all?

53

After the funeral we gather in The Swan, the picturesque pub overlooking the village green. It was the obvious choice for the wake. Like Lisa, Matt, the landlord, grew up in South Langley and was Craig's best man at their wedding over twenty years ago.

The moment Lisa walks in she is swamped by red-eyed villagers offering their condolences. The same phrases drift across the pub towards me. *Taken too soon... had her whole life ahead of her... such a tragedy.* Clichés, every one of them, but they are well meant and Lisa replies graciously, her pale face composed as she thanks people for coming.

Noah disappears in the direction of the bar, and I find a quiet spot by the patio doors that lead out to the pretty pub garden. The rain has finally stopped, and a small knot of Annie's friends are braving the chilly afternoon, sitting at a picnic table, their heads bent closely together. I can't see Josh or Connor. Ethan and Lottie also seem to have disappeared. I'm glad I didn't insist Joe came to the wake. I'm not sure how welcome he would have been.

Back inside the pub, Matt and his wife Kirsty have put on an impressive spread, and people are soon helping themselves to sandwiches and sausage rolls. My stomach is so knotted, even the smell of the food makes me nauseous, so when Billy comes to find me, his paper plate piled high with egg sandwiches and pickled onions, it's all I can do not to rush to the ladies and chuck my guts up.

Even though I've known Billy since he was seven, we've never been close. It's not for want of trying. When Noah and I first got together, I made every effort to include him in everything we did. I organised trips to the cinema and weekends at Center Parcs. I was always offering to help him with his homework or cook his favourite meals. Without fail, my attempts to win him round were rebuffed. Like the time I spent a small fortune buying him tickets to see Chelsea, his favourite football team, only to discover he'd switched his allegiance to Arsenal the week before the match.

There was always a barrier between us, one I never managed to breach. It didn't help that Billy worshipped Noah, and although he never said it to my face, it was obvious he blamed me for breaking up his family.

Maybe if Jenny had had the grace to admit that their marriage was already over before Noah and I met, maybe if the divorce had been amicable and she'd given me her blessing, things would have been different. Billy would have come to see me, if not exactly as a mother figure, as an ally. As it was, Jenny was an embittered, vindictive cow who liked nothing more than to stick the boot in at every opportunity.

I like to think things improved when Joe was born, but only because Joe idolised his big brother from the get-go, and Billy enjoyed the attention.

Despite everything that's happened, courting favour with Billy is instinctive. I touch his arm and say, 'It was nice of you to come today. I know Lisa will appreciate it.'

'Yeah, well, like I said, I wanted to pay my respects. I've known Annie as long as the rest of you.' As usual when he's talking to me, his tone is truculent, and an uncomfortable silence falls between us.

'Oh, look, here's your dad,' I say with relief, spotting Noah approaching with our drinks. 'I'll leave you two to it. I should check on Lisa.'

I find her sitting on a bench overlooking the pub garden. I sit beside her, take her hand and give it a squeeze. 'You've been so brave today. Annie would be so bloody proud.'

She gives a tiny nod, her eyes filling with tears.

'I'm sorry,' I say, horrified. 'I didn't mean to upset you.'

She pulls a tissue from her pocket and blows her nose. 'It's OK. I know you didn't.' She squeezes my hand back. 'The truth is, I'm struggling.' She glances at me. 'I've decided to go and stay with Mum for a while, just until I get my head together.'

'You're going to Cornwall?'

She nods. 'Tonight.'

I can't hide my shock. 'Are you sure that's a good idea? I mean, your work's here, your support networks...' I trail off. *What about me? I'm here, and I don't want you to go. I need you as much as you need me.*

'Being here isn't helping. Annie's everywhere I look. I can't... I can't...' A solitary tear trickles down her cheek and she bats it away with the back of her hand.

Shame washes over me. Lisa has just buried her only child and I'm making her feel guilty for taking some time out to grieve. I smile brightly. 'Of course you must go. Let me know if there's anything I can do. Keep an eye on the house, water your plants, anything.'

'There is one thing,' she says after a moment's hesitation.

'Name it.'

'Find out who gave Annie the ecstasy for me. I need to know who did this to her.'

'I will, I promise.'
'Whatever it takes?'
'Whatever it takes,' I agree.

54

Lisa leaves with Jackie just after six, the tiny boot of her car rammed with cases and her dog Vincent on a blanket on the back seat. I've never been to Jackie's bungalow on Cornwall's south coast, but Lisa took Annie for a couple of weeks every summer, and they always came back tanned and happy and brimming with stories of clifftop walks and surf lessons.

'It'll do her good,' Noah says as we wave them off.

I know he's right, but it doesn't stop me feeling as though I've lost a limb.

* * *

That night I wake to a noise that sends a shiver of unease right through me. Muffled splutters, almost as if someone is choking. Not Noah. He's on his side with his back to me, snoring gently. I glance at the red display on my alarm clock, surprised to see I have been asleep for less than an hour. The noise is coming from Joe's room.

I slide my legs out of bed, pull on my dressing gown and slippers and cross the landing.

Joe went through a stage of having night terrors when he was seven. Terrifying episodes that would see him thrashing and screaming in his bed, his eyes wide with fear and his sheets soaked in sweat.

The first time it happened, I thought he must be in the middle of a nightmare, but when I tried to comfort him, he arched his back and screamed even louder. I'll never forget the way he looked at me. It was as if I was a stranger. The next morning he had no memory of what had woken him. We dismissed it as a one-off, suspecting Joe was overtired after a trip to the zoo with Billy. When he started sobbing at pretty much the same time for the next three nights, I booked an appointment to see our GP.

Dr Bicknell listened carefully as I relayed Joe's apparent night-time wakenings, the way he stared at me blankly or became agitated if I tried to soothe him, the sweat-dampened sheets, the fact he couldn't remember a thing the next morning.

'I don't know what to do to help him. It's terrifying,' I finished.

'Terrifying for you, but not for him,' Dr Bicknell said. 'I'm certain from your description that Joe is suffering from night terrors.'

'Night terrors? You mean nightmares?'

'Actually, they are quite different. Children waking up from nightmares will remember their dreams, but those having night terrors will have no recollection of them the next day. Even the experts don't fully understand what causes them. What we do know is that parts of the brain are in a deep sleep, while other parts, the parts that operate movement and motor functions, are active, hence Joe appearing to be awake when he is not. They are most common in children aged between three and eight and are more likely to happen where there's a family history of them. A lack of sleep can be a trigger, as can illness or anxiety.'

'We're very strict with Joe's bedtime routine. Always have been, ever since he was a baby,' I said a little defensively.

Dr Bicknell smiled. 'I have no doubt, and I understand how distressing they must be for you, but I can assure you that Joe isn't aware of anything when he's having an episode; that's why he doesn't remember them the following morning. Is he anxious about anything at the moment? Any changes in routine? Anything that's worrying him?'

'Not that I can think of.'

'In that case, I'm confident it's a phase Joe will grow out of,' he said.

'There's nothing we can do?'

'There is one thing you can try which sometimes helps, especially if the night terrors are happening at a similar time every night.'

'They're always just as we're heading to bed at about eleven.' I leant forwards in my seat, keen to hear what we could do to help our little boy.

'Try not to wake him up when he's in the middle of a night terror because that'll only disrupt his sleep further. It's a vicious circle. The less sleep he gets, the more likely he is to have an episode. Unless, of course, he's in danger of falling down the stairs or suchlike.'

'Of course.'

'What you can do is to rouse him from sleep about fifteen minutes beforehand. I don't mean by setting an alarm,' the GP added. 'Talk to him or give his shoulder a gentle shake. The aim is to make him stir in his sleep, which can be enough to break the cycle. Try it for a couple of weeks and you should start to see an improvement.'

I crept into Joe's room at twenty to eleven on the dot for the next fortnight. Sometimes, all I had to do was call his name softly and he would stir. Other times, I stroked his forehead or squeezed his hand in mine until he sighed and rolled over. It worked, and Joe never had another night terror after that.

I never knew for sure what triggered them, but I had my suspicions. Weeks later we were on holiday in Wells-next-the-Sea in Norfolk when Joe pleaded with me to buy him a packet of Pokémon cards from a newsagent by the harbour.

'Please, Mum,' he wheedled, turning those big green eyes on mine. 'I really, really need them.'

'You don't need to ask me. You've still got the money Gran gave you for your birthday, haven't you?'

His face had fallen. 'Not any more.'

'I thought you were saving it for the holiday.'

'I was,' he said, a flush creeping up his cheeks.

'Oh, Joe, you haven't lost it, have you?'

'No!'

'Then where is it?'

He tugged my arm, pulling me further into the shop and away from Noah, who was standing on the pavement trying to get a signal so he could call the office.

'Promise you won't tell Daddy?' he said once we were safely out of earshot.

I did my best to hide my surprise. 'I promise,' I said, laying my hand on my heart.

'I gave it to Billy,' he said. 'At the zoo. He said I owed it to him.' His brow furrowed. 'But I don't think I did.' He scuffed the tiled floor with the toe of his trainers and looked sidelong at me, his face pinched. 'I knew you'd be cross.'

'I'm not cross with you, sweetheart,' I assured him.

'But you are cross with Billy.'

When I didn't reply, Joe's eyes grew round. 'Please don't say anything, Mummy.'

At fourteen, Billy knew better than to take his brother's birthday money, but a promise was a promise. I pulled Joe into a hug. 'It's all right, I won't say a word.'

The relief that flooded his face showed me how worried he'd been. That, coupled with the fact that Joe's first night terror had been the day we'd been to the zoo, told me everything I needed to know.

Joe's door is closed. I pause outside, my heart pounding. Could Annie's death have triggered another night terror after all this time?

55

I press my ear against Joe's door. The splutters have stopped but I can hear him moving around in his bedroom. One in the morning is far too late to be playing his Xbox. I open the door without knocking and stride into the room, ready to read the riot act. But he isn't on his Xbox, nor is he on his phone. He is standing by his window staring out into the garden. The curtains are open and the moon casts a silvery light into the room.

'Joe?'

He gives no impression he's heard me, and for a moment, I fear I was right and he's in the grip of another night terror, brought on by the stress of Annie's funeral.

'Joe,' I say again. 'Is everything all right?'

His shoulders shudder. He is crying. Silent sobs that wrack his body but make no sound in the still bedroom. I cross quickly, wrap an arm around him and guide him to his bed. He perches on the edge, clamping his hands over his face in an attempt to hide his tears.

'Oh, Joe, what is it? What's wrong?'

He shakes his head. 'I... I can't—' He cuffs the tears away. I reach into the pocket of my dressing gown for a tissue and he blows his nose, the sound like the blast of a trumpet.

'Joe, talk to me, please.'

'No... I can't,' he says again.

'Is it Annie?'

He nods so faintly I almost miss it.

'Darling, it's all right to be upset. You've known Annie all your life. Of course her funeral has hit you hard, but I mean it when I say bottling it up isn't good for you.'

Joe's shoulders heave again as he is hit by a fresh wave of sobs. I hold out my arms and he sinks into them. In that moment he is not so very different from the seven-year-old boy in the newsagents in Wells, who was more worried about dropping his brother in it than saving his own skin.

'It's my fault she died,' he sniffs.

He's said this before, I remember suddenly. The day I told him the doctors were switching off Annie's life support machine. He cried then too.

'You can't blame yourself for Annie's overdose just because it happened at your party.'

'It's not that, Mum. I... I—'

I take his hands in mine. 'I'm on your side. Whatever it is, we can deal with it.'

He hangs his head. 'You might say that, but you don't mean it.'

'I'm your mum. Of course I mean it. I love you unconditionally, that's the deal.'

'Promise?'

I smile, squeeze his hands. 'Cross my heart.'

'It was me,' he mumbles.

'What was you, sweetheart?'

'I gave Annie the E.'

At first, I think I must have misheard him, because Joe

would never do that. He would never give a class A drug to Annie. He must be mistaken.

Please let him be mistaken.

I keep my voice neutral. 'What are you talking about, Joe?'

'I gave Annie the ecstasy. That's why it's my fault.' He pulls his hands away from mine and shuffles back on his bed, hugging his knees.

Facts and assumptions are reassembling themselves in my mind like cogs in a clock. Annie, my god-daughter, the golden girl who excelled at everything she did, who was destined for great things, took recreational drugs, and Joe, my beautiful boy, supplied them.

It is the evidence I was looking for. Proof that Joe has been recruited by a London gang to push drugs in our postcard-perfect village. I can't pretend any longer, not now he's admitted it to my face. With a sinking feeling I remember Lisa telling me about the raids the police were planning and how officers were confident they'd catch whoever had supplied the ecstasy.

My thoughts jump forwards, my imagination in overdrive. We are at home, asleep, when there is a terrible hammering on the front door. Police in tactical gear are yelling at us to open up before they smash through it with a battering ram. Officers are running up the stairs in pairs and shouldering open the door to Joe's bedroom, hauling him out of bed and slapping handcuffs on him while he's still in his boxers, half-asleep.

I know I'm being fanciful. In reality we'd probably get a phone call from Sergeant Harrington asking us to bring Joe into the police station at a pre-arranged time. All very civilised. It doesn't stop my heart racing.

My focus snaps back to Joe. He is eyeing me warily, and I know I must keep my cool, because if I fly off the handle, I'll push him away.

'Annie shouldn't have asked you to get drugs for her,' I say. 'What was she thinking?'

Joe rests his forehead on his knees and groans. 'She didn't ask me to get them for her,' he mumbles. 'You don't understand.'

He's right. I don't.

'Ecstasy's supposed to be the love drug, isn't it? That's why everyone took it at raves in the nineties, to get loved up.'

'Yes, but—'

'You don't get it, do you? I loved Annie, Mum. Not as a sister or a friend. I *loved* her.'

I cover my mouth to hide my gasp.

56

The revelation is a slap in the face. Once again, all my assumptions are thrown upside down. Joe loved Annie. If I was in any doubt, one look at his stricken face is enough to convince me he's telling the truth.

'I... I had no idea.'

'Why would you? I was hardly going to tell you, was I?'

'How long had you felt like that?'

He rubs his face. 'Since France.'

'Val-d'Isère?' I blink. 'But that was nearly three years ago.'

That winter, Noah and I had offered to take Annie skiing with us to give Lisa a break. I cast my mind back. Joe had been quiet, bordering on grumpy, the whole week. I'd put his mood swings down to teenage hormones. Turns out I was right, although not in the way I'd imagined.

'I told her last Christmas, and d'you know what happened?'

I shake my head.

'Sh-she laughed at me. She laughed at me and told me I was a freak.' Joe's shoulders are shuddering again and the words are coming out in snotty fits and starts. 'Those w-were her exact w-words. "Don't be ridiculous, you f-freak."'

'Oh, Joe.'

'I thought if I gave her an E at my party she m-might change her mind.'

'You offered it to her?'

'I... no... I—'

Understanding rips through me with a force that leaves me breathless. 'You spiked her drink.'

'That makes it sound so c-calculated. It wasn't like that. I thought it would loosen her up a bit. You know what she's like, always Miss Goody Two Shoes. I told her I'd done it once she'd taken it. She was cool with it, Mum, I promise.'

Because the ecstasy was already releasing serotonin into her system, I think. Common sense would have flown out of the window the moment the drug kicked in.

'And it worked,' Joe says, a note of pleading in his voice. 'She was so buzzy, going around hugging everyone. She even told me how much she loved me.' His face darkens. 'Then Josh dared her to kiss Lottie and they were going at it for ages. I kept telling myself it was the ecstasy making her do it, that it wasn't real.'

Funny how Lottie didn't think to mention *that* when we spoke. What else hasn't she told me?

'If Josh had kissed her like that I'd have punched his lights out, but I couldn't, could I?' Joe says a little desperately. 'I couldn't punch a girl.'

I'm picturing the scene as he talks. Annie in her emerald-green dress, her golden hair spinning as she whirled around the room like Tinkerbell in *Peter Pan*. Josh challenging her to kiss Lottie, the others egging her on as Joe watched, crestfallen, from the sidelines. My heart aches for them both.

'Then what happened, Joe?'

He shakes his head. 'Ethan told her she needed to keep drinking water to stay hydrated, so she kept filling up her glass and downing it. We all danced for a bit. She was pulling these strange faces.' He moves his jaw from left to right to imitate gurning. 'Connor and Josh were laughing at her. Ethan said we needed to get more water down her, so I dragged her into the kitchen and made her drink another two glasses. I thought he knew what he was talking about because his dad's a doctor.'

It's heartbreaking. Ethan thought he was doing the right thing, when, in fact, he was sealing Annie's fate.

'You weren't to know,' I say automatically.

'I sat her down on the sofa and told her to take it easy, but that's when she started jerking and stuff, so I put her in the recovery position and called you.' He finally looks me in the eye. 'D'you see now why I blame myself? I gave her the E, and then I made her drink too much water. Whichever way you look at it, it's my fault Annie died.'

A sick feeling rises from the pit of my stomach and for a horrible moment I think I might vomit all over Joe's navy duvet cover. Images of them together through the years flicker through my mind as if I'm flipping through the pages of an old photo album. The pair of them building sandcastles at the beach and feeding the sheep at a petting zoo. Sharing tennis lessons, picnics, bedtime stories. The summer Joe taught Annie how to skateboard. The Christmas holiday they were obsessed with *Pokémon Go*. From the day they were born, their childhoods have been so closely entwined it would have been impossible to untangle them. Yet I had no idea Joe had carried a torch for Annie for the last three years. How the hell did I miss that?

I reach across the bed and pull him close. He doesn't protest, and we sit like that, his head tucked under my chin, my arms wrapped around his shoulders, until his breathing evens and he pulls away.

'Did the others know?' I ask, even though I'm pretty sure I already know the answer.

He nods. 'They promised not to say anything.'

'What, like a pact?'

He shrugs. 'I guess.' He chews the skin around his thumb, a habit I thought he'd outgrown years ago. 'What about you? Are you going to tell the police?' he asks.

I know I should, but what good will it do? It won't bring Annie back. Joe would almost certainly be arrested and charged with spiking Annie's drink. He'd probably end up in a Young Offenders Institution, his future in tatters. I glance at him. He's retreated to the end of his bed again. His whole demeanour is beaten. By not reporting him to the police I might be depriving the justice system of a conviction, but it's clear Joe will carry the guilt of what he has done with him forever. He is already paying his dues.

'Mum?'

'No,' I say.

He nods, stifling a yawn.

I look at the clock on his bedside table. It's almost two in the morning. My alarm's set for five hours' time. Just the thought of it makes me want to crumple into an exhausted heap in the corner of the room. Instead, I push myself to my feet. 'We should both get some sleep.'

It's only when I'm halfway to the door that it occurs to me there's a crucial question I've missed. 'Joe?' I begin.

'What?'

'Where did you get the ecstasy from?'

His gaze drifts upwards, as if the answer is scribbled on the ceiling. I wait, tapping a toe on his rug, pretending not to notice his expression closing down. The intimacy I'd felt just moments ago, that feeling of connection between us that is so rare these days, has disappeared as quickly as it appeared, and when he finally speaks, his voice is not just defensive, it's bordering on aggressive.

'No one,' he snaps.

I gaze at him, troubled by the sudden shift in his mood. 'Joe, please, tell me.' But he shakes his head, avoiding my eye, and I shuffle from the room, a cold weight of dread settling in my chest.

57

By some small miracle I fall into a deep sleep almost as soon as my head touches the pillow, waking groggily when the alarm sounds at seven o'clock. I don't know why I set it, it's not like I have a job to go to any more, but old habits die hard.

Noah's side of the bed is empty, but I can hear the low rumble of a morning TV programme drifting up the stairs.

I shower, pull on some clothes and head down to the kitchen, desperate for a coffee. Noah is sitting at the island scrolling through his phone, a plate of toast in front of him.

'What happened to you last night?' he says, looking up.

'Couldn't sleep.'

I want to share the bombshell our son dropped in the early hours. That he spiked Annie's drink with ecstasy in the hope that she might finally reciprocate his love for her. In the cold light of day, it sounds so much worse than it did last night. Although I gave Joe my word I wouldn't go to the police, it doesn't mean I can't tell his dad. But what if Noah insists we call Sergeant Harrington?

Something else occurs to me as I fill a mug with coffee and drop two slices of bread into the toaster. I promised Lisa I would find out who gave Annie the ecstasy. Lisa, who has already been through so much, who says knowing what happened will help her grieve. If I was her, I'd want justice too. I wouldn't just want someone charged, convicted and jailed, I'd want them hung, drawn and quartered. I'd want them to pay for my child's death.

How will Lisa react when she finds out Joe's to blame? She came to hospital to see him when he was a few hours old. She's had him over for play dates and sleepovers, birthday teas and barbecues countless times in the intervening years. She is closer to him than my own mother is, for God's sake. Once, when Joe was about five, he told me he wished Lisa was his mummy because she was much nicer than me. I'd probably just told him off for something or other, but even so. Just as Annie was the daughter I never had, Joe is the son Lisa and Craig always wanted.

'Eve? Did you hear what I said?'

I look up to see Noah staring at me, one eyebrow cocked. The toast pops out of the toaster, making me start.

'Sorry, what?'

'Billy was very down yesterday. I'm worried about him.'

'Everyone was down yesterday. It was Annie's funeral,' I snap.

'I know, but it was more than that. He seemed rattled. I'll try to pop in to see him later, but I have a meeting with the liquidators at half nine. I don't suppose you could...?' He looks at me hopefully.

'I can't. I'm tied up all day.'

He frowns. 'Doing what?'

I clench my teeth. 'I shall be going cap in hand to the credit card company, the bank and the building society to see if there's a way out of the shitshow you dropped us in when you gave all our money to Billy.'

* * *

I spend most of the day on the phone, glad to have an excuse to push Joe's confession to the back of my mind. I'm not ready to confront it yet. Instead, I talk to mortgage advisers and personal bankers, utility companies and the finance company we bought Noah's car through.

It is stressful and exhausting and by half past four my head is throbbing and my voice is hoarse, but at least I've made progress.

I have managed to wrangle a stay of execution by switching to an interest-only mortgage. I know this is a short-term fix, but at least we can make the lower payments from my salary. I'm still suspended on full pay pending the results of the police investigation into Annie's death. I just hope no one ever finds out Joe gave her the ecstasy, because if I lose my job, we'll be up the creek, but we'll cross that bridge if we come to it. The bank has agreed to a temporary extension to our overdraft, and I've set up payment plans with the credit card, gas, electricity and water companies. The car finance company is extending the period of our loan to keep the monthly payments down. Luckily our council tax is split into ten monthly payments and the next isn't due until April.

Our credit score has been grievously wounded by the late payments and will probably never recover, but that's a problem we'll have to face further down the line. My priority was to keep a roof over our heads, and I have achieved that, for now at least.

I type a message into the family WhatsApp group.

Need to pop out. Be back about six. There's a casserole in the slow cooker if you can't wait till then.

Then I grab my bag and coat and leave the house. Joe may have admitted to giving Annie the ecstasy, but he has refused point-blank to say where it came from. Pact or no pact, I intend to find out.

58

I crawl down Lambhurst Eventing's long gravel drive twenty minutes later, gambling on the fact that Lottie Miller doesn't have time to exercise her horses as well as mucking them out before school. As I let myself out of the car, I see that my gamble has paid off. She's riding her dark-brown horse in the outdoor school.

I suppose I could have quizzed Connor, Josh or Ethan again, but I have the feeling Lottie is the key to discovering who supplied Joe with the ecstasy, which is why I'm here.

Especially now I have leverage.

I lean on the rails, watching Lottie ride. She's trotting her horse in ever-decreasing circles, and just when I think the circles can't get any smaller, they spiral out again, only for the pair to repeat the whole sequence in the opposite direction. It's mesmeric, the harmony between Lottie and her big brown horse. She is totally absorbed, her face a picture of concentration, until she sees me, and her expression turns thunderous.

She wheels the horse around and stops a few feet from me.

'What are you doing here?' she hisses.

'I wondered if we could have a quick chat.'

'I told you I wouldn't speak to you again without my parents present.'

I smile grimly. 'I can pop round to your house later if you'd prefer? Perhaps I'll mention how close you've been getting to your PE teacher lately. It's your choice.'

Her mouth hangs open.

'That's what I thought,' I say briskly. 'I'll be waiting for you by the stables.'

She must have cut her schooling session short, because she appears a few minutes later, jumping down from the horse and fiddling with the stirrups and girth before leading him into his empty stable.

'Give me five minutes,' she mutters.

'I have all the time in the world.'

She untacks the horse, gives its coat a quick brush, then rugs it. 'I need to bring Blue in from the field,' she says. 'You can come with me.'

She grabs a headcollar from a hook and hitches it onto her shoulder. I follow her out of the yard and along a track around the back of the outdoor school.

I decided on the way here to keep Joe's confession to myself. There's always a chance he lied to me and is taking the rap for one of his friends. Let Lottie believe I'm still in the dark. That way, I might actually get to the truth.

'Why are you here?' she asks. 'I told you everything you wanted to know the other day.'

'That's the problem. I'm not sure you did. For example, I think you know exactly what was going on between Connor and Ethan that night.' I stop and face her. 'What was the evidence Connor was threatening to show everyone?'

She chews her lip, then lets out a sigh. 'It was a dick pic. Ethan sent it to Connor thinking he was sending it to a lad called George he met at some school debating competition before Christmas. It was obvious Ethan had the hots for him and Connor thought it would be funny to create a fake Snapchat account and pretend to be George. They messaged for a while, then Connor asked him for some photos.'

'Was Connor blackmailing Ethan?' I ask, shocked. A breath later, a prickly heat rises up my neck to my face, because that's exactly what I'm doing, isn't it? Blackmailing a sixteen-year-old girl because I'm sick of the lies and half-truths. Even though I know it's the only way I'm going to get answers, it's not much of a defence. I start walking again so she doesn't see my reddening cheeks.

'Not for money,' Lottie says, falling into step beside me. 'Connor has this massive chip on his shoulder about being the council-house kid and I think he just wanted one up on the posh public schoolboy.'

Things are beginning to make sense. 'Is that why Ethan told me Connor had taken cocaine, to get his own back?'

She shrugs. 'Probably.' She stops by a gate and whistles. There's an answering whicker, and the big dappled-grey horse she was tacking up the other day appears in the gathering gloom like a spectre. Lottie lets herself into his paddock and fastens his headcollar, and I hold the gate open so she can lead him through.

'Another thing,' I say, clicking the gate closed and catching her up. 'Why didn't you mention the fact that Josh dared you to kiss Annie?'

She stops and stares at me. 'Because it's none of your bloody business!'

'Like it or not, everything that happened that night is my business, Lottie.'

'Who told you?'

'Does it matter?'

'It matters to me.' She sets off again, her shoulders rigid.

'Joe,' I say eventually. 'He was very upset. He was in love with Annie, you see.'

She snorts. 'Tell me something I don't know.'

It's beyond galling that everyone else knows more about my son than I do. My resolve to scale the wall of silence these kids have barricaded themselves behind hardens.

'Why did you kiss her? Are you...?' I trail off, aware I'm tiptoeing through a minefield of political correctness. Any misstep and I'll be cancelled.

'If you mean am I in the habit of kissing girls, no, I'm not. It was the Molly.'

I frown and am about to ask her who the hell Molly is when her mouth curves into a sneer.

'Oh my God, really? You don't know, do you? Molly's another name for ecstasy.'

I stare at her in shock. 'You took an E too?' Yet again the events of that night are re-writing themselves in my head. 'Did everyone?'

'I think so, yeah.' She gives me a sideways look.

'What aren't you telling me?' I demand.

'I... I think Joe gave Annie hers.'

My hand flutters to my throat as I feign shock. '*Joe* gave Annie the E?'

'I think so, yeah. He was with her just before she went all weird.'

A thought strikes me. 'What about Joe?'

'What do you mean?'

'Did he take one?'

'Joe gave them to us,' she says.

Blood rushes in my ears. Gone is the need to pretend I'm shocked. With one breath, Lottie has confirmed my worst fears. Not only might Joe be caught up in county lines, but he's also supplied class A drugs to all of his friends. Could it get any worse?

She watches me closely, the faint trace of a smirk on her face. 'Bet you're wishing you hadn't asked me now.'

We've arrived back at the yard. Without waiting for an answer, Lottie leads her horse into his stable and slides the bolt across the door.

'Do you know where he got them from?'

She plants her hands on her hips. 'If I tell you, will you promise you won't breathe a word about me and Nick?'

I hesitate. Isn't it my duty as a teacher to let the authorities know Green is having an affair with a sixteen-year-old girl? But it's not like I took an oath when I started teaching, like a doctor would. I'm suspended anyway.

'You have my word,' I tell her.

She nods, satisfied. 'Joe said he got them from his brother.'

59

Dusk is falling as I stamp on the accelerator and pull out of the livery yard, my car feeling the full force of my fury as I tear through the quiet country lanes towards home.

Billy.

I should have known.

Of course Joe didn't get himself caught up in the local drugs scene. He was hooked in by his half-brother. While I was haunted by nightmares about a shadowy web of faceless men with gold teeth and baseball bats, the real threat had already infiltrated our lives, our home.

Billy recruited Joe. Billy supplied the ecstasy that killed Annie. And Billy browbeat Noah into handing over our life savings.

It all leads back to him.

Approaching the village, I'm blinded by oncoming head-lights. I flash my lights in warning, cursing under my breath when the driver ignores me. It's a single-track road and the only passing place for half a mile is the track leading to the Langley Manor ruins. I'm nearest, and I move down the gears, ready to pull in. The other driver is showing no sign of stopping and I'm gripped with panic as the car bears down on me.

The passing place is still twenty feet away and I'm never going to reach it in time so I slam on the brakes, my car lurching forwards as the wheels lock.

I scream, bracing for impact, but at the last moment the other car veers across the road and up the track to Old Langley, missing my car by inches. I pull up, heart racing, and turn in my seat to watch the red taillights weaving between the trees.

It'll be a boy racer in a stolen car, and he'll thrash it along the track that circles the old ruins until he runs out of petrol and sets light to it to destroy the evidence.

Adrenaline surges through me and I consider following the car so I can give him a piece of my mind, until the voice of common sense reminds me I'd probably be stabbed for my troubles. So I replay the footage on my dashcam to see if I can identify the car instead.

Even though I play the clip half a dozen times, all I catch is a flash of metallic-white paintwork as it careers past.

I shift into gear and pull away, my legs like jelly. Evidence-wise, the dashcam footage is not enough for the police. Even so, I can't shake the feeling I've seen that car before.

* * *

The house is in darkness, which takes me by surprise, because Joe always leaves every light in the house blazing and he should have been home from school over an hour ago.

I let myself in, calling out as I kick off my boots and hang my coat on the newel post.

'Joe? It's Mum. Where are you?' He doesn't answer.

He'll be on his Xbox in his bedroom, his headset on, having lost all track of time. Except when I look, he isn't there. He isn't in the bathroom either. I check our bedroom and the spare rooms, then head back downstairs. On the island in the kitchen is a half-drunk glass of milk and a plate with a few biscuit crumbs on it. Neither were there when I left for the livery yard. He's been home. Where is he now?

I try his phone, but it goes straight to voicemail. I leave a message asking him to call me, then phone Noah, who does pick up.

'I'm just leaving. I'll be home in half an hour.'

'Have you spoken to Joe?'

'Not since this morning. Why?'

'He's not here. I mean, he's been here, but he's gone again.'

'Don't stress,' Noah says. 'He'll be back when he's hungry.'

'And what if he doesn't come back?' I demand, but Noah has already gone and I'm talking to myself.

I throw my phone on the worktop and start peeling potatoes and chopping broccoli into florets, hoping that if I keep busy I'll stop my thoughts from spiralling, but it's no good. Images of Joe keep forcing their way into my mind. Loitering in a dark alley-way, a hood pulled down low over his face. Dissolving a pink pill on his tongue. Heating a teaspoon of brown liquid over a naked flame. Slack-faced as he sits cross-legged on a stained mattress smoking a crack pipe. Each image exponentially worse than the last.

I tell myself not to catastrophise, that Joe's probably over at Ethan's, or Josh's, and will be home any minute now.

But the time ticks on.

At half six, I hear the click of the front door and rush into the hallway, but it's only Noah. My face falls.

'Oh, it's you.'

'Nice to see you too,' Noah says, dumping his briefcase by the umbrella stand.

I ignore him. 'Joe's still not back.'

'Why are you getting so worked up? It's not late.'

'It's not what time he comes home, it's where he is and what he's doing I'm worried about.'

Noah frowns. 'What are you talking about?'

The instinct to protect Joe whatever the cost is so deeply ingrained in me that I hesitate. Yet I recognise that by constantly shielding him, I'm not doing him any favours. At sixteen, he's old enough to make his own choices. His dad deserves the truth. Before I can change my mind, I nod towards the living room door.

'I think you should come and sit down. There's something you need to know.'

60

Noah listens in silence as I share everything I have learnt over the last twenty-four hours. How Joe admitted giving Annie the E because he wanted her to love him as much as he loved her. How he made her drink more water because Ethan told him it would help. How everyone at the party had taken ecstasy and had made a pact not to tell.

'Everyone?' he croaks.

I nod. 'That's what Lottie said.'

'Could she be lying?'

'I don't think so.' I tell him about her affair with Nick Green and the leverage it had given me. If he disapproves of my methods for extracting the truth, he doesn't say so. Instead, he buries his head in his hands.

'Christ.'

'I know.'

'Does Lisa know?'

'Not yet, but I'm going to have to tell her.'

He nods and we sit like that for several minutes. Noah seems to age before my eyes as the bombshell sinks in. Finally, he looks up at me, as if something has just occurred to him.

'Where did the drugs come from?'

It's the question I've been dreading. Bad enough that his youngest son gave Annie the ecstasy, but to discover his oldest son was the one who supplied it will break his heart.

'Lottie said Billy gave them to Joe.'

'Billy?' He jumps to his feet in such an explosion of energy that I flinch. He pulls his phone from his pocket, stabs at it and holds it to his ear. 'Billy. It's your father. Phone me *now*.'

He paces the room, his phone clasped in his hand, the anger sparking off him. 'And where the hell is Joe?'

'I told you. He's been home and has gone out again. I've tried calling him but he's not answering either.'

'You think they're together?'

'I don't know. Maybe. You said yourself I was worrying about nothing and he'll be home in time for dinner.'

'That's before I knew he and Billy were peddling drugs,' Noah growls. 'Just wait till I get my hands on them.'

'They might not be together—' I begin, but Noah cuts across me.

'I'm phoning the police.'

'No, wait,' I say. 'Why don't we phone round a few of his friends to see if anyone's seen him before we do anything rash?'

He grunts.

'You speak to Ethan's parents and I'll call the Duffys and Connor's mum.' I find him the Curtis's number, grateful I never deleted Joe's primary school's WhatsApp group, and wander into the kitchen to phone the Duffys, praying Greg will still be at work. I let out the biggest sigh of relief when Chrissy answers.

'Chrissy, it's Eve Griffiths. I don't suppose Joe's with you, is he? Only his dinner's almost ready and he's gone AWOL.'

'No,' she says, and I wait for her to elaborate, but she doesn't.

I force myself to sound upbeat. 'Would you ask Josh if he's seen him this afternoon?'

A sigh, then a reluctant, 'All right.' The click-clack of foot-steps across the Duffys' marbled hallway floor is followed by the sound of a door being opened and the low murmur of the television. 'Josh,' Chrissy says, 'Joe Griffiths's mum is on the phone asking if you've seen him this afternoon.'

'Nope. Haven't seen him since Saturday.'

The door clicks shut and Chrissy begins, 'Josh hasn't—'

'It's OK, thanks, I heard.' I ask her to call me if Josh does see him, though I'm not convinced she will. There was a definite chill to her tone that suggests that despite the pact the kids made, she knows Joe's been handing out drugs like sweets.

Sighing, I phone Connor's mum, Lorraine, next. To my surprise, she greets me warmly.

'Our Bobbi-Jo said you came round to the house the other day to see how Connor was doing, you know, after what happened to Annie and everything.'

I don't set her straight. If she knows why I really went to her house to speak to her son, she might not be so amenable. Instead, I say, 'It's my pleasure. It's been such a shock for them all. Which is why I'm calling, actually. I wondered if Connor has seen Joe today. I can't get hold of him.'

'Bobbi-Jo!' Lorraine yells to her daughter. 'Ask Connor if he's seen Joe Griffiths today, will yer?' She comes back on the phone. 'She won't be a sec. And, er, I'm sorry if we was a bit... frosty at Annie's vigil. It was just we was all so upset, and you know how it is...'

'It's fine,' I say. 'Totally understandable.'

'Course, if it ever did come out who gave poor Annie them drugs, there'll be... oh, here she is. What did he say, Bobbi-Jo? Right, I'll tell her. Yes, I'll tell her that too. Now skedaddle, will ya?'

'What did she say?' I ask, my grip on the phone tightening.

'Connor ain't seen him for days.'

'Oh, right.' My shoulders droop. 'Thanks anyway, and I'm sorry to have troubled you.'

I'm about to hang up when she says, 'Wait, there was something else.'

My heart misses a beat. 'What?'

'Bobbi-Jo says to tell yer Maisie's had her kittens. Six of 'em, there are. Bobbi-Jo says you and Joe can have first pick.'

'Thank you,' I say. 'It's very sweet of her.'

I end the call and pace the room restlessly, worry eating away at me. I would give everything for Joe to burst through the door, complaining about late buses and asking when dinner will be ready. Instead, I can't help feeling that he's lost to me forever.

61

Ethan hasn't seen Joe either, Noah informs me as we pull up stools at the kitchen island and decide our next move.

'What about Lottie?' he says.

'I don't have her number. I suppose I could drive back to the livery yard.'

'No. You're better off here for when Joe comes back.'

I make a non-committal noise and Noah gazes at me keenly. 'Just how worried do you think we should be?'

'What d'you mean?'

'Should we call the police?'

I shake my head. 'Like you say, it's not exactly late, is it? And he's sixteen. Old enough to look after himself. Let's leave it till half seven and if he's still not back by then...'

Noah knows as well as I do that reporting Joe missing will escalate everything. As soon as they input his details, they'll see he was released under investigation following Annie's death less than a month ago. If they speak to their Operation Kestrel colleagues, they might even link Joe to the gang they're investigating for supplying drugs in Nesborough.

'I'll try Billy again,' Noah says. I slide off the stool to turn the slow cooker on to low and put plates in the oven to warm. Not that I can face the casserole. My stomach's in knots.

'Billy, it's Dad again. I need to know if you've seen Joe today. We can't get hold of him and we're getting worried. If we haven't heard from him by half seven we're calling the police. So if you know where he is, phone me, OK?'

I run us each a glass of water from the tap and sit back down. Noah fiddles with a teaspoon, tapping it against the palm of his hand until I want to slap his wrist and snatch it from him.

'How did it happen, Eve?' he says. 'How did Joe and Billy end up giving children drugs in our own home? Where did we go wrong?'

'Why must it be something we've done wrong?' I cry. 'It's a knee-jerk reaction, isn't it? When a kid goes off the rails, blame the parents. We can't bloody win. Children are either suffocated or left to run wild. They are starved of love or spoilt rotten. We're too demanding or too lax, too strict or too lenient. You give them everything, let them bleed you dry, and it's still not enough. If they don't get to grammar school, it's your fault for not hiring a tutor. If they have anger issues, it's because you lost your temper one too many times when they were toddlers. Anxious parents have anxious children. You do the best you can with the tools you have but it's still not good enough. It's never bloody good enough!'

Noah listens to my rant in silence, and when I finally run out of steam, he steps off his stool, comes round to my side of the island and holds out his arms. I collapse against him, sobs wracking my body, and he holds me till my tears run dry.

* * *

At twenty past seven, my phone rings. I dart across the kitchen to grab it, my fingers trembling so badly it slithers out of my grip and clatters onto the tiles.

'Shit,' I mutter, snatching it up and staring at the screen. 'Noah, it's Joe!' I accept the call, relief surging through me. 'Joe, sweetheart, we were getting worried. Where are you?'

'I'm fine,' he says, which is weird because I asked him where he was, not how he was. I let it go. I'm just so pleased he's called.

'You're dinner's ready. When will you be home?'

'Um, not sure at the moment.' His voice dips in and out, as if he's somewhere with poor reception.

'Shall Dad or I come and pick you up?' I glance at Noah, who nods and disappears into the hallway.

'No, don't do that. I'm fine,' he says again.

'You sound a bit strange, Joe. Are you *sure* everything's all right?'

'Remember that time I was pretending to be Captain America and I put my pants over my jeans and told you, Lisa and Annie I was off to save the world, only you all laughed and called me Captain Underpants and I sulked for the rest of the day?'

The relief turns sour. Why is Joe rambling about superheroes? He must have taken something. The images are back, only this time Joe is wrapping a piece of rope around his bicep and pulling it tight with his teeth and...

No! I can't think like that. I push the image away.

'Joe, *please*, sweetheart, just tell me where you are and I'll come and get you.' But the line has already gone dead.

Noah is back, coat and shoes on, the car keys in his hand. 'Where is he?'

'He wouldn't tell me. He was wittering on about Captain America and Captain Underpants. Christ knows what he's taken. Jesus, Noah, he could be anywhere!'

As I say this, I realise I do remember Joe, aged about six, disappearing during a walk through the woods with Lisa and Annie. It must have been early May, because the air was thick with the sweet scent of bluebells. Annie had stopped to pick a bunch when Joe jumped out from behind a bush wearing his favourite red pants over his jeans and demanding we all call him Cap, like in the film. Annie, I remember, had got the giggles and told him he looked more like Captain Underpants than Captain America. Joe, his male ego fragile even then, had stormed off in a sulk.

We searched high and low, but it was as though he'd vanished off the face of the earth. I'd been on the verge of calling the police when Lisa suggested we tried the Langley Manor ruins.

'But they must be over a mile away,' I said.

'You know how much Joe loves it up there. It has to be worth a shot,' Lisa reasoned. 'If he's not there, we'll call the police.'

I ran on ahead, stumbling over the uneven ground, barely noticing the whippy branches of the coppiced hazel as they caught my face, my only goal to find my son. The overwhelming terror was like nothing I'd experienced before or since. Sheer panic at the thought that Joe might have run onto the road into the path of a car or been grabbed by a dead-eyed stranger.

When I reached Old Langley, there he was, sitting on one of the tumbledown walls, kicking the stones with his heels.

'Joe!' I cried, sprinting over and pulling him into the biggest hug. 'Don't ever, *ever* disappear like that again.'

Now, I stand on shaky legs, gripping the kitchen island for support. That gut-clenching feeling of panic is back, and just like childbirth, I'd forgotten how terrible it was.

'What's wrong, Eve?' Noah says urgently.

I push my hair off my face and pick up my phone. 'I know where he is.'

62

We take Noah's SUV. It'll cope better with the woodland tracks than my hatchback. Noah tears out of the village as if his life depends on it. I stare into the darkness as the countryside hurtles past.

'Old Langley's where the kids go, isn't it?' he says, crunching up through the gears with such ferocity the engine screams in protest. 'To get up to no good?'

'Yes.'

'You think Joe was out of it when he rang?'

'I don't know. He sounded weird. Robotic, almost. But he wanted us to come. Why would he have reminded me about Captain America otherwise?'

Noah drums his fingers on the steering wheel. 'I don't like this. I don't like this at all.'

'Slow down, it's up here on the right somewhere.'

He slows, and we both peer into the trees looking for the track. 'There,' I tell him, pointing, and Noah checks the rear-view mirror before slowing to a crawl. He indicates and dips his headlights before turning onto the track. It triggers a memory. 'I saw a car drive up here on my way back from the stables. It was white, one of those souped-up hot hatches. It almost hit me.'

'None of Joe's friends are old enough to drive.'

'Since when did that stop a teenage joyrider off his head on booze or drugs?' I scoff.

'But Joe would never—'

'You're sure about that, are you?' I shake my head. 'Face it, Noah, our own son's a stranger to us.' We've been so focused on leading our busy, important lives that somewhere along the way we've lost sight of who he is. I worry we've left it too late to find out.

Noah stamps his foot on the accelerator and I hold onto the grab handle as we lurch forwards. The car hits a tree stump and we're both jolted out of our seats. Noah, hunched over the steering wheel, white-knuckled, grim-faced, swears roundly, then glances at me.

'You all right?'

I nod. The track curves to the right. 'It's not far now,' I say. 'Maybe fifty yards?'

He takes his foot off the accelerator. The track widens into a clearing. The beam of the headlights picks out the shadowy ruins of Old Langley. There's an old sepia photograph of Langley Manor in its heyday hanging in the snug at The Swan. It was a handsome house before the fire. Now, four crumbling stone walls covered in graffiti are all that remain.

Noah pulls up, switching off the ignition but leaving the headlights on. My eyes rove over the ruins, looking for Joe, but there's no sign of him. There's no sign of anyone. Perhaps I read too much into his phone call and I've led Noah on a wild goose chase. Then my attention is caught by a glint of paintwork. A car has been parked to the left of the old manor house, between the wall and the trees, half-hidden from view. A white car. I squint into the darkness. There's that feeling again, that I've seen it somewhere before. I touch Noah's arm.

'Look. That's the car that almost hit me earlier.'

Noah leans across me and reaches into the glove compartment for the torch he keeps in there for emergencies. We unclip our seat belts and jump out.

I know the ruins better than Noah and lead the way, taking care not to trip over the stone steps that are scattered everywhere like forgotten pieces of Lego on a playmat. Noah's not so circumspect and cries out in surprise as his foot catches a slab of sandstone, and he topples headfirst onto the ground.

I dart over and hold out a hand to pull him to his feet. He shakes his head, brushes off his jeans, and we continue on our way to the ruins.

Just as we reach the first of the crumbling outer walls, a figure steps out in front of us, a knife glinting in his hand. Noah lifts the torch to his face and I give an involuntary cry.

'Billy!' Noah croaks. 'What the hell are you doing here?'

63

I stumble forwards, my foot catching on a bramble, and I hold out a hand to steady myself.

'Billy, is Joe with you?'

He doesn't answer, just keeps looking over our shoulders, as if he was expecting someone else.

'Billy! Are you listening to me? Is Joe here?'

'You shouldn't be here,' he cries. 'Why did you come?'

'We're looking for Joe, Billy.' Noah's voice is calm. I glance at him; he is staring at the knife in Billy's right hand. 'Do you know where he is?'

Billy shakes his head. He is agitated, shifting his weight from one foot to the other. He used to do it when he was younger, usually when he'd done something wrong and was about to get a rollicking from his father.

'You shouldn't be here,' he says again.

'Why, who were you expecting?' I ask. His gaze darts to me. A tic is working in his jaw.

'No one.'

'I don't believe you,' I say, stepping forwards.

Billy's right hand shoots up, the knife with it. I hear Noah's indrawn breath.

'Eve, wait,' he whispers, but I ignore him. I just want to find out where my son is. 'Is it the people you owe money to? Is that who you were expecting?'

'Fuck you, step-bitch!' Billy hisses, holding the knife above his head.

'Billy!' Noah says warningly. 'Put the knife down now.'

'No way, man. I need it for protection. They're gonna lose their shit if they find you here. They're gonna go out of their fucking minds.'

'Who are?' Noah says, edging forwards.

Billy's eyes dart between Noah and me. 'Caleb and the others.' He waves the knife towards the track we've just driven up. 'I'm in enough shit as it is. If they think I've set them up...' He drops to his knees, hands laced behind his head, the knife protruding from his palm like Edward Scissorhands. 'This is bad, man. Really fucking bad.'

'Billy,' I say. 'When I came to see you at the unit, you told me you were staying there because you were keeping under the radar. There'd been a misunderstanding with one of your suppliers, you said.'

'My only supplier.'

'Of the gym equipment?'

He laughs manically. 'If only.'

'Who, then, Billy? A loan shark? The bailiffs? Your landlord?'

He cradles his head even tighter. 'I *told* you! Caleb. He said if I don't give him back the money or his gear, he's going to fucking shank me.'

'Gear?' Noah says. 'You mean drugs?'

'Got on the wrong side of some dealers, didn't I? Sorry to disappoint, Father. It was only ever meant to be one job to repay what I owed them. That's what Caleb said. "Do this one drop-off, mate, and we'll be square." So I do the job, only he gets some bastard to rob me on the way back, and suddenly I owe him double.' Billy gets slowly to his feet, his fist still curled around the handle of the knife. 'Next thing I know, I'm trapping for them.'

'Trapping?'

'Selling drugs, stepmother dearest.' He waves the knife in Noah's direction. 'You wouldn't give me any more money, so what else was I supposed to do?'

'There was no more money to give,' Noah says. He takes a step towards Billy. 'Where does Joe figure in all this?'

Billy's face hardens into a sneer. 'I thought he could help me out of a spot. Those private school kids are minted. I knew Caleb would be well pleased.'

Something Emma Bradley said at a staff meeting a couple of years ago comes back to me. The police had sent out a warning to local schools after a dealer was seen hanging around outside the gates of Nesborough High School. The local paper had picked up on it, running a front-page story about drug use in schools.

'I don't know why they're focusing on drugs in state schools when everyone knows the problem's far worse in the private sector,' she remarked tartly.

'The kids can afford a better class of drug for a start,' the head of PE quipped, and I'd laughed along with the rest of them, even though Joe went to a private school, because I was confident in the knowledge that my sporty son would never touch drugs.

How naive can you get?

'We know you gave Joe the ecstasy for his party. Were you supplying the kids in the village with drugs too?' I ask Billy.

'Just a little of what they fancied every now and again. Nothing too heavy, so there's no need to look like that.'

'No need?' I'm incredulous. 'Annie died because of you!'

Billy's eyes narrow. 'Annie died because of Joe, not me.'

Out of the corner of my eye, I glimpse Noah moving closer to Billy, his gaze fixed on the knife. I need to keep Billy talking.

'Where is Joe now?'

Billy's head jerks towards the far side of the ruins. 'In my car.'

That's where I've seen the car before. It's the sporty Golf that was parked outside Billy's unit on the Nesborough Business Park. Bought with the money Noah gave him to set up his business, no doubt.

'Give me the torch,' I bark at Noah. He passes it to me and I follow its beam to the car, my heart crashing in my chest in dread at what I might find when I get there.

64

The moment I shine the torch into the car, I see Joe's prone body lying on the back seat.

'Joe!' I cry, tugging at the door handle, but it won't open. Growling with frustration, I try the driver's door, then dart round to the other side, and finally the boot, but they're all locked.

I peer back inside the car. Joe hasn't moved. He's curled in a fetal position, either asleep or...

'Joe!' I yell, banging on the window with the heel of my hand. 'Wake up! It's Mum.'

I take a couple of steps back, looking for something I can break the glass with. Luckily, rocks are in plentiful supply among the ruins of the old manor house. I find one as big as a brick, weighing it in my hand and flexing my shoulder before hurling it at the window with all my strength. It shatters with a loud crash, the sound echoing through the trees.

'What the hell?' Billy cries from somewhere behind me. 'You crazy bitch! What did you do to my car?'

There is the sound of a scuffle, a body hitting the ground. Noah roars, and I can't tell if it's in anger or in pain, but it's immaterial, because my focus is on Joe. Nothing else matters. I reach through the window to unlock the door, not caring when a shard of shattered glass nicks my wrist.

With trembling hands, I duck into the car and give Joe's shoulder a gentle shake. I think of all the times I have done this over the years. Waking him up for school, for rugby training, for swimming lessons or football practice. When he was little he would open his eyes and gaze at me blearily, a smile creeping across his face when he saw who it was. When he hit his teens he would grunt and roll over, muttering 'go away' while drawing his duvet under his chin and screwing his eyes tight shut.

But tonight there is no smile and no grunt. His body is limp and unresponsive, but at least his eyelids flutter at my touch.

'Come on, Joe,' I urge. 'Wake up, please.'

He mumbles something, but I can't make out what he's saying. I shake him again.

'Joe, you need to tell me what you've taken.'

His eyes flicker open. His pupils are dilated, his gaze unfocused.

'Was it ecstasy?' Even as I say it, I know it can't have been. The night of the party, Annie's jaw was clenched, her body totally rigid, whereas Joe is floppy, like he's made of marshmallow.

Billy will know what he's taken. I smooth Joe's hair off his forehead. 'I'll be right back, sweetheart,' I tell him, and retrace my footsteps back to the ruins. The torch beam picks out Noah first. He's sitting on a low wall, his body angled away from me, his shoulders hunched over. He looks beaten, as if a veil has been lifted and he's finally seen Billy for what he is. In contrast, Billy is pacing up and down, muttering to himself. His movements are jerky, his hands flapping. But there is no sign of the knife, and some of the tension leaves my body.

'Billy, what's Joe taken?'

He spins round, glaring at me. 'You just fucked up my new car!'

'Never mind the bloody car. What have you given Joe?'

His gaze drops to the floor.

'Billy, just tell me what Joe's had!'

He mumbles something, but all I catch is 'K'.

A hot wave of anger rolls over me. 'He is not bloody well OK. He's completely out of it!'

'I mean he's taken K. Ketamine,' Billy says. 'He's probably having a bad trip.'

'Ketamine? You mean the stuff they use to tranquilise horses? Jesus, Billy.' I pull my phone from my pocket. His head jerks up.

'What are you doing?'

'I'm phoning 999, which is exactly what we should have done the moment we arrived.'

'You can't do that! Caleb will go mental!' Billy tries to snatch my phone, but I'm too quick for him and dart out of his way.

'Noah,' I yell, but my husband is still slumped on the wall in his own little world. When Billy goes to grab my phone a second time, instinct takes over. I raise the torch in my right hand and slam it into his temple, dropping it in shock as he crumples to the ground.

I dial three nines, exhaling loudly when the call is picked up on the fifth ring.

'What's your emergency?' the call handler asks calmly.

'We need an ambulance. My son, he's... he's taken drugs. Ketamine, I think.'

'Is he conscious?'

I picture Joe's prone body. 'Barely.'

'And your location?'

'The woods at Old Langley.'

'Old Langley?' he queries. 'Do you have a postcode?'

I want to shout, 'Of course I don't have a bloody postcode!' but instead I take a deep breath. 'No, but it's the woods west of the village of South Langley. There's a track on the right just past the turning to the Langley Fields estate.'

'Do you have What3Words?'

'I don't.' I curse inwardly. I deleted the app before Christmas when my phone was almost out of storage, thinking I'd never need it. 'Wait,' I say. 'My husband does. I'll get his phone.' I snatch up the torch and jog over to Noah. 'Where's your phone?' I demand impatiently. He doesn't react. I drop to my knees, about to start patting his pockets.

That's the moment I see the handle of Billy's knife protruding from Noah's stomach.

65

'Before you say anything, it was an accident,' Noah wheezes.

I can't tear my gaze away from the knife sticking out of his midriff and the darkening pool of blood staining his coat. His hands are clasped around the handle. At least he's had the sense not to pull it out.

'Hello?' says a voice in my ear. 'Are you still there?'

My attention snaps back to the call handler. 'My husband's been stabbed,' I gabble as I fumble through Noah's pockets looking for his phone. I hold it to his face to unlock it, find the What3Words app and reel off our location. 'Please,' I implore. 'You have to send someone as soon as you can.'

For a moment I'm paralysed with indecision. Blood is pooling around Noah's stomach, more than I first realised. I want to check on Joe, but I don't want to leave Noah. I stand, rooted to the spot, aware that it'll be at least half an hour before the ambulance gets here. He could bleed out by then. Panic claws at my chest as I rack my brains, wondering if there's anyone else I can call, but everyone in the village hates us. The only person who would have dropped everything to help is Lisa, and she's in Cornwall, over two hundred and fifty miles away. I'm on my own.

As if sensing my dilemma, Noah clears his throat and croaks, 'Go to Joe. I'm... all... right.'

'No, I can't leave you like this,' I cry, my eyes filling with tears. 'You need me.'

He squeezes my hand weakly. 'Joe... needs you more.'

'All right.' I duck down and kiss his forehead. His skin is cold against my lips. 'I'll be as quick as I can, I promise,' I tell him, and begin making my way back through the ruins to the Golf, the glow of the torch lighting my way. It's just as well I have it. The headlights on Noah's car are starting to dim as the battery drains, giving the ruins a macabre air, the murky shadows and crumbling masonry resembling a film set for a slasher movie.

Billy is still lying on the ground where I left him. I stop and direct the torch over his inert frame, viewing him with dispassion. I'm too numb to feel hatred, although I'm sure that'll come. Right now, Joe and Noah are what matter, not Billy. Even so, I feel a tinge of relief when I see the steady rise and fall of his chest. At least I haven't killed him.

An owl screeches, the harsh sound echoing around the decaying remains of the old manor house. Distracted, I step too close to Billy. His hand shoots out and grabs my ankle, yanking it so sharply I lose my balance and topple to the ground like a felled tree.

* * *

Before I can scramble to my feet, there's a knee on the small of my back, forcing my face into the damp earth. I try to wriggle free, but Billy's weight is like a barrel crushing the air out of me. All those sessions in the gym, honing his physique for his bloody app.

He shifts position and suddenly his face is next to mine.

'Give me Dad's car keys,' he hisses in my ear.

I tense my muscles and arch my back, hoping to buck him off, but he just laughs and pins me tighter.

'Use your own car if you're going to run away, you coward,' I pant.

'I've lost my keys, which is why I need you to give me Dad's.'

'I don't have them.'

He shines the torch into my eyes and I twist my head away.

'Don't lie to me! He said he gave them to you.'

I know for a fact Noah did not give me the keys, but if that's what Billy thinks...

'All right, you win. I'll find them for you. But you're going to have to let me up.'

He hesitates, then releases me. I pull myself to my feet, wipe the dirt from my face and start searching through the pockets of my coat. I frown.

'What is it?'

'I... I must have dropped them.'

'*What?*' he yells, his face inches from mine.

'I'm sorry. They must have fallen out of my pocket. Give me the torch and I'll look for them.'

'There isn't time. Oh, man,' Billy wails, cradling his head in his hands. 'This is so fucked up.'

'Billy—'

'I mean, why did you and Dad have to come here? I had everything sorted. Then you turn up, and Dad tries to grab the knife off me, even though I told him I needed to keep it because of Caleb. I *told* him, but he grabbed my wrist and then we fell, and—' He glances at Noah. 'Oh, man.'

'It's all right, Billy. Your dad told me it was an accident.'

'But what if I... what if he...?'

'He'll be OK. The ambulance won't be long now.'

His demeanour shifts again, his eyes narrowing in suspicion. 'You called an ambulance?'

'Your dad has been stabbed and your brother is semiconscious after taking a horse tranquiliser. Of course I've called an ambulance!'

'What about the police?'

I shake my head.

'But they'll come, won't they? When they hear someone's been stabbed.'

'Maybe. I don't know. Like you said, it was an accident. Give me the torch. I'm going to check on Joe and your dad.' I hold out my hand. Billy rubs the back of his neck and then, as if reaching a decision, slaps the torch into my outstretched palm spitefully. I swallow a gasp of pain. Laughing, Billy turns his back on me and resumes his pacing.

When I reach the Golf, Joe is sitting up on the back seat, his elbows on his knees and his head lolling.

'Joe? It's Mum.'

He looks up groggily.

'How are you feeling?'

He holds his hands in front of his face, staring at them as if he's never seen them before. He's obviously still tripping, but at least he's conscious.

'Can you stand up?' Not waiting for an answer, I lace my arm through his and attempt to haul him to his feet. 'C'mon, Joe,' I coax. 'Stand up so I can take you over to Dad.' But he's a dead weight, and no matter how hard I push and pull, he doesn't shift an inch. Admitting defeat, I lay him down and traipse back through the ruins to Noah. His face is pallid but the bleeding seems to have stopped.

'Is Joe OK?'

I sit on the wall beside him. 'I think so.'

'Thank God.' He smiles weakly at me. 'This isn't your average Tuesday night, is it?'

'It is not,' I agree. 'Give me an evening in front of the TV with a pile of homework to mark any day of the week.'

He chuckles softly, then winces. 'I'm sorry, Eve. About everything. It's all my fault.'

'Don't worry about that now.'

'I love you, you do know that, don't you? I haven't stopped loving you from the day we met.'

'Noah—'

'No.' He grimaces again as he shifts position. 'I need to tell you, in case I...'

I want to shake him by the shoulders and tell him he isn't going to die because I refuse to let him. Not after everything we've been through. But I don't, because I can't risk dislodging the knife. Instead, I reach out and touch his cheek. 'I love you too.'

I check the time on my phone. It's been fifteen minutes since I called 999. 'Will you be all right here if I go and see where the ambulance has got to?'

He nods, and I clamber stiffly to my feet and start picking my way through the brambles to the track.

'Oi, where d'you think you're going?' Billy cries.

'To wait by the lane for the ambulance.'

'Not on your own, you're not.' He crashes through the undergrowth towards me, but I stride on, my head down. I have no wish to breathe the same air as him. He's toxic.

I remember the feeling I had that everything that had happened to us since the night of Joe's party was connected. The sense that someone was behind it all, orchestrating every single calamity. I was right.

Billy catches up with me. He is breathing heavily.

'Your grand plan worked,' I spit. 'I hope you're satisfied.'

'What are you talking about?'

'I get that you hate me, but why drag Joe and your dad into it?'

'Into what?'

'Don't play the innocent with me, Billy. I know it must have been tough for you, your dad moving out when you were little, then starting a new family. But that doesn't give you carte blanche to wreck our lives.'

He glares at me. 'You have no fucking idea.'

'We didn't set out to hurt you.'

He makes a strange spluttering sound, half laugh, half sob. 'Do you know how much I used to idolise Dad?' He doesn't wait for an answer. 'It killed me that he was away all week and I did everything I could to make him stay with us. I used to hide his shoes or his glasses on a Sunday night, knowing he couldn't leave until he found them. I'd help him tear the house upside down looking for them, even though I knew exactly where they were. I tried to hide his razor once, only I sliced through my finger and he had to take me to minor injuries to have stitches. He didn't go to work until the next day. So a couple of weeks later I cut myself again, on purpose this time.

'I pretended to have stomach cramps, or sore throats, anything to make him stay for a few extra hours. During the week when he FaceTimed to read me my bedtime story, I'd string it out for as long as I could. It used to drive Mum mad. I could just about cope with him being away all week because I knew that at the weekends he was all mine. Then you came along and ruined it all.'

Despite everything he's put us through, I feel a stab of remorse as I picture seven-year-old Billy dreaming up schemes to stop his father leaving the house. Anything to keep his dad at home for a few more hours.

'I had no idea,' I begin. And, of course, I didn't, because

Billy was just a concept to me then. A voice on the other end of the phone. A face in a photograph. A reason why Noah couldn't spend his weekends with me.

Truth is, sometimes I resented Billy.

But not, it turns out, as much as he resented me.

66

'I remember the day Mum told me Dad was leaving us. She'd been in a funny mood all week, but that wasn't unusual. She was often in a funny mood.' Billy's mouth twists in the torch-light and for a moment he looks as if he is holding back tears, but then the sneer returns.

'Then one evening she went across the road to borrow a pint of milk from my Auntie Sheila, and when she came back she was crying. I asked her what was wrong but she wouldn't tell me. She just said she had to go to see Dad at his London flat and Auntie Sheila would mind me. I was pleased cause Auntie Sheila always brought sweets and let me stay up late. We were still watching TV when Mum came home.'

I remember the fury on Jenny's face when I'd answered the door to her all those years ago. Her blotchy cheeks. The venom in her voice. Those thin lips curled in a contemptuous smile. She'd said she hoped that one day I'd know how it felt to be betrayed. She believed Noah would cheat on me like he cheated on her, but she was wrong. He lied to me, yes, but only because he thought the truth would tear us apart. He was wrong about that too.

I glance at Billy. Even through the gloom I can see his expression is closed, like he is back there in his childhood home watching television with his Auntie Sheila. There is a vulnerability about him, a sense that if you peeled back the layers you would find a confused, hurting little boy not so far beneath the surface.

'D'you know what Mum said to me?' he asks. 'D'you know how she broke it to me that life as I knew it was over?'

'No.'

'She told me my useless fucking twat of a father was poking his dick into some slag young enough to be his daughter. Her words, not mine.' Billy gives a mirthless laugh. 'And then Dad fucked off and I didn't even get to spend the weekends with him any more.' He shoots me an accusatory look.

'That was down to your mum, not your dad,' I remind him. At first, Jenny had refused point blank to let Noah see Billy at all. It was only when Noah threatened to go to court to get a contact order that she agreed he could have access for two hours every week. 'He took you out every Saturday afternoon,' I add.

'And I was supposed to be grateful for two measly hours a week?' Billy shakes his head. 'Two hours spent in bowling alleys or the cinema because Dad didn't know what else to do with me.' His expression darkens. 'And then my baby brother comes along, and suddenly he has no interest in me whatsoever.'

'Come on, Billy,' I say. 'You know that's not true.'

'From the day he was born it was Joe this and Joe that. I might as well have been invisible. "Look at Joe, walking at ten months. You didn't walk until you were a year-and-a-half,"' Billy mimics. '"Doesn't Joe look the spit of me? Not like you, Billy. You're Jenny through and through."'

The bitterness in his voice chills me. I knew he hated me, but I had no idea how much he resented his half-brother. A memory pops into my head. Billy, aged about ten, running to find me in the garden after two-year-old Joe had shut his middle finger in the kitchen door. I'd rushed my howling son to minor injuries where a nurse had taken one look at the blood pooling underneath his nail and drilled a small hole in the nail plate to release the pressure. Another time, a couple of years later, when Joe sprained his wrist after falling from the top of the slide at the playground on the rec while I'd been busy on my phone. There were other things too. Bruises and grazed knees. Lumps and bumps. At the time I assumed they came hand in hand with the rough and tumble of growing up. Noah and I even used to joke about how clumsy Joe was.

I stop and stare at Billy in horror as the memories slot into place. It's as if I'm seeing the past clearly for the first time.

'You were always ill,' I say slowly. 'Every year on Joe's birthday you'd have tummy ache or earache or a headache. Noah and I would give you Calpol and make a fuss of you while Joe spent his birthday running around fetching and carrying for you. Your little acolyte.'

'Yeah, well, I don't know what that means since I didn't go to a fancy school like my baby brother, but so what?'

'You were putting it on, weren't you? Faking it to get our attention.' I shake my head. How did I not see it at the time?

Billy glowers at me, deep grooves scoring his forehead. 'The sun shone out of Joe's fucking arse. He could do no wrong. I, on the other hand...'

'That's not fair. We treated you both equally.'

Billy stares at me incredulously. 'What actual planet are you on, *Eve*? Joe goes to a private school for posh twats, for fuck's sake. I looked up how much his school costs a year. Thirty thousand! By the time he's finished it'll have cost over two hundred grand! Meanwhile, I had to make do with the local high school. And you say we were treated equally. Don't make me laugh.'

'The only reason we can afford to send Joe to private school is because I work full time,' I say levelly. 'Every penny I earn goes to pay his school fees, and that's fine, because it's my choice. There was nothing stopping your mother from getting off her backside and looking for a job.'

It's the wrong thing to say. I should know by now never to criticise Saint Jenny, because while Billy is happy to slag his mother off, woe betide anyone else who has a pop at her.

He takes another step towards me. He's so close I can feel his breath on my cheek, hot and sour. I force myself not to flinch, not to show even a chink of weakness, because I refuse to let him intimidate me.

He jabs me in the chest. 'Don't you fucking dare speak about my mum like that, you bitch. Don't you fucking dare!'

He turns abruptly and stalks off down the track towards the lane. For a moment I'm rooted to the spot, heart crashing in my chest, ears straining to catch the faint wail of a siren. Then I plunge through the trees towards my stepson.

67

I catch up with Billy a few yards from the lane, grabbing his sleeve and forcing him to turn and face me.

'Look, I'm sorry, all right? But your father loves you, he always has. He lent you the money for your app, didn't he? He was so proud of you when you told him about your plans, what you were hoping to achieve. He risked everything for you. Our house, his business, our marriage. Everything.'

'He did, didn't he?' Billy says slowly. 'Funny how things turn out. That perfect life of yours isn't looking quite so perfect now, is it? Dad's business has hit the skids. You've lost your job. Your son's in trouble with the police. You'll probably end up having to sell up and move.' He tilts his head to one side, watching for my reaction. I try to keep my expression neutral, but it's impossible.

'Happy now?' I hit back.

He shrugs. 'I was only getting what I was due. You and Dad owed me.'

'Even if that is true, what about Joe? He's your brother. You should be protecting him, not dragging him into your seedy world.'

'Bullshit,' Billy scoffs. 'He was happy enough to earn a bit of pocket money running a few errands.'

'Running errands? Is that what you call it?' I shake my head. 'Is that how you got the drugs into the village, through Joe?'

He smirks. 'Why keep a dog and bark yourself? He did all right out of it.'

I think of the designer trainers and the Tommy Hilfiger bomber jacket, the sunglasses and the Xbox games. Joe paid for them with money he'd earned running drugs for his brother. It sickens me.

'Who beat Joe up? Your supplier, this Caleb bloke?'

Billy lowers his gaze.

I stare at him in disbelief. 'Oh my God, it was you, wasn't it?'

He doesn't answer.

'Billy!'

He gives me a surly look. 'It's what you do, innit? Rob one of your own while they're carrying your gear so they end up deeper in debt. It's what Caleb did to me. I was just passing it forward. Course, I jumped him from the back so he had no idea it was me. Tell you something for nothing,' he says, touching his jaw as he waggles it from side to side. 'Joe got off lighter than I did.'

I'm shocked to the core. Billy beat his own brother up so Joe had no choice but to carry on dealing. No, everyone has a choice, I tell myself. Joe could have come to us and told us the whole sorry story and we would have pulled him out of the hole he'd dug himself into. Instead, he refused to drop Billy in it, and by doing so he landed himself into a whole heap more trouble.

I want to rage at Billy, to rant and rail and wipe that smug smirk off his face, but something holds me back. It's guilt, I suppose. Billy has made his own choices, but he's damaged, and I can't shake the feeling that it's partly my fault.

'This Caleb, does he know about Joe?' I ask him.

He shakes his head, the hunted look returning. Whoever Caleb is, he's clearly bad news.

'I was going to tell him tonight.'

'So where is he?'

'Dunno.' He thrusts his hands in his pockets, and I stare up the lane towards Nesborough, willing the ambulance to arrive.

'There is a way you could turn this around,' I say.

He eyes me suspiciously. 'How?'

'By telling the police what you know. Give them the evidence to arrest Caleb.'

His head jerks up. 'Grass him up? You've gotta be kidding me. No one messes with people like Caleb. No one.'

'It's the only way you'd be free.'

'Free?' he snorts. 'I'd be looking over my shoulder for the rest of my life. No way, man.'

'Then will you promise me one thing?' I beg. 'Please keep Joe out of it?'

I'm still waiting for an answer when the silence is broken by the faint wail of sirens. I step into the lane, my arms outstretched, watching for the pulsing blue lights to approach.

'Thank God,' I cry when I see two vehicles in the distance: an ambulance and a solitary police patrol car. I flag them down and point up the track, yelling, 'They're up there!'

As the taillights disappear into the trees, I look around for Billy, but he's gone.

68

By the time I've tramped back up the track to the ruins, Noah is flanked by two paramedics, and a police officer is sitting with Joe in the back seat of Billy's car while a second is talking into his radio. He breaks off when he sees me.

'Mrs Griffiths?'

I nod.

'Do you know the whereabouts of your stepson, Billy? We'd like to ask him a few questions.'

'He's not here.'

'I can see that. Do you know where he is?'

I run a hand across my face. 'Do we need to do this now? I just want to make sure my son and husband are all right.'

'I've spoken to the paramedics. They're taking Mr Griffiths to Nesborough Hospital as soon as they've stabilised the wound.'

'What about Joe?'

'We were told it was a suspected overdose, but he is conscious and talking. My colleague's trying to ascertain what he's taken—'

'It's ketamine. He's taken ketamine.'

If the officer is surprised by this he doesn't show it, but I suppose he sees worse in his job. He must be in his late forties and has a weathered face and piercing blue eyes. 'In that case we'll make sure he goes to hospital for a check-up too. What about yourself? Are you all right?'

Just as I'm assuring him I'm absolutely fine, I'm hit by a wave of dizziness and lurch towards him.

He grabs my elbow. 'Perhaps you should sit down for a moment. Everything's under control.'

I do as he says, before my legs buckle. 'Sorry. It's been a long day.' I lick my lips. They feel dry and cracked and I wish I had my little tin of Vaseline with me, but it's in my bag in the car, and I don't have the energy to fetch it. I glance at him. 'I was beginning to think you weren't coming.'

'There was a big drugs raid in Nesborough this afternoon. With fifteen in custody, it's been all hands to the pump.'

My ears prick. 'A drugs raid?'

'Five simultaneous raids, to be accurate. Four houses and a lock-up. It's the biggest county line we've ever dismantled. The district commander's cock-a-hoop.'

I want to ask if one of the dealers they've arrested is Billy's Caleb, but I don't get a chance because the two paramedics are approaching, carrying Noah on a stretcher. I jump to my feet, my exhaustion forgotten. Although he is still parchment pale, he brightens when he sees me.

'Joe's coming with you in the ambulance. I'll follow in the car,' I tell him.

'You'll need these,' the police officer says, dangling Noah's car keys on his index finger. 'One of the paramedics found them in your husband's coat pocket.'

Once Noah's safely in the back of the ambulance, I go in search of Joe, who's still sitting on the back seat of Billy's car next to the second officer.

'C'mon, mate,' the officer says. 'Time to get you checked over by the docs.'

Between us we help Joe out of the car to the ambulance. Once he's strapped in, I kiss him lightly on the cheek.

'Sorry, Mum,' he mumbles.

I pat his shoulder. 'It's all right. I'll see you at the hospital, OK?'

The two police officers and I watch the ambulance trundle slowly down the track. The blue lights start flashing as it reaches the road and accelerates away towards Nesborough.

'You'll need to come into the station to give a statement in the morning,' the older officer says. 'Although your husband says his injury was accidental, it's still an offence to carry a knife in a public place. We also need to know who supplied Joe with the ketamine. Which leads me to my original question. Where is your stepson, Mrs Griffiths?'

'Believe me, I wish I knew.'

He holds my gaze. 'We'll find him sooner or later, so why don't you speed things up and tell me where you think he might have gone.'

I close my eyes for a moment but am immediately hit by the image of Noah bent double, the knife sticking out of his stomach. I sigh. 'You could try his mother's.' I recite Jenny's address in Essex. 'But he's been living in a house share in Nesborough since before Christmas. Number 27 London Road, I think. Oh, and he rents a place in the Nesborough Business Park. Unit 5B.'

We clamber into our respective cars, make our way slowly back down the track, and I follow the patrol car to Nesborough Hospital, shaken and dog-tired, yet grateful beyond measure that my child, unlike Annie, will live to tell the tale.

69

The sky is tinged pink with the first suggestion of dawn when Joe and I finally step out of the hospital and head towards the car park.

Doctors kept Joe under observation throughout the night but were happy to discharge him after an ECG and blood test results came back normal. Noah will have to stay in for a few more days, but he has been lucky: the knife narrowly missed all his major organs and blood vessels.

It could all have been so much worse.

I wept when the consultant in A&E told me Noah was out of the woods. Tears of pure, unadulterated relief. I'd spent the journey to hospital imagining the worst, picturing myself in widow's weeds throwing flowers on his coffin. It hit me with the force of a sledgehammer that my life would be nothing without him. He is my soulmate, always has been, always will be. Losing the house and our money is incidental.

There were tears for Lisa too, because while I was lucky, she was not, and the sheer injustice of it all is hard to bear.

We reach Noah's car; I blip the lock and we climb in. It's the first time we've been alone since yesterday, and although the questions are burning the back of my throat like acid reflux, I don't want to cross-examine him. It turns out I don't need to. As we pull out of the car park he mutters, 'I've been such an idiot. I should have known not to listen to Billy.'

'What d'you mean?' I ask carefully.

'Telling me I could make easy money by "running a few errands". I said no at first, but you know what he's like. He's got this way of talking you round. He said I'd be giving my friends what they wanted while I earned a ton of cash, like it was a win-win, you know?' Joe picks at a spot of mud on his trackies, then gives me a sideways glance.

I do know. When Billy turns on the charm, he's irresistible. Over the years I've seen him switch it on for Noah and Joe more times than I care to remember, and he has Jenny wrapped around his little finger. He's never bothered to keep up the pretence with me. To him, I will always be his evil stepmother.

I sigh. 'I do.'

'I'm never going to touch drugs again, Mum. I promise.'

'Good.'

'I told Billy I didn't want to take anything last night but he kept going on and on about me being chicken and I just wanted him to stop. I had no idea it was fucking ketamine.'

'Language, Joe.'

'I know my grades have been slipping at school but I'm going to get my head down between now and my GCSEs. I've decided I want to go to university. I... I kinda think I owe it to Annie, you know? She'll never get to go, so I should make sure I do. For both of us.' His voice cracks and I grip the steering wheel as I'm hit by a wave of grief.

'That's a great idea,' I say, once my breathing is back under control. 'I think she'd approve.'

He nods, satisfied. 'What d'you reckon about physiotherapy? I could get a job with the England Rugby team. That would be pretty cool.'

I glance at him and smile. 'It would.'

He goes quiet for a bit, and the next time I look at him, he's chewing his bottom lip.

'What's wrong?' I ask.

'What if the police find out I've been helping Billy?'

Helping Billy? Talk about putting a positive spin on it. Joe should forget about physiotherapy and get a job in PR.

'I—' I begin. I'm about to step into my usual role of Joe's Biggest Advocate and reassure him that there's nothing to worry about. That the police won't connect the dots. That he is safe, and his privileged future is as bright and golden as it has always been. That everything is A-OK.

But the words catch in my throat, because everything is not A-OK. Annie is dead, Lisa's alone, and Noah is lying in a hospital bed with a knife wound that was millimetres away from killing him.

I've babied Joe for too long. He is sixteen. It's time he understood that every action has a consequence, that every stone you drop into the water causes a ripple. He needs to grow up.

'Mum,' he says, desperation creeping into his voice. 'What'll happen if the police find out about the drugs and stuff?'

'You'll have to deal with it, Joe. You know Dad and I will always be in your corner, but we can't cover up a crime. You'll have to face up to what you've done and take the rap. But we'll be there. We'll always be there.'

Because that's the deal, I think, as I fix my eyes on the road ahead. There's no expiration date when you're a parent. No get-out clause. You're in it for the long haul, like it or not.

70

TWO WEEKS LATER

I have downloaded half a dozen podcasts and a couple of audiobooks for the long drive down to Cornwall.

It was Noah's idea that I go. He said it would be good for me to get away for a few days after everything that's happened. I was loathe to leave him, but his consultant says he's doing great and I mustn't worry.

'Text me when you arrive,' Noah says. 'I'd give you a hug, but—' He gestures to his stomach, still sore from all the stitches, and kisses me on the cheek instead. 'Safe journey, and don't worry about us. We'll be fine.'

'I won't,' I tell him. 'You're both big enough and ugly enough to look after yourselves.'

Not so long ago I would have reminded him that Joe has cricket practice after school this afternoon and rugby on Saturday morning, and that he needs to book a slot for the Sainsbury's delivery ASAP, but I don't. Stepping back from micromanaging the household has been surprisingly easy. Let them figure it out between them. I'm on the end of the phone if they need me.

I avert my eyes from the For Sale sign as I reverse out of the drive. I may have recognised I need to let Noah and Joe start looking after themselves, but I haven't quite made my peace with the fact that we're having to sell The Old Vicarage.

Interest from buyers has been insane, the estate agent told us yesterday with almost indecent glee. She's hoping for a bidding war. I just hope we make enough to buy somewhere smaller, mortgage-free. I never want to risk losing my home again.

We've decided to leave South Langley, but we'll stay in the area. It'll be good to start afresh somewhere new, where people don't whisper behind our backs. Somewhere we feel welcome.

The car eats up the miles, and before I know it, I'm turning onto the A30 and following signs for Bodmin and Okehampton.

Lisa's mum lives on the edge of a sprawling seaside village eight miles east of Penzance. I've made good time and it's just after three when I arrive.

Lisa must have been watching out for me because she opens the door as I tramp up the drive past her VW Beetle to the bungalow. We hug, then she leads me inside. Vincent greets me like he hasn't seen me for a year, his stubby tail wagging furiously when I crouch down to scratch him behind the ear.

'Mum's popped to the supermarket,' Lisa says. She is tanned, her golden hair bleached almost platinum by the sun. Only someone who knew her well would notice the shadows under her eyes and the fresh crop of worry lines wrinkling her forehead. 'Want a cup of tea, or would you prefer a walk along the beach? I need to take Vincent out before it gets dark.'

'A walk,' I say decisively. 'I'm as stiff as a board.'

'A walk it is. Annie's wellies are in the garage. They should fit you.'

Lisa shows me the spare bedroom and the bathroom, then disappears in search of Annie's wellies while I change into a comfy pair of jeans.

'Ta-da!' she says, reappearing with a pair of boots with a bright daisy design.

'Annie's Orla Kiely wellies,' I say, blinking away tears. 'She was going to wear them to Glastonbury as soon as she was eighteen.'

'That's right.' Lisa's face clouds, but then she visibly picks herself up. 'C'mon. The beach is stunning. I can't wait to show you.'

She clips Vincent onto his lead, locks the front door behind us, and we wander down the street to the sea. It feels good to be outside with the briny air filling my lungs after the six-hour drive. I listen contentedly as Lisa points out places of interest: the fish and chip shop, the pitch and putt, the beach bar where Lisa, Annie and Jackie used to enjoy mocktails after a day's sunbathing.

The beach is a perfect crescent of golden sand that stretches for at least a mile. This time of day it's empty apart from a handful of fellow dog-walkers and a few dedicated surfers watching for the next swell.

We walk arm-in-arm along the shoreline. Lisa tells me about the art class she's started up in the local community centre and the Hatha yoga class she attends on a Wednesday morning.

'It's funny,' she says, 'but I feel right at home.'

'And there I was thinking you were a South Langley girl through and through,' I joke.

She stops and turns to me. 'That's the thing. I've decided to move down here.'

'For good?'

She nods. 'I'm sorry.'

I squeeze her arm. 'Don't be. Actually, I also have news. Our place is on the market. We're moving too.'

'But you love your house.'

'I know, but we can't afford to stay there any more.'

When I phoned Lisa to tell her Noah's business had gone

bust, she admitted she'd known it had been in trouble for a while. He'd confided in her when she'd found him drowning his sorrows in the pub one night.

'Why didn't either of you tell me?' I'd demanded.

'Noah didn't want to worry you, and it wasn't my place to say.'

It explained why she'd blushed bright red when I first told her I thought Noah was having an affair, I supposed.

'I'm sorry,' she says now.

'It's all right. It's only bricks and mortar. People are still going out of their way to avoid me. To be honest, I shall be glad to leave the village.'

'Things no better?'

'Not really. I've been managing to avoid Greg Duffy, but Siobhan and the other mums give me the daggers whenever I bump into them.'

'D'you think it was Greg who threw the brick through your window?'

I shake my head. A couple of days before I left for Cornwall, Bobbi-Jo Moody knocked on our door and asked shyly if I'd like to come and see Maisie's kittens.

Inexplicably touched, I told her I could think of nothing I'd like more and followed her across the road to her house.

'This one's called Twinkle,' she announced as she scooped up a tiny tabby kitten and placed it carefully on my lap.

'She's gorgeous,' I said, stroking the kitten gently under its chin.

'She is,' Bobbi-Jo said proudly, then her smile faded.

'Is everything OK, Bobbi-Jo?'

She gave a half-shrug, her blue eyes troubled. 'Thing is, I know a secret, and Mrs Emerson says it's wrong to keep secrets, 'specially really bad ones.'

I felt a spark of unease. 'Would it help to share your secret?'

'I... I think so.'

I gave her an encouraging smile. She was quiet for a moment, then said, 'Connor threw a brick through your window.'

'*Connor* did?'

She nodded as the words tumbled out of her. 'I followed him and saw him do it. He was cross with Joe, cause of what happened to Annie. I know I should have told someone but I didn't want him to get into trouble with the police in case they locked him up in prison like my dad. They won't, will they?'

Connor threw the brick, not Greg Duffy or one of the other villagers. Connor. A sixteen-year-old boy dealing with the death of his friend the only way he knew how. A knot of tension somewhere deep in the pit of my stomach loosened.

'They won't,' I said, reaching across and squeezing her hand. 'Because we won't tell them.'

Her eyes widened. 'But what about your window?'

'The window's not important. I understand why Connor was cross with Joe. I was cross with him too, because of what happened to Annie.'

'That's all right then,' she said, her narrow shoulders sagging with relief. 'I'm glad I told you. I don't like secrets.'

'Me neither,' I said.

Lisa listens as I recount the conversation.

'You're not going to report Connor for criminal damage?' she asks.

'No. Those kids have been through enough.'

'You're right.' She pauses. 'Is everything OK between you and Noah?'

'Yes. God knows how, but it is.' I shoot her a mischievous look. 'He's promised to buy me a whopping great eternity ring for our twentieth wedding anniversary to replace my engagement ring.'

'I always told you he was a keeper. What about Joe? Is he staying at Elmwood?'

'Mum's offered to help us with his final term's fees and he's going to apply to Nesborough Sixth Form College for his A levels.'

'Bet Noah's pleased about that.'

'He is. It's certainly been a wake-up call for Joe, which is no bad thing. He announced this week he's going to look for a summer job as soon as his exams are finished.'

'Good on him,' Lisa says. 'Talking of jobs...'

'There's a governors' meeting after Easter. I'm hoping I'll be back at work before too long. If not, there's always The Swan.' We both chuckle.

'And what about Billy?' she asks.

We are circling ever closer to the truth, and the closer we get, the stronger my urge to unburden myself becomes, because I know how Bobbi-Jo felt. If I keep Joe's secret much longer, I fear it'll start dividing and multiplying like an aggressive cancer, taking my healthy cells with it.

'Billy was picked up by a patrol car hitch-hiking back to Nesborough. He's been charged with possessing a knife in a public place. His brief reckons he should get a suspended sentence as it's his first offence.'

'What about the fact he stabbed Noah and gave Joe ketamine?' Lisa is indignant.

'Neither Joe nor Noah would incriminate him, so the police took no further action. I think he'll be keeping his nose clean from now on.'

We've reached the end of the beach. It's time.

'Let's sit for a bit, shall we?' I say, and we make ourselves comfortable on the sand and stare out to sea while Vincent snouts around by the rockpools. My mouth is dry, my heart pitter-pattering in my chest. This is going to be harder than I thought.

When I promised Joe I wouldn't tell the police he gave Annie the ecstasy, I meant every word. But I also made a promise to Lisa, one I intend to keep. What Lisa decides to do with that information is up to her. Maybe she'll tell the police and Joe will be arrested. If he is, we'll deal with it. Maybe she'll understand why he did what he did and forgive him.

It is her decision and hers alone.

I take a deep breath. 'Lisa, there's something I need to tell you.'

71

I leave nothing out. I describe how Joe loved Annie and only gave her the ecstasy so she'd reciprocate his feelings. How he and Ethan made her drink so much water because they thought they were helping her. How the five teenagers had made a pact not to tell anyone what really happened that night.

'Joe is so very sorry, Lisa. I'm not sure he'll ever get over it,' I say finally.

'If he's so sorry, why isn't he here telling me this himself?' Lisa asks. Her voice is cold, and a feeling of dread seeps into my bones. But what else could I expect? Whichever way you look at it, Joe was responsible for Annie's death.

'He doesn't know I'm telling you.'

She looks up sharply.

'I wanted it to be your decision,' I explain. 'If you want to tell the police what really happened, I'll understand.'

'Even if it means Joe's arrested?'

'Even if it means he's arrested,' I agree. 'He did what he did out of love, but it was still a reckless, stupid thing to do, and he should have known better. If you think he should pay for what he's done, I won't stand in your way.'

Vincent ambles over, a piece of driftwood in his mouth. He drops it by my feet and cocks his head, looking at me with hopeful eyes. I pick the stick up and throw it as far as I can. It lands with a splash in the shallows and the Jack Russell darts after it, barking excitedly.

'You really think he's sorry?' Lisa asks after a while.

'I do.' It's true. I have no doubt that guilt will be a burden Joe will have to carry for the rest of his life. 'He did something bad, but he's not a bad person.'

'I know.' Lisa rests her chin on her knees and stares out to sea. 'He always looked after Annie, didn't he? Remember the time he thumped that kid for pushing her off the slide at the rec?'

'You told him he was a legend.'

She smiles. 'He was.' She falls silent again, then says, eventually, 'I knew he loved her.'

My eyes widen. 'You did?'

'I'd always harboured a secret hope they might fall in love one day. Get married, have kids, the whole works. It would have been perfect. The pair of us, proud grannies.' She bites her bottom lip. 'I knew he'd fallen for Annie the day we went to Brighton. I could see it in his eyes. He was head over heels. I should have told you. Perhaps if I had...'

'Don't—' I begin.

'I guess what I'm trying to say is that I think I understand why Joe did what he did. He wanted Annie to love him. It's what we all want, isn't it? To love and to be loved?'

'It is.'

Lisa turns to me. Her face is tear-streaked, but her eyes are clear, her voice determined. 'I won't be going to the police.'

'You won't?'

'I keep thinking, what would Annie want? She'd hate Joe to be arrested. What if he was convicted? He'd be sent to a young offender institution, and she'd never want that. He was her best friend and she loved him. Maybe not in the way he wanted her to, but she did, nonetheless.'

Lisa pauses and I hold my breath.

'It wouldn't change anything anyway,' she continues. 'Nothing will bring Annie back. It'd put you through hell, and I'd never do that to you. I think you've all suffered enough.' She nods to herself. 'Not knowing what happened that night was intolerable, but now I know the truth, at least I can start to come to terms with it.'

'Thank you.' My own eyes well with tears of relief. 'I'm so sorry I didn't tell you sooner.'

'You're telling me now, aren't you?' Lisa stands, brushes sand from her jeans, then holds out an arm and pulls me to my feet. We embrace for a moment before she breaks away and links her arm in mine.

I can understand why Annie loved it here. The big skies, the vast beach and the pounding surf are exhilarating. For a moment, I let myself pretend she's walking beside us, chattering about her day – a golden girl on a golden beach. Joyous, vivacious, *alive*.

Lisa stops to face me, tears streaming down her face. 'Tell me you can feel her too?' she says urgently.

'I can. I *can*!'

Laughing and crying, we retrace our steps towards the bungalow as gulls wheel above us and the sea crawls inexorably towards the shore.

EPILOGUE

JENNY

Jenny Griffiths pushes a trolley along the aisles of her local Waitrose, deciding what she and Billy will have for tea. Her eyes are on stalks at the prices. Who on earth can afford two pounds fifty for a packet of shortbread biscuits, for goodness' sake? Jenny normally shops at Aldi or Lidl because she's had to watch every penny ever since the day Noah walked out.

For eighteen years she has scrimped and saved. Buying yellow sticker food and showering every other day. She and Billy have lived hand to mouth in their cramped two-bedroom terrace while Noah and the bitch swan about in their former vicarage living the life of Riley.

Jenny made the mistake of looking up her ex-husband's home on Rightmove not long after they bought it. She'd scrolled through the photos with a growing anger, noting the spacious, light-filled rooms, the original features and the huge garden overlooking the church. It was exactly the kind of house Jenny had always pictured herself living in one day.

Fat bloody chance.

She stops in the meat aisle and peruses the steaks. She picks up an organic ribeye and reads the label. The marbled cut is from cattle reared on grass, grain and forage. It is almost eight pounds, an obscene amount of money, but she and Billy are celebrating, so she drops two in her trolley. Heading over to the desserts, she chooses a salted caramel and chocolate tart and a tub of clotted cream. In the freezer aisle she adds triple-cooked chips and a bag of organic petits pois to her haul. Finally, she makes her way to the drinks aisle, deciding on a bottle of Cabernet Sauvignon for her and four cans of Stella Artois for Billy.

Jenny has a wobble when the shopping comes to almost fifty pounds. She is on the verge of asking the white-haired woman on the checkout if she can swap the steaks for a tin of corned beef when she stops herself. She bets Noah and the bitch eat steak all the time, and if it's good enough for them...

Jenny pays for the food and tramps down the street to the bus stop, the bags of shopping feeling heavier with every step. While she waits for her bus to arrive, she texts Billy.

Don't be late for tea tonight. I have something special planned. Xx

She's on the bus, halfway home, before he replies.

K.

It's about as much as she can expect from him these days. They used to be so close, but when he hit his late teens, he started to withdraw from her. Once, during a row, he told her she was suffocating him, but she's sure he didn't really mean it.

Trouble is, she's had to be both mother and father to him ever since Noah left her for that woman.

Jenny stares out of the window as the town whizzes by. As

her thoughts drift, a memory comes to her, one she's re-lived so many times over the last seventeen years it's almost comforting in its familiarity.

She'd left a seven-year-old Billy at home and had popped across the road to her sister Sheila's for a pint of milk when her phone had rung. She'd answered without checking the number, worried it was Billy, surprised when a woman whose voice she didn't recognise asked for her by name.

'Before you ask, I haven't been involved in an accident at work,' Jenny was about to say, but the woman cut across her.

'It's Bernice,' she announced, and a band of fear had tightened around Jenny's chest. Why would Bernice, Noah's office manager, be phoning her at six o'clock on a Thursday evening?

'Has something happened?' Jenny gasped. 'Is Noah all right?'

'Noah's fine,' Bernice assured her. 'That's not why I'm calling.' She paused. 'I thought long and hard before phoning you, Jenny, but I'd want to know if I was in the same boat.'

'In the same boat? What are you talking about?' she asked, confused.

'If my husband was playing away.'

Jenny was silent as the older woman's words sank in.

Bernice cleared her throat. 'I'm sorry to have to tell you this,' she began, though it struck Jenny that she didn't sound sorry at all. In fact, she sounded self-righteous, even smug.

'Noah's been sleeping with one of his clients. A woman called Eve. She's become a permanent fixture lately. If you were to turn up at his flat unannounced, you'd probably find her ensconced in there like she owns the place.'

Jenny could hear the sour note to Bernice's voice over her own hammering heart. She'd always suspected Noah's matronly office manager of harbouring a secret crush on him. It seemed like her suspicions were correct. But if what Bernice was saying was true...

'I don't believe you,' Jenny said.

Bernice tutted, a clicking sound that seemed to reverberate down the phone. 'Believe what you like. It's no skin off my nose. Just don't say I didn't warn you.' The line went dead.

Jenny collapsed on Sheila's sagging sofa, her phone clutched in her hand as her life imploded around her.

Bernice could have been lying, but Jenny knew in her heart she was telling the truth. Noah had been preoccupied for months, his mood only lifting on a Sunday evening when it was time for him to head back to London. She'd taken her eye off the ball and suddenly everything she cared about was being snatched from under her nose.

Sheila appeared in the doorway, a pint of milk in her hand, but Jenny was already rushing from the room and sprinting across the street. Their front door was ajar, just as she'd left it, and she pushed it open, shivering in her thin cotton top. The suffocating silence hit her, as thick and as solid as a wall.

Jenny staggered through the house, reeling from shock. Everything looked the same, yet she knew nothing would ever be the same again. After promising to love and cherish her till the day he died, Noah had betrayed her in the worst way imaginable, tearing their little family apart.

She found Billy watching television and gathered him up in her arms so tightly that he complained she was hurting him. But she hadn't let him go. He was all she had left.

Now, as she rests her forehead against the cold glass of the bus window, memories slam into her with enough force to knock the breath from her lungs, even after all these years. Eve answering the door to Noah's London flat: proof, if she needed it, that Bernice's claims were true. The day Noah told her the dewy-eyed bitch was pregnant. Billy announcing that she'd had the baby. He'd been so excited to have a little brother. Jenny suppresses a smile. Until she poisoned him against them all.

Turning Billy against Eve was easy. Even aged seven, he

could see his stepmother was responsible for breaking up their family, and a few carefully chosen observations from Jenny cemented his enduring distrust of his dad's second wife.

Jenny thought Noah would be a tougher nut to crack because Billy had always hero-worshipped his dad. In the event, the erosion of trust had been easier than she'd thought.

A question here, a lie there. False memories planted, history rewritten to suit Jenny's narrative. *Do you think your dad would have left if he really cared about you? Can't you see he's using you to get back at me? I know you think you love him, but you're better off without him.*

Drip, drip, drip.

Billy soon saw she was right: that Noah was unreliable and manipulative. That the bitch only cared about her brat, and that the brat would stop at nothing to monopolise his father's love, like a cuckoo in the nest.

Suggesting Billy ask his father to invest in his new fitness app had been a genius move. She knew the start-up wouldn't amount to anything; Billy's hare-brained schemes never did. She also knew it wouldn't take long for him to burn through his father's cash. And Noah's pockets had proved deeper than either Jenny or Billy could have imagined. His generosity was borne from guilt, of course. It was his way of making amends for walking out on Billy when he was a boy. A debt that needed repaying.

Such a shame Noah lost his business and is about to lose his house in the process. Hah!

The bus turns into their road and Jenny pulls herself to her feet and reaches up to ring the bell. Dealing with the cuckoo – Joe – became her next fixation. She could see Billy was torn between wanting a brother and having Noah all to himself, but why should he have to share his father?

She dripped yet more poison, telling Billy that Joe was a parasite sucking their father dry and that no matter what Billy did, he'd always be second best. It wasn't so far from the truth, was it? Look at the small fortune Noah and Eve spent sending Joe to a school for toffs while Billy had to make do with his local high school.

Jenny spotted another opportunity when she found a stash of drugs and cash hidden under a loose floorboard in Billy's bedroom last summer. She sat him down and made him tell her exactly what he was up to, trying to hide her shock when he admitted he was involved in county lines. Although she knew he dabbled, she had no idea he'd started dealing. There was a tiny dart of something else too. Fascination, certainly, because this world of burner phones, cuckooed homes and drug deals was about as far removed from her own life as it was possible to get. Pride? Maybe a little. Jenny would always be Billy's staunchest supporter, but even she had to admit he was a bit work-shy. However, he'd taken his new role with his latest boss, Caleb, very seriously. And, finally, excitement, as an idea began to form in her head…

What if Billy recruited Joe into the county line that Caleb and his gang were operating in Nesborough? The possibility that Eve's brat could end up with a drug conviction made Jenny fizz with anticipation. So, she'd started dropping hints. Hints that Billy, always so suggestible, had picked up and run with, bless him.

Soon, an idea for a money-making enterprise of her own popped into her head. An idea that would take planning and patience but, if successful, would ensure she could buy organic ribeye steaks fifty-two weeks of the year.

Jenny thanks the driver as the bus comes to a stop. She steps onto the pavement and fishes in her pocket for her keys. As she walks up the path to her front door, she spots her neighbour Hazel's tortoiseshell cat squatting in the flowerbed. She drops the shopping bags and claps her hands loudly, but she's too late. The cat has finished its business and, giving her a disdainful look – a feline 'fuck you' – jumps over the wall between the two houses and disappears.

Gritting her teeth, Jenny stabs her key in the lock. As soon as it's dark, she will come out with a trowel and throw the crap into next door's garden. With any luck, Hazel will tread right in it. Revenge, as they say, is a dish best served cold.

Jenny unpacks the shopping and makes herself a cup of tea. She takes it into the living room and sits down on the sofa with a grateful grunt. She checks the phone tracker and location app on her phone. Billy was heading to Dagenham today to scope out some clients for her new business venture. Judging by the moving dot, he's on his way home.

At first, she'd been horrified when she'd discovered Billy, not Joe, was in custody at Nesborough Police Station. When the custody sergeant had explained exactly what had happened in the woods that night, she'd burst out laughing.

Only after she'd hung up, mind.

Not that she wished Noah dead, but there was a certain poetic justice to it all. He stabbed her in the back, metaphorically speaking, when he walked out on her and Billy. Now Billy had returned the favour. It was some recompense for the hell Noah had put them both through.

Jenny borrowed Hazel's car to drive down to Nesborough the next day to pick Billy up from the police station. One of his bail conditions is that he lives with her in Essex. She's been making the most of having her son at home.

Billy has been subdued these last couple of weeks, like all the stuffing has been knocked out of him. Jenny knows he feels bad about what happened to that girl, even though it wasn't his fault. He's also living in fear of the police knocking on their door and arresting him for drug dealing because if Caleb or one of his lackeys implicates him, he'll be in the cells quicker than you can blink. What has surprised Jenny the most is how guilty Billy's felt for the way he treated Noah.

'For the first time in my life, Dad really believed in me,' Billy said. 'And what did I do? I screwed up big time. I'm going to repay him, you just watch me. Every single penny.'

Jenny rolled her eyes inwardly before she realised Billy's determination to pay his father back could work to her advantage.

The unpalatable truth is that they're stony broke. The final straw was losing her rainy-day fund to the nice young roofer who claimed her chimney needed repointing.

He turned out not to be so nice after all, charging her three thousand pounds for the repairs to the chimney and for replacing the loose tiles he found while he was up there. When a gormless-looking Police Community Support Officer turned up the very next day warning that a gang of rogue traders were operating in the area and advising her never to agree to work on the doorstep, Jenny had been incandescent.

Not least because Eve, her nemesis, had told her it sounded like a scam.

Now, Jenny can't even tap up her ex-husband because he's as skint as she is.

Jenny heads back into the kitchen to rinse her mug under the tap, then takes the key from the silver chain around her neck and unlocks the narrow door to the cellar. There's no need to flick on the light switch because the subterranean room, which measures 10 ft by 10 ft, is already brightly lit. Learning how to circumvent the electricity meter is just one of a dozen new skills Jenny has mastered in the last couple of weeks. It's amazing what you can learn online if you know where to look.

A pungent smell hits her as she climbs down the steep stone steps, taking care not to trip over the cabling that runs from a double socket in the kitchen. There's a hose too, leading to a hydroponic system that keeps the plants watered 24/7.

It's perfectly legal to buy cannabis seeds in the UK, Jenny discovered when she began researching her new business venture. It's germinating them that's against the law. Growing twenty plants to maturity is definitely frowned upon by the boys in blue.

Not that Jenny has any intention of being caught. That's why she's keen to keep the operation small for the time being. Just the twenty plants which, when mature, will each have a street value of around £1,000.

They are a way off maturity yet. Jenny reckons they'll start flowering in a month or so. She'll need to wait until the buds ripen before she can harvest them. Then comes the drying process: she's already picked up some tips and tricks on how to do that from videos online. Finally, four months after planting the seeds, the crop will be ready to sell.

Luckily, Billy is perfectly placed to shift the stuff for her.

He'd taken some persuading to come on board. Jenny had had to pull every emotional trick in her not inconsiderable arsenal to wear him down. Gallingly, it was the fact that he'd be able to use his share of the profits to pay Noah back that was the tipping point. You can't have everything.

It's funny, Jenny thinks, as she rubs one of the spiky green leaves between her thumb and forefinger, inhaling the distinctive sweet smell. If someone had told her even two months ago that she'd be setting herself up as a small-time cannabis dealer to help pay the bills, she'd have thought they were barking mad.

Who knows, if her side hustle proves profitable, she might even look to expand.

She smiles to herself. Nesborough is under-served now Caleb and his county lines cronies are behind bars. Maybe Billy can talk his little brother into joining the family business. It would be good to have a lamb they can throw to the lions should the police come knocking. Seeing Joe behind bars where he belongs would be rather gratifying. It might even go some small way to make up for the disagreeable fact that Noah and Eve's marriage seems stronger than ever.

As far as Jenny's concerned, Joe is fair game. Perhaps Eve should have thought about that before she stole Noah from her all those years ago. You reap what you sow.

Jenny's smile widens into a grin. No, she's not quite done with Eve and her perfect little family.

Not yet.

A LETTER FROM A J MCDINE

Dear Reader,

Thank you so much for reading *Everyone Has Secrets*! I hope you enjoyed it. If it's the first of my books you've read, welcome! If you've been with me from the beginning, a huge thank you for sticking around. Your support means the world to me.

If you would like to keep up to date with all my latest releases, just click on the link below and I'll let you know when I have a new book coming out. Your email address will never be shared and you can unsubscribe at any time.

www.bookouture.com/a-j-mcdine

Everyone Has Secrets is my eighth psychological thriller and is based on an idea that's been knocking around in my head for a couple of years: how would a loving mother cope if her son was accused of a crime he didn't commit?

Enter Eve, a typical helicopter parent whose son Joe is the centre of her world. When Eve's goddaughter, Annie, ends up in hospital after a party at their house, Joe is implicated. I was keen to see just how far Eve would go to protect her only child. Obviously, if you've finished the book, you'll know that nothing is straightforward – especially in a psychological thriller!

Writing about mother-teen relationships is a passion of mine, and as a mum of two boys, now aged twenty-two and twenty, I have plenty of material to draw on. I hope Eve and

Joe's relationship resonates with everyone who's experienced the joys and challenges of living with a teen, not least the perpetually empty fridge!

If you did enjoy Eve's story, it would be amazing if you could leave a review on Amazon or Goodreads.

Reviews help new readers discover my books, and I'd love to hear your thoughts.

But, please, no spoilers!

Please feel free to drop me a line at amanda@ ajmcdine.com, visit my website or come and say hello over on Facebook or Instagram.

All the best,

Amanda x

www.ajmcdine.com

facebook.com/ajmcdineauthor

instagram.com/ajmcdineauthor

ACKNOWLEDGEMENTS

Once again, I would like to thank the brilliant team at Bookouture. After being an indie author for many years, when I was author, editor, proofreader, formatter, publicist, marketeer, chief finance officer and general dogsbody, it is so nice to be able to spend all my time writing, knowing that all those other jobs are in extremely capable hands. I love being a part of the Bookouture family!

Special thanks go to my editor, Natasha Harding, whose insight and encouragement have made this book the best it can be. I can't wait to work together on my next twisty thriller.

I would like to thank my copy editor, Jane Eastgate, and proofreader, Lynne Walker, for their eagle eyes and expertise, and my publicist, Noelle Holten, for spreading the word about *Everyone Has Secrets*.

I would also like to thank Harriet Monday for being an absolute star and always dropping everything to give my books a final, final read-through, and Dr Penny Davies, for answering all my strange medical questions. Any mistakes are my own.

A huge, heartfelt thank you to all the bloggers and reviewers who take the time to read and recommend my books. Some of you have been with me from the start, and your support means the world to me.

I would like to give a special mention to Emma Bradley from Wales, who won a reader competition to have a character named after them. Emma, who works in a school as a teaching assistant, has been promoted to head teacher in *Everyone Has Secrets*!

Finally, I'd like to thank *you*, for choosing this book. I hope you enjoyed it!

PUBLISHING TEAM

Turning a manuscript into a book requires the efforts of many people. The publishing team at Bookouture would like to acknowledge everyone who contributed to this publication.

Audio
Alba Proko
Sinead O'Connor
Melissa Tran

Commercial
Lauren Morrissette
Hannah Richmond
Imogen Allport

Cover design
Lisa Horton

Data and analysis
Mark Alder
Mohamed Bussuri

Editorial
Natasha Harding
Lizzie Brien